WITHDRAWN

D0016025

SUMMER OF A THOUSAND PIES

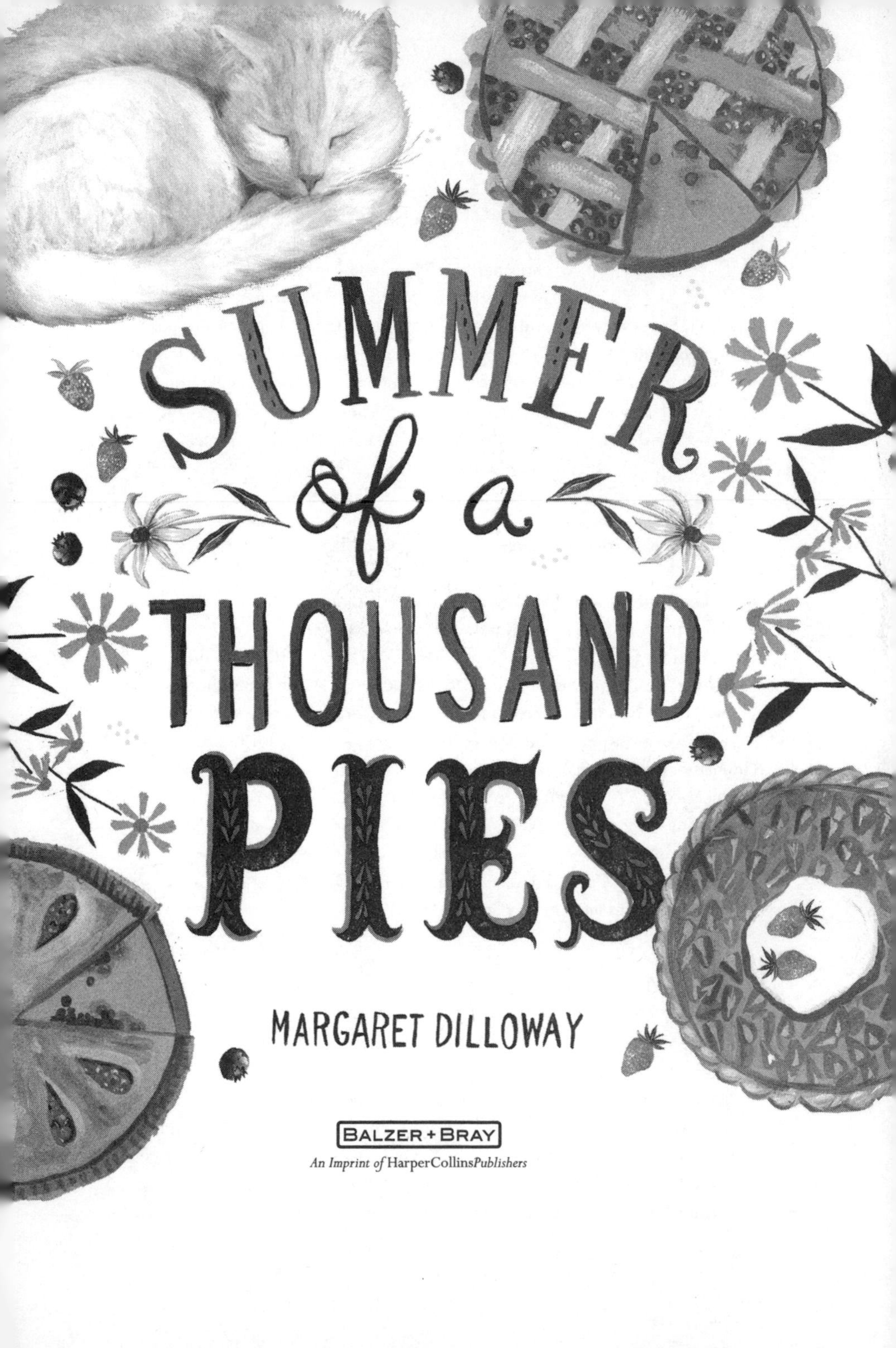
SUMMER
of a
THOUSAND
PIES
MARGARET DILLOWAY
BALZER + BRAY
An Imprint of HarperCollinsPublishers

Balzer + Bray is an imprint of HarperCollins Publishers.

Summer of a Thousand Pies
 For information address HarperCollins Children's Books, a division of HarperCollins Publishers, 195 Broadway, New York, NY 10007.
www.harpercollinschildrens.com

Library of Congress Cataloging-in-Publication Data

Names: Dilloway, Margaret, author.
Title: Summer of a thousand pies / Margaret Dilloway.
Description: First edition. | New York, NY : Balzer + Bray, an imprint of HarperCollins Publishers, [2019] | Summary: After her father goes to jail, Cady Bennett, twelve, is taken from foster care to spend a summer with her estranged aunt Michelle, trying to save her failing pie shop.
Identifiers: LCCN 2018014219 | ISBN 9780062803467 (hardback)
Subjects: | CYAC: Family problems—Fiction. | Aunts—Fiction. | Baking—Fiction. | Pies—Fiction. | Friendship—Fiction. | Family-owned business enterprises—Fiction.
Classification: LCC PZ7.1.D563 Sum 2019 | DDC [Fic]—dc23 LC record available at https://lccn.loc.gov/2018014219

Typography by Jessie Gang
19 20 21 22 23 PC/LSCH 10 9 8 7 6 5 4 3 2 1
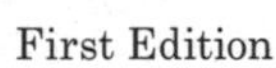
First Edition

When cooking, it is important to keep safety in mind. Children should always ask permission from an adult before cooking and should be supervised by an adult in the kitchen at all times. The publisher and author disclaim any liability from any injury that might result from the use, proper or improper, of the recipes and activities contained in this book.

For DREAMers everywhere

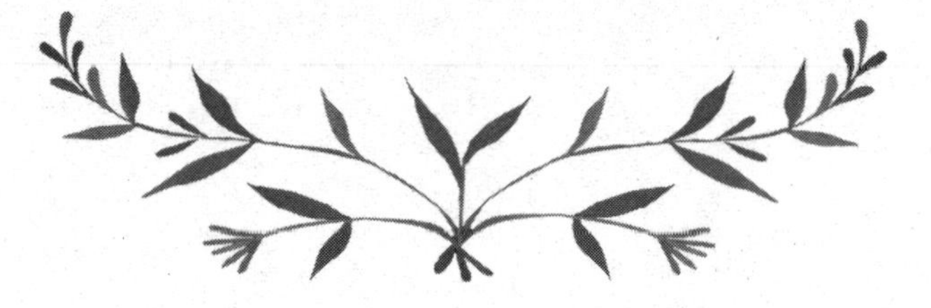

MAY

0 Pies Down

1,000 to Go

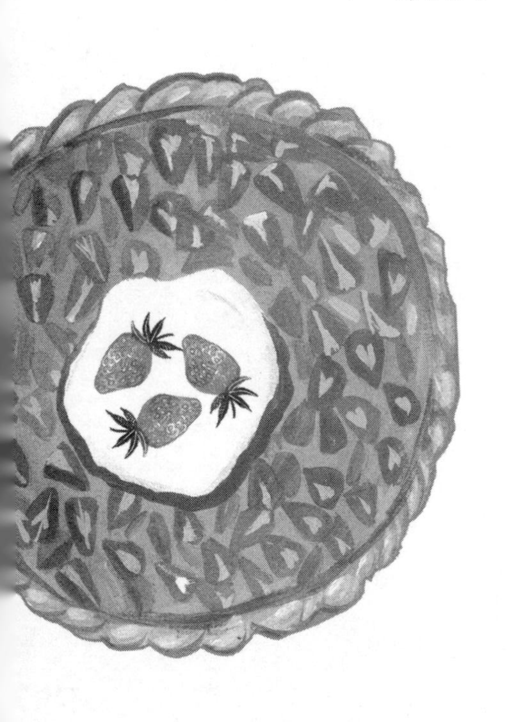

CHAPTER 1

I open my eyes, expecting to see the inside of our van, Dad snoring next to me like a half-broken engine. But I'm in a small bedroom covered in bright posters. Another bed's just beyond my arm's reach, in case someone has a brother or sister. Which I don't.

This is the San Diego County Children's Center. They took me here the day before yesterday, and it still seems unreal. I've been hoping it was like one of those cheesy TV shows where everything bad that just happened *was all a dream*.

Dad. My heart thumps hard. I grab the stuffed animal the police officers gave me and squeeze him so hard I'm surprised his seams don't pop. His name is Bear, from the book *Found*. Jenna, my honorary little sister and reading buddy, loved that book in kindergarten. It's about this bear who finds a stuffed bunny and falls in love with it while he looks for the owner. And now here he is, in stuffed animal form. I'm twelve and getting too old for stuffed animals, but I've got to admit that Bear makes me feel a tiny bit better.

My stomach growls. I look at the clock—it's already eleven. No wonder I'm so hungry. I couldn't fall asleep until after the sun came up. I just didn't feel comfortable enough, though it was my second night here.

I use the little bathroom, then tuck Bear safely into bed and slide on my ratty Vans. I need food. And answers about my father. Somebody has got to know what's up.

The day before yesterday, my dad showed up at my school because I got into trouble. Which is a normal parent thing to do, right? Except my dad—he wasn't normal. He came into the office swaying his body, slurring his words. He blamed it on medication. But everyone from Jenna to the principal could see he was lying.

I've known he was lying for a long time.

So the principal had to call the police. Child endangerment, they said. He broke the law. No way he could take care of me. I don't see why anybody cared *this* time. I was okay with how things were.

Long story short, that's how I ended up here.

I hope Jenna isn't worrying about me. Maybe I can write her a letter to tell her I'm okay. Even though I don't really feel all that okay. I can lie a tiny bit, if it means Jenna won't be anxious. It won't be a big lie, like Dad's.

There's a knock and before I can say anything, the doorknob starts turning. Someone's trying to break in! I gurgle out a half scream. In a panic, I slam my shoulder against the door, shutting it tight, the way Dad taught me. I've seen him do it before at one of the motels where we stay. "What do you want?" I say in my meanest, most grown-up voice.

"It's Marleen," the person says, and I sag against the door. She helped me when I got here—a social worker who asked me a bunch of questions I didn't want to answer.

I open the door an inch. Marleen smiles anxiously, scrunching her shoulders, her blond corkscrew curls bouncing. "Good morning," she says fake cheerfully. The walkie-talkie on her waist mutters with voices, and she mutes them. "Did you sleep well?"

I shrug. This Marleen seems nice enough, but I'm not in the mood to be particularly nice back. Number one, she could have said who she was before she opened the door so I didn't have a heart attack. And number two, I'm *hangry* now, as my dad would say. That means hungry *and* angry. I scowl and step out of the room, shutting the door. "I'm starving. Do you guys have any oatmeal?" I'm hoping for one of those instant packets. Blueberries and cream is my favorite.

"I'll get you a snack in a second." She stands there twisting her mouth around.

A snack? Does that mean a package of crackers, oatmeal, a bowl of cereal? My stomach rumbles. Now only Marleen and her mission are standing between me and my food. I'll do anything she asks. Almost anything. "What do you want?"

Marleen clears her throat, then rattles off her next words so fast I barely understand. "Cady, your aunt is here."

"My what?" I forget about everything else.

"Your aunt. Michelle." She says this like I'm supposed to know who that is.

But the name makes my heart beat a little faster. "I don't have an aunt Michelle."

Marleen opens and closes her mouth in a way that reminds me of a goldfish. Who on earth is she talking about? Then it hits me.

Michelle. Could that be Shell? My mother's sister, the one who didn't want to see us? "Shell? She's here? But why?"

"Oh, good." Marleen lets out a little titter. "For a second I thought I had the wrong kid."

Then another woman appears in the hallway behind Marleen and starts toward us. She looks down over the top of Marleen's frizzy head, her eyes lasering straight toward mine.

She stops in her tracks.

My breath catches in my chest. Because for a second,

I think my mom is there. Same tall build, same kind of face. The black brows above dark brown eyes, the cheekbones. Her skin's the color of Mom's too, a light tan.

But then that passes. This lady is bigger, broader, as if she can plow a field and bench-press a thousand pounds. And older than my mother, with gray streaked in her black hair. Of course, my mom died when I was five. Maybe Mom would have gray hair, too, by now. I wipe my eyes and frown, looking down at where the faded brown linoleum floor meets the dirty white wall trim.

"Is this Cady?" the woman says. Her voice is deep, gruff. Marleen nods. This lady continues toward me. She seems to fill the entire hallway, wall to wall, floor to ceiling.

What Dad said about Shell—it was nothing good. Pretty much the opposite, in fact. From what I know, Shell didn't really care about my mother. Or me.

I immediately go full-on cactus prickly. Dad would be so mad that they called her. "Aunt Shell, I presume. Well, well, well." I clear my throat. "Never thought you'd show your face to me."

This sounds like something Dad would come up with. She looks at the floor, then back up, her expression now uncertain.

We stare at each other, her sizing me up, me sizing her up. I recognize her mouth, thin but with a Cupid's bow on the upper lip. It's the same as mine. So weird to see it on a stranger. She frowns. The same frown I see in my mirror, with the number eleven–looking lines between the brows. "I'm here now, young lady. And you're coming with me."

I stick out my proud Bennett chin, inherited from Dad. That's something she doesn't have. "What if I don't want to?"

"Then I guess you can stay here." Her voice is even. She doesn't care if I stay or come. This stings, but I pretend it doesn't.

"I think I'll stay, thank you." I open my door to make my point. "Can I still get food, though?" I say to Marleen. My pulse hammers as though I finished a fistfight. Worse than when I thought Marleen was breaking in.

I move partly into my room. I totally don't care if Shell leaves. Dad will get me sooner or later. He always has before.

I'll stay here and then they'll find me a foster home until Dad is ready. It'll be fine. But my stomach goes all wobbly. Not to get into gory details, but the foster homes I've been in are definitely not fine. And the last time I was in one, it took months for Dad to get his act together.

Not to mention, I'll miss promotion at school. What will my teacher, Ms. Walker, think? How will I finish the year?

Dad promised he'd never put me through this again. But here I am.

"Wait a second." Marleen steps between us nervously, puts her hand on my shoulder. It's literally undead-cold. I shrug it off. I don't like people touching me in general, much less people with ice cubes for fingers. "Hey, wow, Cady, I didn't realize you didn't know your aunt. At all."

"I told you that when I got here. I said she probably doesn't even know she has an aunt Michelle." Aunt Shell rolls her eyes at the same time I roll mine, because I *also* told Marleen I didn't know about any aunt. This makes me like Shell a tiny bit more. But only a bit.

"It's okay, Cady," Marleen says, her voice too sunshiny bright. "Your dad put her on the emergency contact sheet at your school. We vetted her."

I don't know what "vetted" means. It sounds like something you'd do to an animal. And wait—what? Shell is on my emergency contact list? Shell, my dad's number three enemy? (Number two being this one convenience store security guy who gives him a hard time, and number one being the sun because it's always in his eyes when he doesn't want it to be.)

Not to mention—my dad knew where Shell was this entire time and didn't bother telling me? *And* put her on the emergency list like he actually trusts her?

I mean, what the actual heck?

I think I knew a lot more when I woke up yesterday morning than I do now.

Shell sighs. "Listen, Cady, I know you don't know me

from Eve. But I'm your mother's sister, and she'd want me to take care of you. Okay?"

But do you *want to take care of me?* I want to ask. *Or are you just getting paid for this like other foster parents?* But I don't really want to stay in unicorn la-la land, either. Or go to some completely strange home.

Shell, at least, *looks* like family. Kind of sort of.

Besides, it doesn't seem like Marleen's going to do anything else useful. Not even get me a snack. At last, I give Shell one tiny nod.

Shell takes that as a yes and ducks past me into my room, hauling out my trash bag full of stuff. "Is this all you have?"

"All my worldly possessions." That's what Dad calls it. My throat's so dry I can barely squeeze out the words.

"Traveling light. I like it." She walks out of the room. "Let's roll."

I'm frozen. Roll where? Right now? Before I eat? My stomach growls. "Do I still get a snack?" I remind Marleen.

The walkie-talkie at Marleen's hip crackles. She glances at me. "I'm sorry. You'll be okay. Shell will feed you." She holds out her hand. "Good luck."

I shake it a little too hard. No snack, after she promised? Typical. It probably would have been a lame snack anyway, like fake cheese and crackers.

I take in a deep, deep breath. I have to go with Shell,

even though I want to hop back into bed and pull the covers over my head until my whole life is fixed. Because the earth might stop spinning before that happens. "You gotta deal with what's in front of you," Dad likes to say. This is what's in front of me.

I grab Bear and follow Shell out of the building into the bright May morning.

CHAPTER 2

It's not every day you find out you have a brand-new aunt. Much less one who drives a really old truck so fast it feels like we're going around the curves on only two wheels. Which is not helping my stomach situation. I grip the side of the seat as my aunt accelerates into the other lane around a slow motor home, muttering about how it would be courteous of them to pull over. The truck rattles, as if it's an elderly lady being forced to sprint.

I stare so hard at where the hills meet the sky that I'm surprised the whole thing doesn't burst into flames. My dad says doing this stops motion sickness. "Buckle up, Buttercup," he'd tell me. "Fix your eyes on the horizon, and take ten deep breaths. It'll pass. Always does for me." But it's not working today. My stomach makes a gurgling noise and I turn toward the door, in case I've got to lean out the window really fast. Hurling in someone's car an hour after you met doesn't seem as if it's the best way to get that person to like you. I tuck Bear behind my back so he'll be safe.

My aunt's taking me to her house in Julian, wherever that is. She said it's still in San Diego County. It could be the lost city of Atlantis for all I know, except we're driving inland, not toward the ocean. She drives us farther and farther away from the city, through the mountains, until I'm pretty sure she's taking me to Mars and not to Julian.

Forty-five minutes or so after we left, the curves settle down somewhat, and the road winds between squat mountains dotted with leafy trees, opening up to meadows. Cows and horses swish their tails on either side. I roll down my window some more, stick my head out. The cool air blows over my face, and finally my belly settles.

Everything looks like a museum painting. It sure doesn't smell like a museum painting, though. I wrinkle my nose. Who knew horses and cows were so stinky? The most impressive countryside I've seen before this was the school sports field, where the only wildlife were the tubby squirrels, food thieves who left a trail of ripped-up backpacks behind.

I steal a look at Aunt Shell. I wish I knew anything about her. Shell looks a heck of a lot like me, at least in her build. I poke at my stomach. Some kids call me plain old fat, but Dad says I'm solid like my mother was.

Shell drives with her head resting on her hand, her elbow on the open windowsill. She's got purple circles under her eyes. When Aunt Shell woke up yesterday morning, she probably didn't guess she'd be bringing home a kid today.

She glances over and I pretend I was looking past her at a cow grazing in the brown grass. After all, my father told me Aunt Shell had pretty much written off our family a long time ago. Some kind of fight. That's why we hadn't heard from her. But that doesn't explain why Dad wrote her name first on the emergency contact list. Or why she'd agreed to be my guardian. "Here we are." Shell makes a sudden right into what looks like a bunch of trees.

I gasp, but Shell maneuvers the truck expertly through the miniforest. The tires churn and squelch on the gravel. It's darker here, the trees growing close together, and cool. The trees are tall, with no branches close to the ground, and the tops are thick with leaves. "What kind of trees are those?"

Shell looks startled. I haven't spoken since we left the shelter almost an hour ago. "Quaking aspen." Shell slows down. "My father—your grandfather—planted them as a fire- and windbreak. They don't burn easily, like pine."

My grandfather? This was his house, then. The house where my mother grew up. I didn't know. Is it going to be one of those countryside farmhouse mansions like on

TV? Did we have a super-rich relative this whole time? I look at the truck's ripped seats and decide: probably not.

For a second, though, I picture my mom as a little kid, running down this path between the trees. If she'd been around, I bet she would've taken me to visit. We would have had Christmas here every year, and we'd make lots and lots of food. My heart squeezes with an unfamiliar homesickness I've never felt before.

I sniff the air. No more cow stink. I actually do smell some pine, along with dirt and pollen that make my nose itch.

My stomach cramps and makes another noise like a broken garbage disposal. I hope we can stay on this mountain for a while, because I don't think I can take another trip on those roads anytime soon.

Shell seems to be waiting for me to say something else, so I do. "The trees make it too dark." Being good doesn't mean I can't have my own opinion. I press Bear against my stomach to make it feel better.

"You won't think that when the weather heats up." She pulls up to a chain-link fence with a gate in the middle. Two dogs, a golden retriever and a black Lab with a white spot on its chest, run up barking. I shrink into my seat—I don't much like dogs. Not that I've met many. Shell leaves the truck running, gets out, and opens the gate. She drives slowly through, the dogs kicking up a fuss the whole time. "Your turn," she says to me. "Close it, please."

Um, I don't think so. I open the truck door, eyeing the dogs warily. I can smell their not-minty-fresh breath from five feet away. The animals put their front paws on the seat and pant at me. I flinch and put Bear safely out of reach.

"Meet Jacques and Julia." She spells out Jacques for me. "Jacques is the golden, Julia's the black Lab. Let 'em smell you and you'll be fine."

I hold out my leg uncertainly. The dogs nuzzle either side, making me giggle. "Their noses are wet!"

"Your hand." Shell demonstrates. "Make a fist and hold it out. Haven't you ever met a dog before?"

"Only when I didn't want to," I mutter, thinking of the last dog I met on the street, who growled and tried to bite my leg. I offer them my fist. The dogs smell my knuckles, then wag their tails. Phew. I climb out of the truck. The golden jumps up, putting his paws on my chest. I hop back into the truck, scared, and I swear the dog looks like I hurt his feelings. Maybe he was trying to hug me.

"Sit, Jacques!" Shell says in a no-nonsense tone, and Jacques sits, his tail wagging, doggie-grinning.

"Go on, Cady. Get out and close the gate." Shell gestures at the rusty latch. "Jacques's young and kind of crazy. If he jumps, push him away and tell him to sit, like I did." Shell nods at Julia, who waits calmly, her eyes darting from Shell to me. "Good girl, Julia."

I swallow, eyeing Jacques. His tail's wagging so hard it makes his whole bottom half wiggle. I cautiously put my feet down, and Jacques stands.

"Sit!" I say, too quietly, and Jacques bounds forward. "Sit, sit!" I yell, and his paws skitter to a halt. He plants his bottom on the ground, eyeing me. I pet Julia, then Jacques, who slobbers all over my hand. I'm surprised at how soft their fur is. Julia has a lot of it, too, but it's silkier, like a seal's. Then I finally close the squeaky gate, the dogs following me like I'm a famous person and they want my autograph.

These dogs aren't so bad. They're just big. I pet Jacques on the head and Julia looks jealous so I have to pet both of them. "You're kind of cute, but you could use a bath," I tell them. Like me. Ha.

Jacques woofs and bounds away. I get back in the truck and Shell slowly drives around a bend until a building comes into view. The house. There it is.

It's definitely not a castle or cave. It doesn't look like my best friend Jenna's house, which kind of reminds me of a spaceship taking off. This is much plainer. It's two stories with windows that seem to be winking saltily, painted in a peeling creamy yellow. The upper windows stick out past the roofline. A sagging wraparound porch surrounds the lower portion, along with a yard that's mostly dirt with some patchy areas of grass. In another area to the left of the house, chickens peck inside a wire fence. More trees shade the house. To the right and behind the house are neat rows of shorter trees, maybe only eight feet tall, that seem to stretch on for miles, with small fruits hanging from spidery branches.

I want to *oooh* and *ahhh,* but I don't want to get too happy about all this, in case things change again. Which they will. Things always change. Besides, I *want* Dad to come get me. I hug Bear.

"This is my home," Shell says, and I notice she doesn't say *our* home, and my stomach cramps again. She takes the key out of the ignition. "Come on in."

I get out again, hauling my trash bag and Bear.

CHAPTER 3

The entrance hall is a covered porch that's been walled off, lined with racks of shoes and dog leashes and coat hooks. Shell opens a screen door, then a wooden door, and we enter the living room.

The inside of the house is dim and slightly musty smelling. The floorboards are spaced wide enough to drop quarters in between. It reminds me of the houses in Old Town, where we went on a field trip last year. All of them were built more than a hundred years ago. Maybe like this one.

The house slopes, as if we're on a ship that's in rough water. If I put a ball on the floor, it would roll. I'm hoping it won't bug me. Dad always says Mom was of hardy stock, which means she was tough. Like I want to be.

At the thought of Dad, my heart squeezes. I hope he's okay. I'm sure he is. I imagine him lying in a warm bed, covered with white sheets, getting the rest that he needs. I don't really know if that's true, though, because I'm not a hundred percent sure where my father is.

"You're going to be just fine." Those were his last words before they took him. "You're a smart girl and your daddy loves you."

I stomp down that memory and take a deep, shaky breath. I need to focus on Shell. Do what she says. Within reason, anyway. Being here feels disloyal to Dad—he wouldn't want me trusting Shell too much. Anyway, if she really cared about what happened to me, she would have shown up a long time ago.

I concentrate on the house, its maze of rooms. I glimpse hallways and pieces of other spaces. It kind of feels like someone built one small house and then kept on adding random extra parts.

I follow Shell through the living room, past over-stuffed brown couches covered with quilts, bookshelves, and an ancient small TV. My stomach makes yet another weird noise, like it's generally freaked out. I always say my stomach's got a mind of its own, a little pet I carry around in my midsection.

Shell hangs up her purse and keys, then turns to me with a tired sigh. We stand there in the living room for a second, looking at each other.

Since I've never had an aunt or anyone auntlike, I'm not sure what I'm supposed to do now. Thank her? Hug her? No thanks. I'm not a huge hugger. I don't know why, but it makes me feel like I might break apart. Like I'm giving them something that I need to keep for myself, something I need to survive. My friend Jenna will hug everyone and everything. I've seen her hug at least three library books and a potted plant.

Shaking hands is okay, though, so I hold out mine. If my manners are really good, then Shell can't say anything bad about me. "I would like to express my sincerest thanks for coming out today."

Shell looks down at my hand and her mouth twitches. She takes it and I shake it firmly, the way Dad taught me. So the other person knows you mean business. "No problem." Her hand is twice as big as mine. Shell's not a small lady and I'm not a small girl. I'm about the size of a fourteen-year-old, though I'm barely twelve.

Shell's thick black brows meet momentarily. "You do look like your mother."

I already knew that. I don't look much like my dad, who's got stick-skinny legs and a scarecrow kind of body. I stick my chin out. The proud Bennett chin, with a dimple in the middle. Dad says that Bennetts have dignified jaws. "Except for this."

"Yup. That's definitely not a Sanchez chin. We tend to be a bit weak there." She smiles as she says this, but then we're both quiet again. I wonder if Shell's normally a big talker and if she's nervous too. But grown-ups aren't supposed to be nervous, are they? Grown-ups aren't supposed to be lots of things that they are.

"I want to *be* just like her too," I inform Shell. I want to do something with food when I grow up.

Shell gives me a funny look, opens her mouth, then closes it. "Come on. I'll show you where you'll sleep." She turns abruptly and goes to the back of the kitchen, up a flight of steep stairs, Jacques and Julia practically knocking me over with their overenthusiastic tails.

The room's the first one at the top. I follow Aunt Shell inside and set my bag down, taking it all in. The bed's brass, not shiny but dull, with dark spots and a curlicue, swirly kind of thing on the headboard. The quilt's made of all kinds of patterns and materials, cut into not-exact squares. A white nightstand with two drawers holds a lamp shaped like a fat purple urn. A brown wood dresser with six drawers sits against the wall. In a corner of the room, plastic boxes are stacked up to about half my height. The walls are paneled with white-painted horizontal boards.

It's amazing.

I put Bear on the pillow and sit on the bed. It squeaks and I bounce experimentally. It's a big bed, at least as big as the one in the motel room and bigger than the one at Jenna's house. I've never had a whole room to myself. This is smaller than Jenna's bedroom, which had a couch and a gaming system and a big TV, but it's the right size for me. I can't help comparing this house to Jenna's because that's the only other real house I've visited. Shell's house isn't as fancy, but it feels cozier somehow.

I stare up at the pictures on the wall. A black silhouette of a lady in a big skirt getting her hand kissed by a man wearing a long suit jacket. A small oil painting of a mountain. A faded color photo of two young girls and an older couple.

"This is my guest room," Shell says. "Also known as the junk room, until yesterday. I cleaned out most of the stuff, but there are a few odds and ends left." She opens the closet. Half of it's filled with coats and more boxes. It's a little musty smelling. "This half is yours. The dresser drawers are empty. Feel free to use them."

I bounce some more. "Okay." I have enough stuff for one drawer, maybe. I look around the room again, eyeing a spiderweb in the far corner. It's not spooky, though—it's kind of homey. "Was this my mom's room?"

"Yeah. This was our room." Shell's voice cracks.

I try to imagine Shell and my mom as kids. What kinds of toys did they have? Did they draw a line down the middle like sisters in the movies do? Thinking about them makes my chest feel light. "Did you guys get along?"

Shell frowns and glances away. Oops. She doesn't want to talk about my mom. "Yeah. We did." She clears her throat. "Cady." The silence goes on and on. Awkward. There's so much more I want to ask her. *Where's my dad? Is he going to be okay? What's going to happen to me?* But the way she reacted makes me clam up tight, and I'm back to being lonely. Maybe she doesn't want to talk because she knows I'm not going to be here that long.

I need to be tough. "Yes, Aunt Shell?" I cross my arms. I should look her in the eye, the way my teacher told me to, but it's easier to stare at her chin.

"Get settled," she says instead, "and come downstairs so you can have something to eat." She turns and I hear the stairs creaking, the dogs' nails clattering close behind.

Yeah. Shell's definitely not planning on having me here for long. That's okay, though. We're never in one place for more than a couple of days. This will be no different, except Dad's not here.

Besides, he left me alone a lot. He was always busy. Or not feeling well. Anyway, at least I can appreciate that this place is way nicer than where we usually stay.

I open my black trash bag and dig out my stuff. A small photo album goes into the nightstand. I've got five spiral notebooks full of recipes I copied down from TV shows or the internet or even made up by myself. Mostly Italian food. Spaghetti with meatballs and marinara is my favorite. We used to eat that a lot when I was younger and Dad was still friends with people at the restaurant where he used to work. He'd bring me an aluminum pie tin full of it, flecked with fresh basil and garlic.

I also have one notebook for dessert recipes. So far they're for things that can be made either on a hot plate when we have a motel room or in a microwave. I can do a pretty good oatmeal-and-fruit kind of thing with canned peaches and instant oatmeal. Pudding is also no problem—I make one out of hot cocoa mix and cornstarch. The cooked kind that gets that delicious skin on top, which feels so fancy to me. I could eat just pudding skin forever and be happy.

I write all these recipes down for two reasons. One, because my dad told me that's what my mom used to do. She'd write them down and make up her own, too. And two, *just in case*. Just in case Dad and I really do get an apartment. Just in case I get to cook them all.

It's nice to think about both.

I put the notebooks in one of the dresser drawers. My most prized possession, though, is probably my *Culinary Arts Institute Encyclopedic Cookbook*. It's thicker than the Bible. Not only is it full of recipes—though a lot of them are bizarro 1950s recipes, like one for clear Jell-O with hotdogs floating in it—but it also has pages of cooking tips. Like it says what happens if you use too much sugar in a cake (it'll either be heavy, fall, or crumble) or too little (be too pale or tough).

Also, this book belonged to my mother, and to her mother before that. There are all kinds of notes written in the margins. *Add more salt. Cook at 425, not 400.* Things like that. Like that potions book Harry Potter had in *The Half-Blood Prince.* They're tricks someone learned, and I can't wait to see if they'll work.

My mom would have told me the tips herself if she was still around. Dad always says that Mom was the one who made him do stuff, who was the steady one. Without her, of course, he couldn't handle anything, he'd said. Mom was our family glue.

I put this in the drawer, too. It sticks when I try to close it, and I accidentally slam it.

"Meowrrrr."

Under the bedspread, between the pillows, a big white cat head pokes out. It has flame-colored ears and bright blue-violet eyes. Slowly, it wriggles free, leaving a trail of snow-like fur in its wake, then yawns, squinting. Whoa. It's easily the largest cat I've ever seen, the size of a bed pillow, with huge paws. "You are one big cat."

"Mawwww," it whines crankily, and plods across the bed. It has an orange tail and some orange along its body, too. I sit down next to it and it rubs on me as if it knows me. "What's your name, big cat?" I scratch the side of its head.

"Meow." It drools on my fingers. I wipe my hand on my pants.

"That's not a good name." It's got a collar on and I turn the tag over. Tom. "Tom? That's a funny name for a cat."

"Mew-rawr." The cat settles down, purring. I scratch Tom's ears. All my life without any pets and suddenly

I'm in a house with three. But Dad said since we stay in motels, pets wouldn't work. "As soon as I get us set up, Cady," he'd promised me. Everything was "as soon as." I put my hand over Tom's head—my palm barely covers his skull, and I'm pretty sure I'm already in love.

I should write to Jenna. I can still feel her bony arms squeezed around me, see her splotchy face. When I left, her mom practically had to peel her off me with a crowbar. I get out a notebook and open it to a blank page.

Dear Jenna,

I hope you're doing okay. I'm sorry I had to leave before the Reading Buddies party, but I'm sure Ms. Walker will make sure you have a good time. Maybe Anna-Tyler will even read to you, if she can climb down from her high horse! (Ha, ha, right!)

Everything's fine. My Aunt Shell (short for Michelle!) got me. She's so nice! Her house is super cool even though it's in the middle of nowhere. And she has lots of animals. Tom, Jacques, and Julia. Maybe more.

Anyway, don't worry about me. I'll write again soon.

Love, Cady

I draw pictures of all the animals for good measure. I'm not the world's best artist, but you can tell what they are, and that's all that counts.

There. I tear out the letter and fold it into thirds. Now I have to get an envelope from Shell and a stamp. Jenna's mom says she's too young to have an email account, but her mom did give me their home address before I left, and I promised Jenna I'd write. Besides, I've always wanted a pen pal.

CHAPTER 4

I head down to the kitchen, Tom trailing me. It's straight through the living room. The room's bright, with a whole wall of windows. The cupboards are white, old but clean. Yellow linoleum lines the floor and the countertops match. There's a really wide stove top and a double wall oven. The appliances in here look way newer than anything else in the house.

I lean against the doorway, not sure where I should sit. Shell is washing a pan at the sink. "You must be hungry." She rinses the pan, puts it on a drying rack, then rubs her eye. "Want a sandwich to tide you over until dinner? Grilled cheese or ham?"

My stomach makes another noise at *sandwich,* so I figure that's what it wants. "Ham sandwich." Jars of flour and sugar are lined up along the counter and I sort of gasp at how pretty they look. Maybe I can finally try making a cake, if Shell will let me. Or cookies. Or who knows what.

The dogs rush up to the cat, rubbing his fur with their wet noses. Tom jumps onto a kitchen chair and cleans his fur where their noses touched, as if he's highly offended. I can understand that. Getting dog snot on your fur probably feels gross.

"I see you met Thomas Patrick Colicchio, the biggest cat in all of Julian. Well, except for the bobcats." Shell gestures at the table, which is almost entirely covered in stacks of papers, and I sit at the one cleared spot. "Tom's twenty-five pounds, and he stays inside. Too many coyotes."

"Tom—Colicchio?" The name sounds familiar. Then I remember it from an ad during my YouTube recipe watching. "That guy on *Top Chef*?"

"You bet." Shell's mouth turns up. "Jacques and Julia are named after chefs, too—you might not know them. The names were my partner Suzanne's idea. She's a cook for a yacht charter company. She's coming back tonight."

"Suzanne?" This is interesting. I didn't know there were two grown-ups in this deal. I wonder what Suzanne's like.

A plate clatters onto the table. Thick pieces of multigrain bread and slices of ham and cheese. Real ham, not lunch meat ham. "I hope you like tomato," Shell says. "If you don't, you're wrong."

Who tells someone they're wrong for not liking something? "Huh. It's not my absolute favorite, but it's okay." I only like tomatoes in sauces. My mouth waters, though, when the tangy-sweet smell hits my nostrils. I forget about trying to argue and bite into the sandwich. This tomato tastes like the sun, if the sun had a taste and was also juicy. Not like tomatoes from the school cafeteria or on burgers. Mayo balances the saltiness of the ham and cheese. I try to chew slowly, but it's difficult because I'm cramming it into my mouth as fast as I can.

"Milk or water to drink?" She hands me a small package of plain potato chips.

I suppose this means Dr Pepper's not an option. "Milk." My dad lets me have Dr Pepper. Sometimes a liter of soda is cheaper than a liter of bottled water, so then he'll let me get some.

Dad. My throat kind of closes for a second and I stare down at the table. It's painted white wood, chipping on the top.

"Ahem." Shell looks at me expectantly from her post at the kitchen sink. "Manners?"

I blink, still lost in thought about Dad. Then I figure out what Shell wants. "Milk, please," I say finally. Dad doesn't make me say "please." When we eat together at a motel, we're watching TV and eating out of bags. I guess I'll have to treat Shell's house like school. Ms. Walker does like a good *please* and *thank you*.

She pours me a tall glass. I start in on the chips. The dogs crowd around my side, drooling and whining softly.

Tom watches me from the opposite chair, his pupils almost disappearing into his blue-violet eyes in the bright light. "Sorry, pooches. This is all mine." I finish the last bit of my sandwich, patting the crumbs up with my fingertips and eating those, too.

"You were hungry," Shell observes. She opens a white bakery box. "Do you have room for pie?"

Room for pie? Does the sun set in the west? Is my name Cady Madeline Bennett? "Yes, please," I remember to say, and Shell puts another plate down in front of me.

The box says SHELL'S PIE. Shell's Pie? I sit upright like a bolt of lightning hit my bottom. "You have a pie shop?" I try not to sound too impressed, but I don't succeed. Because I definitely am.

Shell nods. "Yep. That's my business."

"What's your business?" another voice says. A woman with short, wispy blond hair, and a tote bag over her shoulder, appears in the doorway.

"It's your aunt Suzanne! I didn't expect you until tonight." Shell hugs her. Suzanne is only as tall as Shell's armpit. She reminds me of some kind of woodland fairy.

"Today's a bit different, yes? I'm here to help, so you can spend more time with Cady." Suzanne's brown eyes crinkle. "I'm so happy you're here." She extends her arms for a hug, and I hold out my hand.

"Pleasure to meet you." I shake her hand as if we're two businesspeople.

"Well. The pleasure's all mine." Suzanne's eyebrows shoot up and she laughs. Her voice is high and lilting where Shell's is low and earthy. "You have a most excellent handshake, Miss Cady."

"Thanks," I say modestly. I poke at the flaky buttery crust with my fork, then lean over it and sniff. "Cinnamon?" I've had cinnamon in oatmeal.

"Yes! And some nutmeg and a couple other things." Suzanne claps her hands. "Oh, she's good, Shell. Do you like to bake, Cady?"

Yes, I want to say. *Yes, let's make something right now.* I look at the canisters of flour and sugar. "I don't know," I admit. "I haven't actually done it."

"Well." Suzanne's eyes sparkle. "We'll have to remedy that, posthaste. We can start with cake. It's easier than pie."

I'd like that. Love that, actually. But I kind of shrug. "Maybe." I figure Suzanne will forget about it anyway. I sink my fork into the pie and scoop a bite into my mouth. The butter and the pastry melt on my tongue. The sour apple goes just right with the cinnamon and nutmeg spices. Forgetting everything else, I shovel the pie in, not pausing between bites until I'm done. Then I gulp my milk. "Do you make other kinds, too?" Because I want to try them all, right now.

Shell takes the plate away. "We make a pretty mean apple cherry."

"Two flavors? That's it?" I haven't been to that many

bakeries, but even the doughnut shop's got more varieties than that.

Suzanne laughs again, clapping her hand over her mouth. "See? I've been saying that *forever*. Listen to Cady, Shell. She's got you pegged."

"I do those two better than everyone else." Shell's mouth turns down and I stare at my plate. Have I offended her? But Suzanne's still giggling, so it can't be all that bad.

"Oh, you do those the best. But we should do more." Suzanne raises her brows. "In fact, the bike shop next door is available. It would make a great extra space. It's not too big."

"Yeah, yeah, yeah. We're not ready for that." Shell shoots me a tired smile. "Cady, why don't you go out and play for a little while? Just be back when it starts getting dark."

"Like at sunset?" I frown. I look out toward Shell's vast property, stretching farther than I can see, and think of the bobcats and coyotes Shell mentioned. "Are there mountain lions and bears too?"

I'm only half-serious, but Shell cocks her head as she considers my question. "Some people saw a black bear a few years ago, so the answer is maybe on those. They're not native to the county, but a few made their way here. Cougars and coyotes will be out after you come home. Bobcats pretty much leave you alone. You should watch out for rattlesnakes, though."

"Rattlesnakes?" I hear the quiver in my voice. "What do those look like?"

"You know. They're the ones with a rattle on their tails," Shell says dryly. "I thought you grew up in San Diego."

I blush, look at my feet. "I don't go around in the *great outdoors*."

Suzanne makes a tsking noise at Shell. "Okay," Shell says, her tone gentler. "They won't bother you if you don't bother them. But you still have to look out, because they'll bite if they're scared." Shell sort of sighs and moves her neck so it cracks. "Now, Cady, I know you just got here, but I'm almost a one-woman operation. I have got to pay these invoices or there will be no pies tomorrow."

Watching them pay bills doesn't sound very exciting. "How far can I go?" I stick my hands into my armpits.

"As far as you can go and be back when the sun starts setting." Shell keeps her head down.

As far as I can go. I have no idea what distance that might be.

CHAPTER 5

Jacques and Julia meet me in the yard, tails beating against each other. "I don't have any treats. You might as well stay here," I tell them, but they pant, their chocolate eyes shining, and I shrug and let them follow. Are they supposed to be on leashes? I guess not, since this is Shell's property.

It's cooling off, with a breeze whipping up that feels good but also makes me shiver a little. I decide to do a loop of the whole property, beginning with the chicken run. The chicken-wire fence is about eight feet high, with an entrance gate framed in wood at one end. A big coop sits at the other. The birds, in various shades of red or white and everything in between, squawk and run up to me on their spindly legs, like cotton candy balls teetering on toothpicks. They must think I have food, too. Once the chickens figure out I have nothing, they turn around and go back to pecking the dirt. "Hey, birds."

Beyond the coop are several large garden beds, built

on raised wood and covered in black netting, to keep out critters. I pop off a strawberry and put it in my mouth. The sweet tartness of it makes me tear up. I swipe at my eyes and eat another, and then three more. I could eat a whole bushel of these, but I'd better not. Shell might miss them.

I walk the perimeter of the boxes. They're filled with rich black soil, not the dead brown dirt of the yard. Soaker hoses entwine the plants. Beans climb up poles, and purple-black eggplants and dark green cucumbers and zucchini hang off their bushes. Giant tomatoes, supported by cone-shaped wire cages almost as tall as I am. One box contains only herbs—I recognize basil, cilantro, and mint. Another's filled with different types of lettuce, covered with a shade cloth. Six boxes in all.

Sitting on the herb-box ledge, I lean over, close my eyes, and inhale. I don't know the names for all of these plants. I don't even know whether I've eaten all of them. I just know they smell awfully good.

"Am I in heaven?" I ask the dogs, and they stop panting and look at me as if they're seriously pondering my question. I wonder why I was ever afraid of them.

I wish Dad could see all this. Maybe he could come live here, too. He can't hate Shell that much if he put her on my emergency form, can he? Maybe they made up and they forgot to tell me. That could be totally possible with Dad.

He could work in her pie shop. I can imagine him

mixing dough, rolling out crusts. I bet Shell would let him. She seems, if not crazy rich, at least a little bit rich, with a house and a pie shop and all this land.

Where's Dad now? The question I haven't let myself think about for too long seeps into my head. I push it away again.

I stand up off the ground in Aunt Shell's garden and take a deep, cleansing breath, exactly the way the PE teacher told us to when she taught us yoga. In through the nose, out through the mouth. Filling my lungs. I do this until the churning, upset feeling I've stirred up settles, dirt at the bottom of a clear pool. "There's no changing things," Dad would tell me. "Onward and upward." I stand completely still for a moment, my eyes closed, feeling the warmth of the sun on my face. Bees buzz in the distance and birds trill their songs. The dogs pant and pace. I breathe deeply some more, until my lungs hurt.

"Ruff," Julia barks. I open my eyes and she's standing there wagging her tail. She bows down like she wants to play. *"Woof!"*

Jacques dances around her, nipping at her bottom. Julia returns the favor, and they wrestle for a second in an endless circle of fur and excited yips. I laugh—I've never seen dogs do this before. Then Julia breaks away and romps toward the orchard, Jacques following.

I follow them and explore that area next. The branches

hang low, the beginnings of apples on them, tiny green nubs. Black soaker hoses touch the base of each, tracing the entire grove.

To the left of the orchard the land turns wild, a jumble of bushes and trees. I wonder where Aunt Shell's property ends and if I'm supposed to go beyond the apple orchard. Nobody said. It must be fine. I head that way.

I hear a rustle in the shrubs. A bird? A dog? I look down at Jacques and Julia to see if they're alarmed—aren't animals supposed to be protective or something? But they're eyeing a squirrel. *"Woof woof woof!"*

Boom. They go after the squirrel, who of course is long gone by the time they get to it. They chase its scent anyway, heading out the orchard's rear and disappearing into a grassy yellow field beyond.

"Come back!" What if they disappear, and Aunt Shell is really mad at me for losing her dogs? Not to mention, I like them. My stomach does a drumbeat of panic. "Jacques! Julia! Get back here!"

The grass is chest high and goes on for a long time. Beyond that, a forest studs a hill. I have to find the dogs. What if they run into a bear? I wonder if bears are afraid of dogs. I'll have to look that up.

The grass makes me itchy. The wind moves the stalks, the seedpods on top making soft rattling noises. Is this grass or some kind of wheat? I sure don't know. I hit the tops of the stalks with my hand. They crackle.

"Jacques! Julia!" I try to whistle, but I'm not good at it so it sounds like a weak balloon letting out air. I stand still, searching for the dogs in the meadow. The grass moves in a hollow wake, as if there's an invisible boat on top of it. That's where the dogs are. "Here, boy! Here, girl!" I call, but they keep going. "Come back at once!" I yell, trying to sound commanding, like Aunt Shell said, but still they ignore me. I run blindly through the grass toward them.

I feel it before I hear it. My foot comes down on something solid and round. Something that's not wood but has some give. Something kind of spongy, but harder than that.

Something alive. I freeze in place, my body knowing what to do even if my mind has no idea.

There's a rattle, like the rattle of the grass. Only louder.

I look down and see a shiny tan hose covered in darker brown diamond shapes. *Snake,* my mind tells me. That's a snake. I've heard about blood turning cold, and I'm pretty sure that's what mine does.

What do I do? I can't keep standing on it. Slowly I take my foot off the snake's body and it coils itself into an S, its triangular head opening in a hiss as it rears back to strike.

Then something big bounds out of the grass, coming right at me. I scream.

Ooof! A hard blow hits my stomach and I fall backward, the wind knocked out of me. I open my mouth, gasping for air that won't come. What just happened? I keep my eyes screwed tightly shut, in case it's a bear. Play dead—that's what you're supposed to do, I think. I don't actually know. Another thing to Google later, if I survive.

Then Jacques and Julia are licking my face—I hope it's them, anyway; my eyes are still shut—and I hear a boy's voice. "It's only a gopher snake," he says. "I thought it was a rattler too, for a second. Sorry I knocked you over."

I reluctantly open my eyes. The sun seems too bright and the world spins for a moment before it mostly rights itself. I take a deep breath, the oxygen filling my lungs as if I've never breathed air before.

The boy sits next to me, casually petting the dogs. They lick his face and he scratches their chests, cooing at them. "Jacques and Julia, how are my puppies? What a good boy and girl." He barks and the dogs bark back.

I shake my head to get rid of the rest of the dizziness, which makes it worse. "How . . . how do you know?" I ask. To my amazement, my voice doesn't quaver as much as I think it will.

"Glossy body. Head not triangular." He points at the snake slithering out of our sight, only the end of its tail visible.

"That head was definitely a triangle." I squint at the animal, trying to remember.

"They imitate rattlers, so they puff their heads out. Believe me, if you saw them next to each other, you'd be able to tell the difference. But better to be safe than sorry." The boy pushes his dark, curly hair back so it poofs out all over his head in a cloud. He shoots me a dimpled smile, showing white teeth in his bronzed face. "Mostly, though, I can tell it's not a rattler because it has no rattle."

I feel dumber than I did when I forgot how to simplify mixed fractions. "It rattled!"

"It pretended because you scared it. You're lucky it didn't bite you. It's not poisonous, but man, it still hurts. Believe me, I know." He holds up a shorts-clad leg. "One got me in the calf right there." He points.

I squint. His skin is smooth. "There's not even a scar. What are you showing me?"

He lowers his leg, looking embarrassed. "There is so a scar. I can see it. Just not in this light."

I snort.

"I'm Jesús," he says now. *Hay-zeus.* "But everyone calls me Jay. Jay Morales."

Morales. I wonder if his grandpa is also from Mexico, like mine. I try to figure out what kind of kid he is. My school has a lot of Hispanic kids, some who wear fancy designer clothes whose parents drive Mercedes, and some who wear thrift store clothes and ride there on the bus. I can't tell which group Jay's in. Maybe he's in neither group, like me. Just because kids look kind of the same doesn't mean we're automatically friends.

"I'm Cady Bennett. I'm, um, staying with my aunt Shell."

"I know." Jay squints at me from under his brows. "My mother works for her. We heard the whole story."

My cheeks go hot and I really wish I were molten lava, so I could melt into the earth's core and never be seen again. "Oh."

Jay stands and offers me his hand. "I can show you around if you want."

I almost don't take his hand. I can stand up by myself, thanks very much. Instead, I don't know why, I reach up. He grabs my hand and hauls me up as he steps backward. Suddenly I'm standing. "Thanks. What are we going to see?"

He grins. "How 'bout everything?" He turns and runs.

I follow, watching for snakes this time.

CHAPTER 6

We head under a canopy of tree branches and emerge into a different field. A couple of old dead trees stand guard nearby, with other old logs scattered around. Cows graze here, chewing with morose expressions. The dogs dart around, sniffing everything. "This is parkland," Jay says. "Your aunt's property is right against it. Basically there's nothing but wilderness behind us."

"So these cows aren't hers?" I pant. I hope Jay doesn't run all the time.

"Nah, they belong to other farmers who pay the park to let them graze." He points vaguely to the east. "There's a ranch that way, with a gate. The rancher opens it so the cows come out here." The cows eye us warily. The closest one to us has black spots in a sort of U-shaped pattern and a brown calf under her. The dogs bark and Jacques pretends to rush at one, and they skitter back.

"Quiet! Lie down!" Jay commands them in a

deeper-than-usual voice, and the dogs reluctantly settle to the ground. "They make the cows nervous." Jay produces an apple from his pocket and squats. "Here, Ida. That's what I call her. I don't know if that's her real name. She probably doesn't have one." He shrugs. "I'm pretty sure farmers don't name their cows if they're going to, you know, eat them later."

Ida wobbles forward on her skinny calf legs. She takes the apple from Jay's hand and nuzzles him. I hold out my hand. "I bet if the farmers have kids, the kids name all the animals."

"Probably. But could you eat something you'd named?"

"If I were hungry enough, I guess." I don't tell him I've definitely been hungry enough.

"That's a good point." Jay nods.

Ida's eyes are huge. I scratch under her chin. Suddenly Ida's mother moos forcefully and steps forward. I automatically back off. "Why's she making that sound?"

"You're a stranger. She doesn't trust you." Jay hands me an apple. "Don't worry. She will. Give her this."

I hold out the apple. Who knew cows could be like people? Like my dad, who never trusts anyone. I remember the school principal asking me how long it had been like this. How long we had been sleeping in the van or in motels and with Dad "under the influence."

Since I was five. Seven years.

He hadn't always been like that. Back before my mom died, I remember my dad was somewhat normal.

Sure, he slept a lot back then, too. But he'd had a job in a restaurant downtown, a pretty fancy place, doing prep work for the chef—mostly chopping vegetables, from the way he tells it. My mother had been the one on the rise, working her way from a busser to the *rôtisseur*—or roaster—the cook that prepares meats. *Row-TIS-yeur.* I like saying that word.

Dad told me stories of my mother and the wonderful meats she'd prepare for us. How I'm so big and strong because she fed me lots of delicious roasts while she was pregnant. And how the pastry chef, Mom's friend, would send her home with lots of pies and cakes.

This explains why I like food so much. It runs in the family.

If Mom were alive, none of this would have happened. She'd be a chef at a fancy restaurant and we'd have a place to live and everything would be perfectly fine.

The cow takes the apple from my hand and crunches, spraying juice and apple bits all over my arm. "Do you have any brothers and sisters?" Jay asks.

I shake my head.

"Lucky. I've got two sisters."

Envy tugs at me. "I wish I had a sister." Like Jenna. Then again, if Jenna were my sister, I'd be pretty worried about feeding her, so maybe it's best that I'm an only child.

Jay rolls his eyes. "Well. The little one's all right, mostly. But my older one—she's like the Final Boss in a game—practically undefeatable and knows everything."

I laugh. "Is she also a giant monster or something?"

"Pretty much." Jay produces another apple, feeding it to the cow. "Did you know Julian is the only place in San Diego County where apples grow?" he says. "Apples need more than three hundred hours of temperatures below forty-five degrees."

"That's not true, actually. Granny Smith apples don't need so many days." I can't keep the smug note out of my voice. I know things too, even if I don't know much about snakes. "Many species of apples don't require that much low-chill." We learned it in science this year.

Jay blinks slowly. "But they grow better with colder days. Did you know Julian's the apple pie capital of San Diego County?" He sounds as if he's personally responsible for the title. "And Shell's Pie is the best."

My mouth waters, remembering the pie. "I've only ever had her pie, but I believe it."

"Well." Jay gets up. "We'll definitely have to go on a pie-tasting tour of Julian so you *know* it."

"That sounds fantastic." It does. I wouldn't mind going on a pie-tasting tour right this second. We continue across the fields. "So how long has your mom worked for Aunt Shell?"

"Basically forever." He stops moving suddenly and I run into him. He's so solid I bounce right off his back.

"Sorry," I say awkwardly. He might be the first boy my age I've ever met who's taller than me.

Jay smiles. "You know what?"

I shake my head.

"I've never met anyone from outside who knows about apples. You're pretty cool, Cady Bennett."

I have to turn my face away so he won't see the beginnings of a smile. Maybe he's like me—not really in any group. Maybe he and I can be friends. "Well, everyone at my school knows about apples because of science class, so you'd have to be friends with all of them, too." My voice sounds super gruff, so gruff he might change his mind and run home.

Jay laughs, though. "I doubt it."

I meet his eyes this time and his gaze is steady. By now, I know when people are telling me the truth. I can tell Jay's not lying like Anna-Tyler. I swallow. *But maybe this time it's okay,* a voice inside me says. *It's safer to say no,* I tell it.

The sky's beginning to turn a soft shade of pink. Time to go back to Shell's. I start running and so do Jacques and Julia, who leap up at me as if I'm playing. "I've got to get back."

"You coming to the pie shop tomorrow morning?" Jay calls after me.

I raise my hands up, not turning, secretly happy. But I don't want him to think I'm too enthusiastic, in case he really doesn't like me that much. "Maybe. Maybe not." I'll be there even if I have to hitchhike.

CHAPTER 7

We eat a delicious meal Suzanne calls pasta alla Shell (mini pasta shells with a creamy sauce, bacon bits, and asparagus). Suzanne asks me some of those "getting to know you" questions that grown-ups ask. "How do you like school? What's your favorite subject?"

Suzanne is way too eager. She reminds me of a morning TV person, and also of a social worker, and I haven't had a good experience with those. I want to believe Suzanne's being sincere. I really do. But I can't. I don't want to trust her and Shell because if I get disappointed again, I don't think I can handle it. None of this matters, though, because in the end, I'll be back with Dad. And everything will be like how it was.

I say as little as possible. "School's okay. I don't know."

"What do you like to do?" Suzanne opens her eyes big like she's super-duper interested in my answer. *Nobody's* that interested in what anyone likes to do.

"I don't know." I've eaten all the pasta on my plate. I wonder if I can get seconds.

"Do you know any other phrases besides *I don't know*?" Shell points at the salad bowl. "Eat some greens and then you can get more pasta."

I stare at the salad. This doesn't look like any kind of lettuce I've ever eaten. There are leaves that look jagged, leaves that are kind of ruffled, and red-purple leaves that I think are red cabbage. At school, you get the whitish kind that comes on burgers. "Why is it all those different colors?"

"It's called spring mix. It's arugula, baby spinach, baby romaine, baby kale, frisée." Suzanne says it like *free-ZAY* and picks up the ruffled one. "And this one is radicchio." *Ra-dee-kee-oh.* She points at the red-purple piece that looks like cabbage.

"What's the kind that's almost white, then?" I regret asking as soon as I say it because Suzanne smiles and straightens up like she's ready to give me a lecture in Lettuce 101.

"You're probably talking about iceberg. That has almost no nutritional value, so we usually don't eat it. It's almost all water." Suzanne spoons some greens onto my plate. "These are superfoods chock-full of the good stuff. Go ahead. I'll let you drown it in dressing. What kind would you like? We have ranch, Thousand Island, Russian, honey Dijon . . ." Suzanne leaps up to the refrigerator. "I didn't know what you like, so I got everything."

"None." I like ranch, but I want her to leave me alone.

Suzanne sits, disappointed.

I pick up the radicchio and chew. It's really bitter. I swallow that and go on to the next leaf. Everything but the spinach tastes pretty awful. Now I wish I'd taken the dressing, but I've already turned that down, so I'm sticking to what I said. I take a big gulp of milk.

"You'll get used to the taste." Shell squints at my salad. "Sure you don't want dressing?"

"No thanks."

"It's okay to change your mind."

"I'm fine."

"Cady. Just get the salad dressing." Shell leans over her plate. "That kind of stubbornness is only going to hurt yourself. Not us."

I shovel the rest of the greens into my mouth. "I'm good." I'll show her.

Suzanne snorts, then starts giggling.

"What?" Shell says.

"*You're* lecturing about stubbornness." Suzanne works herself into a peal of laughter. "Oh my goodness. That's the funniest thing I've heard all year."

Shell's lips twitch. "Hey. Do as I say, not as I do."

Suzanne laughing makes me want to giggle, but I control myself into a stone mask. I point to my empty plate. Shell nods. I dump the rest of the pasta onto my plate and take my huge mound of food back to the table, to Suzanne's open mouth and Shell's raised brows. And I eat every bit.

After dinner, I help clear the table and Suzanne shows me how to load the dishwasher, and then I go upstairs to take a hot shower.

For the first time in forever, my nerves stop jangling. I liked looking around Shell's land and hanging out with Jay. Maybe—this tiny bit of hope springs up—maybe he can be a friend. Maybe the pie shop will be the greatest place ever. Maybe I'll be the best pie maker ever born.

I'll try not to expect too much, though. That way I can never be disappointed. Anyway, this is all temporary, I remind myself.

I put on a fluffy white robe that somebody left in the bathroom, digging around my drawers for some cleanish clothes. Which I don't have. I think again about Mom growing up here. Wouldn't Dad like to see this room? He misses her so much.

This all started three days ago, during lunch. I had to sit next to Anna-Tyler, who was texting somebody about being stuck next to *stinky Cady Bennett*. Whatever. I decided to ignore Anna-Tyler as hard as she was ignoring me.

I waved to Jenna at the next table over. She's in

second grade and I'm in fifth, but I call her my Sister from Another Mother.

Other kids think it's weird that Jenna's my best friend since I'm so much older. But no matter how many lectures Ms. Walker gives about "being kind to *everyone*," most kids either act like Anna-Tyler or ignore me. At recess, when other kids are playing games, I always say I want to read or help Ms. Walker. It's because even if kids let me into their kickball games, nobody says a word.

Two years ago, when Jenna got assigned to me, I thought she'd ask for a different reading buddy. I sat on the floor scowling as she bounced up to me with the *Found* book in her hand. But Jenna only said, "Yay, I got Cady!" And then I couldn't help but be happy around her.

Jenna waved back. "Reading buddy party after lunch!" she yelled. The other second graders dwarfed her like redwood trees next to a sapling.

Jenna's small and frail because she has celiac disease. What this means is she can't have wheat. She can't even eat from a pan that cooked wheat once before. It'll make her sick, scrape up her insides like a piece of rough sandpaper on smooth wood. She might barf, or worse. She tells me she can only eat things made in a gluten-free kitchen, where everything's kept separate from the regular ingredients and utensils.

I scooped my dessert, half-frozen blueberries, into a baggie the girl next to me had discarded and pocketed it for later. Time for recess. I raised my hand to be excused.

I stood. The boy next to Jenna was standing up, too—that was weird. He was holding something by her head. I thought they were playing. I hoped they were playing.

Then I heard Jenna's voice. I can always hear Jenna in a crowd, because a) she's my best friend, and b) her voice is like a flute in an orchestra of off-key trombones. "Stop it!"

The boy shoved a wadded-up piece of bread against Jenna's mouth, holding her head with the other hand. It was this kid who'd said Jenna made up her disease. She shoved at him, but Jenna weighs about as much as a cat, so he didn't move.

Before I could think it through, I lunged over and grabbed the boy by his shirt, lifting him clean off the bench. I was the second-biggest kid at this school, not only because I actually should be in sixth grade, not fifth. He dropped the bread, Jenna cried, and the next thing I knew I was in the principal's office.

The principal was only slightly surprised to see me. I've gotten into plenty of fights at school over the years. Most of the time other people start them by saying mean stuff or trying to hurt me, but a few times, I admit, I could've walked away.

Jenna told her what happened, so I didn't get into

trouble. But they wanted me to go home for the rest of the day and called my dad.

While I sat in the office waiting, a great creaking and clacking and clattering sounded outside. The principal and Jenna's mom and the office ladies all looked out the window. "Is that the trash truck?" Jenna's mom asked.

I almost crawled under the chair. Of course it wasn't the trash truck. I knew exactly who it was. Dad, in the legendary van.

See, it was not an ordinary van, though it used to be. Once upon a time, it was a regular big white delivery van, until Dad got hold of it. Now it's completely painted, covered in red and black words. JESUS SAVES. PRAISE THE LORD. Quotes from the Bible and things like REPENT, SINNERS. Some words are big, some are so tiny you have to stand right next to the vehicle to read it all.

And though it had all those quotes on it, we never went to church. The churches we tried were never strict enough for him. We prayed and read from the Bible as Dad told me his theories on what the stories meant, his mind scrambling like eggs in a too-hot pan. It never made sense, and it scared me.

I can't tell you how many times people have vandalized the van. The dirty looks we get when we drive around. The kids laughing at me or shaking their heads, saying, *I'm glad I'm not Cady.*

Dad carefully locked it up, as if anyone would want to steal it, and ambled up the walkway to the office. His thick glasses hid his watery eyes, and his skin shone red brown from all the time he spends in the sun. I flinched at how skinny he'd become this year, but his thin hair was combed, and he'd tucked his stained denim shirt neatly. That, at least, was good. I relaxed.

He slammed the door open, then smacked the counter with both palms. "What's this going on around here?" He was having trouble moving and talking. I could smell the sour scent of him.

Dad leaned over and put his head on the counter. "Mr. Bennett?" the secretary said. But he was asleep standing up, drool coming out of the corner of his mouth. The secretaries gave each other alarmed looks.

I knew I'd picked the worst possible time to get into trouble. Whatever happened next was not going to be good.

And it was all my fault.

Somebody knocks on the door. "Wait!" I stand up and retighten the belt on my robe before I open the door. Suzanne, holding a hair dryer and flowered cotton pajamas. I stand aside so she can come in.

"I think these will fit. Do you need anything else?" Suzanne puts the pajamas on the bed and plugs in the dryer. "You can keep this up here." She turns it on and off. "This hot setting works best."

"I like to let my hair air-dry." Most motels have hair dryers that don't work well. I'm not sure how to use one.

Suzanne tsks. "I don't want you catching a cold."

"That's not how you get colds." I cross my arms. Another thing we learned in science. Colds come from viruses, not from actually getting a chill. "A common misconception," Ms. Walker had said. Seems like lots of people have common misconceptions about lots of things.

"But your immunity can get lowered that way, so let's play it safe." Suzanne turns on the dryer again and pats the quilt. "Let me help you."

I reluctantly sit on the bed with my back to her. It feels weird to have someone else touching my head, and I keep flinching. But Suzanne has a soft touch, and pretty soon I relax as the warm air blasts my scalp. Tom purrs away on the bed, not at all afraid of the noise.

Suzanne turns it off and produces a brush. "Has this happened before, sweetie?" She works the bristles through my hair—she's untangled most of it with her fingers so it doesn't pull. She's good at working with long hair for someone with such short hair.

"Yes, I have brushed before." I know she's talking about Dad, but I don't really want to get into it. I concentrate on moving my finger in front of the cat, who pats at it with a soft paw.

Suzanne chuckles. "It's okay if you're not ready to discuss it." Tom gets up and rubs his head against my hand, demanding petting. I tickle under his chin. "Just know I'm here for you."

I swallow what feels like a small pebble. "No, it's not the first time." My voice is so quiet I can barely hear it. When I was six, and we still had an apartment, Dad didn't come home one evening. I was alone until the next afternoon, waiting for him, until a social worker came instead and took me to a foster home. That was the most scared I've ever been.

"Did he leave you alone a lot?" Suzanne keeps brushing in the same rhythm as my Tom petting.

"Yeah." There was another time, too, at my old school, when Dad never came to pick me up. I sat on the curb until it was dark and some parent going to a PTA meeting asked if I needed help, and the next thing I knew, I was at a foster home.

I move away from Suzanne. At least I know I can take care of myself no matter what. "But it's fine." I don't want her to start crying over me or something. And hey, I'm alive, aren't I? So how bad could it have been?

Suzanne goes to the door, pausing to give me a searching look. "Come downstairs and watch TV with us after you put on your PJs."

I nod, shaking myself out of the memories. I put on the soft, clean-smelling pajamas and wrap the fuzzy robe around me again. Wearing the robe's practically like cuddling one of the dogs.

I might as well go watch TV. It's too early for bed, and the shower made me hungry. I rush down the stairs. "Am I allowed to have a snack?"

Suzanne squints at me like I'm speaking Russian. "Of course! Take whatever you want. Always."

I go into the kitchen, Suzanne ahead of me. She opens the pantry. "I went to Costco when I found out you were coming." Inside are huge boxes of granola bars, Pop-Tarts, a big bag of popped popcorn, three kinds of chips, and Oreos. "Plus there's fresh fruit and veggies." She flits around pointing to each item as if she's a fairy godmother pointing with her wand. And that's what she feels like to me.

I'm so overwhelmed that for a few moments, I just stand there.

"Isn't this any good?" Suzanne asks. "Do you see something you like?"

"It's okay." I want to eat everything right now.

"Well, grab whatever you like." Suzanne pats me on the shoulder. "It's all for you." She goes back into the living room.

I look to make sure nobody's watching. Then I get three apples, a handful of granola bars, and two cans of black beans and take them upstairs. I put the food in the dresser drawer, covering it with clothes, my heart pounding the whole time.

I'm doing this just in case. Just in case Dad magically

shows up. Just in case something happens and I have to leave. I definitely don't want to explain myself to Suzanne or Shell. I know they'd tell me I don't need to hide food. Or maybe they'd even tell me I was stealing.

But it makes me feel safer. And relieved, like I got a good grade on a test I thought I'd fail. I'll only hide a little bit at a time, until I have enough to last for a month or two.

I run back down and grab a bag of premade sour-cream-and-onion popcorn and a tall glass of water. Nobody says anything. Phew.

After I settle down into a Shell-shaped divot on the overstuffed couch, Jacques and Julia lie at my feet, and Tom sits beside me.

"They've adopted you into their pack." Suzanne comes into the living room.

I shrug. "They probably like me because I gave them some of my dinner." But I'm secretly pleased. A pack is close to a family. I scratch Tom's chin, which makes Julia huff jealously, so I pet her with my foot and Jacques with my other foot. Or they like me because I'm a sucker for petting them.

"What kind of shows do you like to watch?" Suzanne shows me the remote buttons to get to the TV menu.

"Cooking. And, um, nature documentaries." I like *SpongeBob SquarePants,* but I want Suzanne to think I'm mature.

"Let's see what's on Food Network." Suzanne reaches out as if to ruffle my hair, but I pull away. I'm not one of the dogs. She puts her hands in her lap. "I'm sorry we were busy today. We're really glad you're here. There's just . . . a lot going on with the shop right now. Stuff we *have* to deal with."

"It's fine." I don't tell her I'd rather not talk, because it'd probably hurt her feelings. Shell and Suzanne only took me in because they *had* to. I'll try not to bother them while I'm here.

The show that's on now isn't too interesting. Some kind of grocery store food competition. If I were on that show, I'd fill up my cart and run out the door. I'd also lose the contest because I don't know where anything is in a grocery store. My dad and I mostly shop at gas stations.

My stomach wobbles. I cross my arms over it. "Suzanne?" My voice is smallish. I try to speak up. "Where's my dad?"

I want the truth. Instead she gives me the same answer the other adults have. "I don't know right now, but I do know he's getting the help he needs."

I focus on the grocery game. If I look at an actual human person, I might start crying. "Okay. How long do I have to stay here?"

"I don't know."

So it's the same not-real answer. Typical. My anger

makes those bubbling tears dry up. I change the channel. "This show is boring."

She reaches out as though she's going to pat my knee and then thinks better of it. I don't meet her eyes, but I know they're oozing with sympathy. *Poor Cady.* I hate that.

Suzanne's voice is upbeat. "Try not to worry, okay? Everything's going to be fine."

I feel a little bad for her then. Suzanne reminds me of my teacher, Ms. Walker. A really nice person. I look up at her. "Thank you for dinner. It was delicious." I should have said it at the table, but I didn't think of it. I guess I was too busy being sorry for myself.

Suzanne holds her hand over her heart. "You're welcome. Oh, that makes me happy."

She's not going to cry just because I thanked her, is she? Embarrassed, I turn up the volume.

I scroll down the DVR list. They've saved a bunch of episodes of a show called *The Great British Bake Off* from the BBC. The British Broadcasting Company. *Twelve amateur bakers are on a quest to be named the U.K.'s best baker.* Baking? I want to watch that. I scroll down to the oldest one on the list and hit play. Season six, episode six.

Shell appears with a canvas bag. "Do you mind if I sit there, Cady?"

Suzanne makes a small noise.

“It’s the only place I can put my feet up so my back doesn’t hurt,” Shell says. “I need the arm.”

“I didn’t say a word,” Suzanne says.

“You made a noise.”

I scoot over. “It’s fine.” That explains the Shell-shaped divot. She sure is particular about stuff. I hope I can do everything correctly. Where to sit. To say “please.” It’s a lot to remember.

Shell takes out a long pair of wooden knitting needles and perches a pair of reading glasses on the tip of her nose. Part of something forest green hangs off the end—a sweater or a scarf—it has no shape yet. “This is my favorite competition show.” The needles fly as Shell works. “You should watch ‘Bread Week.’ You’d never guess bread could be sculpted into, like, the head of a lion.” Shell seems way more relaxed with this show on TV and her knitting needles in her hands.

Two perky British ladies named Mel and Sue start talking and a huge white tent appears on the greenest green lawn I’ve ever seen, surrounded by trees and baa-ing sheep. It’s a circus. A *baking* circus. I sit up, taking my feet off the dogs.

The contestants are all ages and genders and sizes and races, which is pretty cool. This week, the challenge is pastries. The first part is the Signature Bake—they all have to make something called a “frangipane with shortbread pastry.” *FRAN-gee-pane.*

I lean forward. "That seriously just looks like a tart to me." They're all topped with fruit and have something they call a shortbread crust.

"Frangipane has an almond cream filling." Shell's fingers continue.

"And this first challenge is the one they get to practice at home," Suzanne adds. "Thus, the term 'Signature.'"

We each say which frangipane looks the best to us. I forget to pretend like I don't care about anything. This show is too interesting. I eat my popcorn.

The frangipane made by the contestant named Nadiya looks good to me. It's got pears and something called Rong tea in it, plus bay leaf.

"What's a bay leaf?" I say.

"I love how she combines the sweet and savory," Suzanne says. She gets up and returns with a packet of leaves. "This is bay."

I smell it. It's familiar. "What do you usually use it for?"

"You cook it with soups and sauces. But you don't eat the leaves—you just want the flavor." Suzanne crumbles one under my nose. It definitely doesn't smell sweet, but sort of like eucalyptus, which grows all over San Diego. "Nadiya's my favorite, too."

The judges are two more British people named Paul Hollywood and Mary Berry. The name Mary Berry sounds musical and I doubt it's made-up, but "Paul

Hollywood" most definitely is made-up. He has grayish hair and bright blue eyes and seems slightly grumpy for no reason. I can't tell how old he is—pretty old, but younger than Mary Berry.

Mary Berry has a nice grandmotherly smile. Her hair is very neat and smoothed into a blond bob. She reminds me of the librarian who erased all my late fines because she said she wanted me to read, so I automatically love her.

It's time for the judges to try the frangipane. I hold my breath. Now's the part where the judges will rip into all of them. That's what usually happens on competition shows. Nadiya's worried about her bottom not being done. Mary Berry will yell at her. Paul Hollywood will throw the pastry on the floor and stomp on it. Nadiya will cry.

I hate this part. I get ready to cover my eyes.

The judges eat Nadiya's frangipane. They compliment her pear arrangement, the flavors. Then Mary pokes at it with her fork. "It's got a bit of a soggy bottom," she says. And that's it.

Then Paul adds, "Your pastry's underdone."

The "presenters," Mel and Sue, comment on everything and go around and talk to the bakers as they're working. These ladies do things like stealing contestants' bowls and licking them clean, or pocketing extra chocolate for later, as if they're two kitchen elves. The kind of stuff I'd probably do.

Paul Hollywood usually tells them exactly what's wrong, but Mary Berry always finds something positive to say, no matter what. "It just didn't work for her today," she says about one baker, instead of saying that lady had no talent. It's like she believes in them.

I wish Mary Berry were my grandma.

One of the contestants, Alvin, made a plum frangipane that didn't turn out so great. They interview him afterward. He says, "Failure is not an option. You need to move on."

I think if it were me, I might have run away.

In *The Great British Bake Off* tent, everything is clean. Everybody helps each other, even though they're in a contest. They always have lots of treats to eat.

Most important, everything is fair. Not like the real world. I want to live *there*.

We watch the end of the show in silence. I notice Shell and I both make noises at the same parts, either a chuckle or little grunts. I wonder how else we're alike. Suzanne's head tilts back as she falls asleep.

"You ready for bed, Cady?" Shell yawns. It's nine already.

"Do I have to?" I decide I'm going to watch all of the episodes. Who knows when I'll have the chance again?

"I suppose not. You don't have school tomorrow, but you do have the work packet to do."

"It'll take me like five minutes to do that whole packet." I'm only half joking. Schoolwork is a lot easier to get done without a bunch of kids making noise.

"Don't stay up too late. Turn out the light when you're done." Shell nudges Suzanne awake.

"Good night, Cady. I'm leaving early, so I may not see you in the morning." Suzanne bends down like she's planning to give me a kiss, but I lean away and she stops.

"Good night," I say. Who knows how late *too late* is? It could mean *all night*. Suzanne and Shell leave me alone. I cuddle up on the couch and get ready to watch as many episodes as I can.

The show's organized the same way every time. One person wins the title of Star Baker each week, and then one person wins the whole season. Each episode has a different theme, like "Cakes" or "Pies" or "Breads." On every episode, the contestants have three baking challenges. The first challenge on the show is always one where they use their own recipes: the Signature Bake. So if it's "Cake Week," they get to bring their very best cake recipe. Then comes the Technical Challenge, which is a surprise. Then the Showstopper Bake, always something grand that has to be whatever they're doing that week.

For a second, in between shows, I wonder what Dad is doing. Where he's falling asleep. Then I start the next show so I don't have to think about that. I watch and watch until I fall asleep on the couch.

Sometime later, somebody tries to wake me up. "Cady. Go to bed." It's Shell.

"Huh?" I roll over.

Shell grunts. "Come on." She lifts me up and carries me upstairs. I haven't been carried forever. A part of my brain wants me to fight the sleep, but the other part tells me everything's okay. That I can relax.

I listen to brain part number two.

CHAPTER 8

It turns out I don't have to hitchhike to the pie shop, because one of their helpers quit a couple weeks ago and Shell says they could actually use another pair of hands. Shell's Pie sits on a road off the main street, in a small strip of stores that also houses a Realtor's office. The shop next door is permanently closed, like Suzanne said. I wonder why Shell won't listen to Suzanne about expanding.

Suzanne already left for the harbor. "I should be back in no more than two days," she told us. She tried to give me another hug, but I stepped away from her and stuck out my hand.

Shell doesn't say a word about how she carried me upstairs last night. I'm glad. How awkward is it that she had to do that with a twelve-year-old? But remembering how I felt, how my brain told me I was really safe, makes a warmth flicker in my stomach.

The dogs and Tom looked like they thought we were abandoning them when we left. Tom slept with me last night, his soft purring body warm and reassuring. I've only been here a day and already I think I'd do anything for those animals.

Shell told me the pets always look like that when people leave. "Whether you're gone for three minutes or three hours, they're tragically pitiful. Don't worry. They're fine."

In town, there are only a few cars around. Shell says those are other bakers, like us, who get to work before dawn. The lights are already on inside, casting slivers of brightness onto the asphalt behind the store. We're going in the back way, through a narrow alley with Dumpsters at one end.

Shell fiddles with the key. Jay stands beside me. It's Monday, so he'll walk to school from here. Both of us shiver. I'm wearing one of Shell's overcoats, and the sleeves hang down past my hands. "We're going to have to go shopping for you." Shell eyes the coat. "It gets real cold here in the fall."

The fall? Will I be here that long? It's May now, so that's a few months away. It depends on what happens with Dad—when I got taken away before, it took a whole year for him to get me back. It feels like I'm turning my back on Dad to wish I could stay until then. Plus, I don't want Shell to think I'm a burden. "I'll be fine."

Shell doesn't respond, still working the stubborn dead bolt, and for a moment I'm disappointed that she believed me.

I hold back a big yawn. That baking show was worth me being tired, though.

"You'll meet my mom. She gets here at three in the morning to make the crusts." Jay unzips his coat and hangs it on a wall hook, then takes a big apron off another hook and puts that on. I do the same. I decide I'm going to imitate Jay all day, since he's done this before. "Shell makes about one hundred fifty pies a day. Some go to restaurants, and also a few grocery stores, but we sell most in the café." He hands me a hairnet and puts one on his head. I struggle with mine until he expertly snaps it over my thick hair. I probably look like a dork, but Jay doesn't look so bad, so maybe I'm okay.

"Wow." I'm beyond impressed. How many slices does the shop have to sell every day, to stay in business? My brain hurts a little, trying to do the math. Mostly because I don't know all the facts yet—how much the slices sell for, for example. My stomach flutters a bit, same as it does when I read an exciting book.

I turn and get my first glimpse of the pie shop. We're in the back kitchen space. In the middle sit six gleaming, long stainless-steel tables, heavily scratched. Huge silver-colored mixing bowls are stacked on the shelves underneath. One long wall is covered by three units that look like grocery store refrigerators with clear glass fronts and multiple shelves, but there are pies inside, and I realize they're actually ovens. Along the opposite wall is a big stainless-steel door, and next to that is a counter with big electric mixers and some other machine on it that looks like an extra-large printer. On a short wall are shelves full of bags of flour and sugar. In the back is a sink and dishwasher area.

A woman who's not much taller than Jay appears from near the sink. Her curly hair is also bound under a hairnet. "Good morning, sleepyheads." She gives Jay a kiss on the cheek, hugging him to her.

"Ma!" He makes a big show of wiping his face, but I think he secretly likes it. A small stab of jealousy tears at me. "This is Cady."

Jay's mother smiles at me. She's small and trim, with very white and slightly oversize teeth, which makes her look like she's about to smile even when she's not. "Cady! Welcome!" She has a thick Spanish accent, so maybe she's the one who came from Mexico, not Jay's grandparents. I'll have to ask Jay sometime.

I hold out my hand. "Nice to meet you, Mrs. Morales."

She pulls me in for a hug. "Call me María." I stiffen awkwardly. "I'm so glad you're here." She pats my back and I relax a little. Her hug is different, like she's giving me some of her energy or something. Plus she smells like sugar and butter and apples and cinnamon. They should make a perfume of that. I relax as if I'm in a warm blanket. I step away. "I was about to put some more dough in the machine. Want to watch?" She points to the printer-looking contraption next to the mixers.

"That's boring." Jay sighs.

She waves him off. "Don't be a naysayer all your life, Jay." A ball of dough sits in a bowl on the table. She flips a switch on the machine and it roars to life. She feeds the dough into one end and it starts up, then squeezes the pastry through into a thin sheet. It sort of looks like a metal printer, except instead of paper, pastry dough comes out. María cuts a huge circle in the dough with a big cookie cutter. "Voilà," she says. "The bottom crust." She presses this into an aluminum pie tin. "Now it's ready for filling. We don't make all the pies at once, unless we have a big order. We wait until we're running low."

My mouth has dropped open. Jay nudges me. "Cady, it's pie. Not a rocket to Mars."

"I don't care. It's cool!" I grin at Jay's mom. "Can I try?"

"No." Shell appears from the front. "Don't mess with the dough roller. It's expensive. I want you to learn how to make crust by hand before you use that machine."

"But the machine is easier," María points out.

"Cady needs to do it by hand first. Like I learned," Shell says firmly. She leans against the door frame.

"Learning to bake is like anything else. If you're learning how to draw, you don't start with Photoshop or oil paints. You start with pencil and paper. You learn the basics. Then you repeat and repeat until you're good at it."

I've never actually done anything enough to get good at it, though. I look longingly at the ultrasmooth crust. There is zero chance I can make a crust this good. "I guess." I sigh, kind of dramatically, and Shell and María exchange an amused look. "How many pies do I have to make, anyway, before I'm good at it?"

"A lot. You need hours of practice before you're really good at anything." Shell's mouth works as she considers my question. "But let's say, conservatively, you need to make . . . about a thousand pies."

My mouth drops again, this time in dismay. A thousand pies? "That will take me forever."

Shell relents. "You don't have to make all *thousand* of them by hand, Cady. Just a few. Then María will show you the machine."

"But a thousand?" I squeak.

"It's not too bad. Ten pies a day for a hundred days." María smiles at me encouragingly. "I make more than that, if business is good."

Am I going to be here for a hundred days? That seems like a lot, but it is only a little more than three months. My gut seesaws. I don't know if I should be happy or sad about that.

"We'd better get to work, huh?" Jay slaps my back. "Come on."

The phone on the wall rings, and Shell answers. "Hello?" Her face drops, like she bit into a mushy apple. "Yes, I'll accept the charges," she says, and glances at the clock. It's six thirty-five. Who's calling so early?

Shell puts her hand over the mouthpiece. "Cady."

She doesn't have to say who it is. Only one person could be calling for me. My armpits sweat. Dad!

I leap forward and grab the phone out of her hand. "Hey!" This phone has a wire attaching it to the wall so I can't move very far. I face the wall. The others keep working, but they're quiet. I hope they don't listen, but they probably can't help it.

"Buttercup." His voice is super scratchy and tired sounding, but it's him. "How's it going? Is your aunt Michelle treating you good?"

I look around at the pie shop. I don't want to seem too happy or it might upset him. "It's all right." I lower my voice. "I didn't know you still knew Aunt Shell."

"Well. She was a last resort." Dad sounds like he needs to blow his nose. "If those jerks at your school hadn't called me in . . ."

My muscles freeze. Ms. Walker was one of those jerks. They were *worried*. But I don't want to make Dad mad. I still want him to get me. I shouldn't have gotten into trouble—if I hadn't, I wouldn't be here. "Yeah."

"Well, Buttercup. Don't you worry. I'm going to be

getting you soon. This social worker says he knows of a program that can help get me a job, you know? It's going to be great."

"Social worker?" Maybe he's not in jail for real, then. "Where are you?"

"Don't you worry about that. Now, Buttercup, I want you to be a good girl and do what your aunt says. Except don't let her take you to church. Got that? You say the prayers like I taught you." Dad starts babbling and I stop listening.

He hasn't even asked how I am.

I squeeze my eyes shut and lean my forehead against the wall.

I want to believe him. But I remember too many times when he's made promises he had to break. Promising to come back at a certain time and then not showing up for two days. Promising to get clean. He always apologizes, and he always has reasons, but it doesn't make it any better. I feel tears starting, hurt and anger that I can't show him. I kick the wall.

"Got that?" he says again. "No church."

I'm pretty sure Shell doesn't go regularly, but now I just want to hang up, not argue. "Got it." *Please get fixed this time.*

"Good. Put Shell back on, please." Dad's breathing like he's run a race, and I imagine how he looked a few days ago, all pale and skinny, and he doesn't seem better at all. I hand the phone to Shell.

I walk back to Jay, who's measuring flour. I want to run out of the pie shop and into the mountains, as if I could outrun these feelings, but instead I put my hands on the counter and lean against it. He does a double take at my face. "You okay?" he asks.

"Yeah. That was my dad. He's going to get me soon." I sound like a total robot to myself. Inside I'm churning like a river after a storm. With Dad, at least I know what will happen. Not like here, where every moment brings me something new. I'm not sure how much more *new* I can handle. I fidget anxiously. "I don't know when."

"Oh. That's cool. I guess." He hands me the measuring cup. "I hope you'll come visit us." Jay sounds more polite than friendly now, and it tears at me.

"Probably not." There's no way Dad can drive the rickety van all the way up here. And really, I should be happy—right? My dad's okay and he's going to come for me.

So why do I feel so mixed up?

"Cady." Shell hangs up. I wasn't paying attention to what she was saying to Dad. "You got to talk to your dad. Do you feel better now?"

"I don't think she'll feel better until she gets to see him." María acts like she's going to put her arm around me, so I dodge to the other side of the island.

"I'm fine." I look at Shell. "Pretty soon you won't have to worry about me." I wait for her reaction—will she be relieved? Sad?

Shell opens and closes her mouth. “I’m—I don’t know.” She exchanges a glance with María, and I don’t know what that means either. Apparently nobody knows anything. I dump flour into the bowl, a cloud of dust poofing into my face.

“Well.” Shell stands there awkwardly. “If you need anything, I’ll be out making deliveries.”

I nod. My words and emotions are all gummed up inside me and I can’t unstick them. I’ll deal. That’s what I do.

I concentrate on the flour mixture in front of me. There’s one thing I can try. I’m going to be the best baker they ever saw.

CHAPTER 9

While María finishes making the store pies, Jay demonstrates a crust. I've seen people make crusts on *Bake Off*. But watching, it turns out, is a lot different from doing.

Jay's got sort of big hands, but he handles the knife delicately, cutting the butter into small cubes, his tongue sticking out of the side of his mouth as he concentrates. Then he adds it to a bowl of flour. He picks up a thing that looks like it has four blades to mash stuff. "This is a pastry cutter." He holds it up, reminding me of Ms. Walker showing us how to do a science experiment.

He cuts the butter into the flour so there are butter pieces sprinkled all over the mixture. Then he drizzles a little ice water from a cup onto the flour and butter and starts cutting it all together with the pastry cutter. "You have to work the butter and water into the flour. But you don't want the butter to completely melt, or it'll be tough. Just do it until it holds together, like Play-Doh." He hands me the pastry cutter.

I understand what he's talking about—I saw that on *Bake Off* too. "I know that." I press and press the cutter down into the flour, watching the butter pieces get smaller and smaller. I think about Dad's phone call and smoosh harder.

Jay watches with a raised brow. "Don't do it too much."

"It's fine." I'm embarrassed that I'm not paying attention. But these look pretty good to me, actually. Besides, everyone on *Bake Off* has a slightly different technique, so maybe I just work differently from Jay. Maybe I'll be the only person ever who got to be an expert after one try! Won't Shell be impressed?

"Now you should let it rest in the fridge for a half hour."

"Should, or have to?" My stomach growls. I skipped breakfast, thinking I'd have pie right away. I don't want to wait another half hour.

Jay considers. "I guess you don't *have* to. . . ."

"Then I want to roll now." Suddenly there's nothing more important in the world than for me to see this pie crust all finished in the pan.

He purses his lips in that way he has. "Are you sure?"

"Yes, I'm sure," I snap. Now that I insisted, I have to show him I'm right or Jay will think I'm dumb. Dad's phone call flits into my head again. If I have to stand around doing nothing, I'll start blubbering. I rock back and forth on my feet. "Come on. I want to roll."

"Fine. Put a little flour on the table so it won't stick." He hands me a wooden rolling pin. "You want it to be an eighth of an inch thick all around. Roll like the crust is a clock—roll toward twelve, then six, then nine, then three. Go in one direction."

I stop listening to him spouting out the details, concentrating on my crust. It sticks to the table and has more holes than Swiss cheese. My cheeks get hot and I steal a look at Jay. But his face is neutral. It reminds me of Paul Hollywood's face when he's watching contestants make things wrong.

I start sweating for real, my shirt sticking to my ribs and armpits. I roll it again, forgetting to roll like it's a clock, pushing the pin back and forth. I don't want to fail. It feels like everything in the world is at stake.

"Stop!" Jay puts his hands on the pin. "Cady, you're killing the dough."

I peel it off, dropping my head to my chin. He's not very helpful. "Well, what am I supposed to do?"

Jay tsks. "You should have let it chill, like I said."

He really is turning into Paul Hollywood. "You're the one who needs to chill." It's as smooth as a bedsheet and it looks good to me. "It's perfect."

"It's *your* pie. Come on."

I hate the way he says that, like he doesn't want to

have anything to do with my pie. I follow Jay to the big stainless-steel door. He opens the levered handle. "This is our walk-in fridge." Inside it's like a really cold closet. There are shelves stacked with bowls and some extra crusts wrapped in cellophane. I like how magazine-neat and clean everything is. "If we need more pies, we get the crust from here." He takes down a large metal bowl filled with cut-up apple and spices and we go back out. He hands me an aluminum pie tin. "Time to bake."

I sniff the apples. "What's in here?" I smell cinnamon and sugar for sure.

"Granny Smith and Gala apples, cinnamon, nutmeg, brown sugar, white sugar, cornstarch." Jay nods at the tin. "Put your crust in there."

The bossy way he says it makes me want to crush the pastry into dust, just so I don't have to follow his directions. I liked Jay better when we were playing around outside.

My crust lies crookedly across the tin, not quite big enough to completely cover it. He touches the dough doubtfully. Now I see how uneven it is, fat in some places, thin in others. "Do you want to make a new batch?"

He's got to be joking. My shoulders ache and I'm starving. "I thought you said it's *my* pie." *It'll turn out fine,* I say to myself, like I can will that into happening. Like when I don't know the answers on a math test and just bubble in random responses, hoping it will be all right. Even though, deep down, I know it won't be.

"Whatever." Jay sniffs. "You do what you want."

"I will." I hurriedly spoon in the apples.

"Where's your top piece?" Jay looks around like I've stuck it under a table.

I glare at him. "What top piece? You didn't say anything about that."

"You've seen the pies. They have top pieces. That recipe was enough for top and bottom." Jay twists his mouth up impatiently. But wasn't *he* teaching *me*?

I let out a groan the size of Kentucky. I should have stayed home watching television. But I make another piece of dough, faster this time. This one is dry, with pieces of flour flaking off onto the counter, but it holds together okay. The butter will melt and make it pretty.

At last my pie is ready to go into the oven. It's super-lumpy, and the neat pinched-crust edge that the other pies had is nonexistent. It'll be fine when it's cooked.

I know, just like with the math test, that I'm telling myself a lie.

We sit at the back table, eating fresh apples. My head's pounding and I really want to go back to bed. But now I have to see how the pie turns out. Besides, Shell's not here to give me a ride.

I have a sour Granny Smith while Jay has a sweeter Gala. Jay explains that not every apple is good for pies because some of them, like Red Delicious, turn mushy, so it's like eating applesauce. "Did you know these apples were probably picked over a year ago?" Jay says, eyeing me. I can tell he wants me to say, *No, I didn't, Jay. Tell me more.* I'm getting sick of being lectured. But I shake my head anyway. "They stick them in a cold storage unit that's oxygen controlled so they last all year. That's why we can buy apples even when they're out of season."

"That's nice." I wish I could tell Jay something he doesn't know, but I can't think of anything. Jay grins at me and continues eating his apple. This guy. Nothing seems to bother him.

The timer pings and I race to get my pie out. It's a nice golden brown, bubbling under the crust. It's much better looking than I thought. And it smells delicious, warm and sweet. My mouth waters. Maybe I will be Star Baker!

Jay sets it on the cooling rack. "I don't want you to drop it," he says, and I want to push him over. Maybe he and I won't be friends after all. It's probably good that I'm leaving. "Now we really have to wait a half hour," Jay says. "Or you'll burn your tongue."

I roll my eyes and sit down on a stool.

"What?" Jay says.

I shake my head, refusing to answer. My stomach growls so loud María looks up from her work. "Are you all right, Cady?"

I nod. Just wait until Jay and María and Shell taste my pie. Then Jay will be sorry.

And Shell—Shell's going to be so impressed. She'll want me to stay here forever. Not that I want to. I just want her to want me to. I want her to like me so much that she'll drive down and get me, take me to Julian to visit whenever I want.

Pretty much everything depends on this pie. I swallow hard against the knot in my throat.

Aunt Shell gets back from her deliveries, hanging up her key on the hook. That didn't take her very long—she must not have had to go to many places. "How's it going?"

"Shell! Aunt Shell! Look what I did." I pick up the pie from the cooling rack and pretend like it doesn't burn my fingers, setting it on the counter. It steams into my face. I pick up the knife. "Ready?"

"We should let it cool some more," Jay says.

I stick out my chin. "It's fine."

Shell leans over it and sniffs. "I could use some nourishment."

Jay shrugs as if to say, *It's your funeral.*

I slice into the pie. Or try to. It's hard to get the knife through the crust. Like, I have to start sawing as if the crust is a tree branch. I glance up at Shell and she's frowning, but her lips turn up when I catch her eye. "Keep going, Cady."

María claps my shoulder. "Not bad for a first try."

"She didn't listen to me," Jay complains. "I've been making crust since I was three years old and she thinks she knows better."

"I did so listen to you." It's a punch in my gut that Jay's been making pies since he was three. *Not fair.* He's known Shell so much longer than I have, it's like he's her nephew and I'm the stranger. Well. This pie will prove that I'm Shell's niece. I keep cutting.

"It's nobody's fault, Jay." María glares at him.

Finally I manage to get a piece of pie out. The crust pretty much falls apart. I dish the pie onto plates, the filling oozing out with steam, and Jay gets us some plastic forks. "We're looking for sheer perfection," I say, like Mary Berry, and Shell chuckles. I blow on the pie, then finally work my fork in and chew.

And chew some more. The apple flavors are good—I didn't make that part—but the pastry is as tough as beef jerky. The worst part—the bottom of the pie is soggy. Mary Berry always says, "We don't want any soggy bottoms." My shoulders sag. This is far from sheer perfection.

Jay and Shell and María are all chewing bravely. "It's a nice color," María offers.

"The apples are good, at least," Jay says. Of course they're good. I didn't make them.

I narrow my eyes. "If someone had told me to make

two crusts, then the bottom crust wouldn't be so thick."

"If someone had been listening instead of doing whatever she wanted, then maybe the pie would be perfectly fine," Jay counters. "Don't blame me."

"Don't blame me if you're a bad teacher," I say.

"Stop, you two!" María says. "It's only a pie crust."

I shovel another piece into my mouth and gnaw away. It's not only a pie crust to me. It's everything. I pull the hairnet down over my face.

Shell doesn't say anything. I know what she's thinking. The dough's overworked. I made the butter melt with my hot hands and Hulk-grip on the rolling pin. I developed the gluten! It's as tough as bread. Paul Hollywood would tell me how wrong I was. Even worse, I bet Mary Berry would look at me sympathetically and give me a tiny compliment, like "The cinnamon is very cinnamon-y." Which means your baked good is horrible.

I spit the piece I'm chewing into the trash can. I can't believe I've wasted my whole morning. And for what? Nothing.

I'm nothing.

I shove the pie tin hard across the table. It flies off, landing with a splat and a clatter on the floor.

"Cady." Shell's voice is calm. "That is an unacceptable reaction. Clean that up."

My eyes fill with angry tears, and I almost walk out of the store. Shell regards me solemnly and Jay and María don't say a word. My face heats. I stomp over and pick up the tin, hurling it into the trash can. I try sopping up the apples with paper towels, but end up smearing the stickiness farther across the floor. Great.

"You need to use wet paper towels." Jay tries to help me, but I muscle him aside. "Hey, let me show you." He sort of pushes me back. "You're doing it wrong."

I can tell I'm doing it wrong. I'm doing everything wrong and Jay does everything right. I shove him with my shoulder so he skitters sideways. "You've shown me enough, Jesús Morales!" I yell. "Why didn't you make me do it right?"

He glares at me, his hands on his hips. "You wouldn't listen!"

"All you do is lecture and act like a know-it-all." Snot's coming out of my nose, and I sniffle it back in.

Jay gets in my face. "That's because I actually do know more about this than you do!"

"Cut it out!" Shell makes the safe signal like an umpire and both of us go quiet. "Jay, use some cleaner for the stickiness. Cady, you're on dish duty. Maybe that will teach you how to control yourself." Shell gestures to the deep sink at the far end of the workshop, on the other side of a half wall, stacked with pie tins and mixing bowls and small white plates.

"Fine. I love doing dishes." I go behind the wall to the sink. It doesn't matter. I'm never going to be a baker. I'll be leaving soon anyway.

I stack the tins noisily. Shell can't actually make me stay here and clean all day. I'm a kid. I don't want to clean dishes. I want to go to Shell's and watch TV. But *not* the *Bake Off*.

Jay whispers behind me, "My first pie was so bad, we had to give it to the pigs."

I'm too cranky to respond. My skin is on fire. "Leave me alone."

He claps a hand on my shoulder. "Look, I couldn't catch a baseball the first time I tried. Or dribble a basketball. But I kept trying. And now I'm good at both. Haven't you ever been bad at something, then gotten better?"

"Huh," I grunt. I've never played a team sport, only the things they have you do in PE, which are more like fooling around. I've been good at reading for a long time and never had to work at it.

I think about the kids at school being picked up in their shiny new SUVs and driven to their fancy lessons and sports practices, and a pit of jealous rage opens up in the center of my chest. "Not all of us have had the *privilege* of doing sports." I move away from Jay, ashamed of the bitterness in my voice but unable to keep it out.

Jay gives an incredulous snort. "*Privilege?* Who do you think I am?" His face, under its brown tone, turns red. "We live on your aunt Shell's property, you know. Me and my sisters and my mom and *mi abuela,* all in that tiny house. I sleep on the couch."

I cross my arms, not wanting to admit I'm wrong. That fire leaps from my skin straight to my tongue. "At least you have a house. At least you have a mother and a family. My mother's dead. My father's in jail."

Jay's face changes, goes mad. As mad as I am. He takes off his apron. "That's true. But do you know where my father is? What happened there? Or do you even care? You're not the only one bad stuff happens to, you know." He pivots on his heel and walks away from me, calling to his mother, "I'm going to school."

"It's too early!" Jay's mother cries.

"I'd rather sit outside the school than stay here." Jay leaves out the back, slamming the door.

María gives me a questioning look. I stay by the sink, staring at the cracked dough stuck to the tins, and a memory comes to me of Jenna trying to read to me in kindergarten and getting frustrated. "I don't care!" she'd cried, and flung the book. I'd picked it up and told her to try again. I'd encouraged her, like Jay was encouraging me. Jay's being a good friend and I'm not.

Remorse floods through me. *Wait!* I want to yell. Nothing comes out. I stay where I am, staring at the scummy water. I wish I hadn't thrown a fit or been mean to Jay. Biting my lip hard, I pull on a big pair of orange rubber gloves and do a really good job washing up.

CHAPTER 10

It takes me over an hour to get through the weekend mess. María shows me how to rinse the plates and coffee mugs and stack them in the big industrial dishwasher. I wash the mixing bowls by hand. Then I clean out the sink until it's gleaming. After that, I mop the floor. This place probably hasn't been so clean since it opened.

A while later, Shell comes into the sink area. I'm hoping she'll tell me I did a good job, but instead she says, "Cady, let's talk about what happened."

I hunch my shoulders up to my ears. "What about it?"

"That kind of behavior is unacceptable. There are better ways to manage your anger." Shell begins a mini-lecture about what those might be, but I'm not listening. My blood thumps around my temples.

I bet Shell's thinking about calling the foster people or whoever and telling them to come get me. Maybe she already called. I nod once. Am I supposed to apologize? I think I am, but saying sorry makes me feel like *I'm* bad. I've only ever said sorry if a teacher or principal made me. Otherwise, I pretend like nothing happened. It's worked okay before.

She gestures at the dishes. "Looks like you're done. Why don't I run you home?"

Shell still hasn't said I did a good job, but I sure bet she'd tell me if I messed it up. "Can I stay?" I want to see Jay when he comes here after school. Besides, the thought of being alone in the house all day makes me super anxious. I'll just be watching the clock, waiting for someone else to get home.

"Why don't you go out front? Your face is all red and sweaty." Shell leans against the wall. I can't tell what she's thinking any more than I can tell what a piece of stone thinks about our current president.

I release a breath I was holding for too long. "Can I try to make another pie instead?"

"Not today."

I sag, trying to hide my disappointment.

"How about later, at home?" Shell suggests. "No big mixer, but I have the basics, and a recipe."

I nod. "I guess that would be okay."

Shell's face softens. "Cady, I was your age when I started baking. And I can tell you getting every pie right, every time, then trying to make each one better than the one before, takes longer than one day."

I know she's right. Of course I do. On *Bake Off* they mostly show them during the competition. They don't show much of the contestants before they got there, when they were practicing baking their breads and desserts hundreds or thousands of times. "It's too bad that pie went to waste."

"That's not the first time some pie ended up on the floor, and it won't be the last. Don't worry about it." Shell boxes up a pie.

And Jay—he'd tried to help me and I'd said all those mean things to him. What had happened to his father? "When does school get out?"

Shell's eyes crinkle. "Jay doesn't hold grudges. He gets out a little after two and he usually stops by here."

I swallow, thinking of school. "Will I go to school here now, too?"

"Not this year." Shell cocks her head at me. "You just have to finish the packet with this year's work."

I remember Ms. Walker's neat classroom. The bookcase stuffed with board games we can play during free time. The baskets and baskets of books she has from fifteen years of teaching. The beanbag chairs on the carpet that you have to earn the privilege to sit in.

Ms. Walker had been my favorite teacher ever. She'd give me granola bars and apples to take with me. If a field trip required a fee, other teachers wrote on the permission slip, "Please see the teacher if paying this is a problem." Dad would never admit to needing help. "We are not a charity case, Cady," he'd say, and throw away the form no matter how much I cried about it. He'd call me in sick that day, or I'd have to go sit in another classroom.

This had happened only once with Ms. Walker. She knew. Maybe the other teachers talked, but Ms. Walker knew. After that, she always paid for me. I was grateful for it, though I never told her so. Because of her, I got to go on the *Star of India* overnight trip, the zoo, the county fair, and the tide pools—all places I'd never been. It makes my stomach ache to think of all the field trips I missed out on.

I wish I could tell Ms. Walker thank you. "Can I go to my promotion, though?"

Shell gives me a half smile. "I'll ask."

The front of the store consists of a small café, with wooden benches and tables and yellow cotton half curtains hanging on paned windows. Cartoony-looking apples splatter across old-fashioned wallpaper. A glass display case full of pie divides the eating space from the cash register. A pretty teenage girl stands there chomping gum, doodling a cartoon figure of a man on a motorcycle in a little notebook. She's got long black hair pulled into a ponytail and covered in a hairnet. Her brown eyes are covered in thick black liner that look like sharp apostrophes on her lids.

"Cady, this is Jay's older sister, Claudia." Shell puts her hands on my shoulders, making me flinch. "She'll show you what to do."

Claudia sighs, a long-drawn-out sound that begins in her lungs and seems to come out through the top of her head.

Shell gives her a look.

"What?" she says.

"Spit out the gum." Shell returns to the back.

Claudia leans over the trash can, spits, then stands there looking at me. Not in any kind of mean way, but like I'm a particularly boring plaid couch.

"I'm not going to have to do the register, am I? I mean, I could. Though I'm not that good with change. But I don't even know if it's legal. Is it legal?" Something about her silence is making me babble. Maybe I'm a little scared of her. Maybe I want her to like me. I haven't decided yet.

Claudia's mouth turns sideways. "Yeah, no, I'll do that. You'll clean the tables when people are done. And you can serve them more coffee. They get free refills." She gestures to two coffeepots on burners. "The orange handle is decaf. The other is regular. Don't confuse them or you'll give one of these old people a heart attack. Okay?"

I swallow. That seems like a lot of responsibility. "Okay."

María brings a pie in and puts it into the case. "Ma." Claudia leans against the counter. "I'm going to take the bus into town this week. There's a concert."

"You know I don't want you on the bus." María slams the slider closed.

I wonder why. "I ride it all the time. It's not bad." I think I'm being helpful, but Claudia shoots me the death stare.

"That's not why, Cady," María says gently. She takes a breath, like she's going to tell me something, but instead she goes back into the kitchen.

"I can't take the bus, and you don't want me on the motorcycle! How am I supposed to do anything?" Claudia yells after her.

"You should have gotten yourself a boyfriend with a car!" María yells back.

On cue, a motorcycle roars outside. The bell on the door tinkles, and a young man enters. His brown hair is shaved on the sides and thick and long on top. He's wearing button earrings with roses on them and swings a plastic grocery bag. "Claudia! Here are your paints."

"Thanks, baby." She leans over the counter and he kisses her on the lips. For way too long. I have to look away.

He notices me anyway. "Who's this kid staring at us?"

I draw myself upright. Watch out. Here comes my

chin. "I'm Cady. It's not my fault you're doing that right in front of me. I was already here."

Claudia laughs. "Oh, snap. She told you, Gable."

"Great. Another sassbucket to deal with." Gable smiles at me, though, and I see why Claudia likes him. In his skinny black jeans and white T-shirt, he reminds me of some lead singer in a band. He's got tattoos all over his arms, roses winding around and disappearing up into his T-shirt. He and Claudia kiss again.

"No PDA in the store!" Shell booms from the back. "Gable, don't you have to go to work?"

Gable and Claudia break their smooch. "Yes, Miss Shell." Gable wipes Claudia's lipstick from his mouth. "My parents said thanks for the eggs."

"Tell them they're welcome." Shell sticks her head in. "You staying out of trouble?"

He nods vigorously. "Yes, ma'am."

"That's what I like to hear." Shell nods back at him and disappears again.

Wow. Gable seems like he's afraid of Shell. Or maybe not afraid, exactly—like he respects her. He rubs Claudia's shoulder. "I'll see you later." He turns and leaves.

Claudia watches him with a dopey, dreamy smile, as if he's Prince Charming on a motorcycle.

"So that's your boyfriend?" I say.

She lifts her head up. "We're artists. We belong to no one."

I check out her lovesick expression. She's lying. I

shrug. "Why's he wearing flower earrings?"

Claudia kind of blushes. "Roses are his thing. He uses them in his paintings."

I gesture at the paint. "You're an artist, too. I saw your drawing. It's really good."

Claudia sticks the bag under the counter. "I'm not as good as he is."

I remember what Shell said. "You probably need to practice more."

She snorts. "You don't know my life."

The bell tinkles again and an elderly man with white hair and a cane comes in. He's wearing rough-looking pants and a plaid shirt and vest, old-timey pioneer clothes. "What's the word on the street, Miss Claudia?"

Claudia perks up to the point where she almost looks normal. "Good morning, Mr. Miniver! Your usual?"

Mr. Miniver nods, easing slowly into a chair, as if his bones are very fragile. "It's going to be a hot one today. Dry as an old skeleton left in the desert for a dozen years." He winks. "Better add some ice cream to my order. I'm volunteering at the museum today and I need my strength. The good thing about being my age is you can have pie à la mode for breakfast and nobody can tell you not to!"

Claudia opens the pie case and slices out a piece of apple, then puts it in the microwave. She pours a mug of decaf. "Take that to him." She turns to help another customer.

Carefully I carry the mug to the table, trying not to spill. A little sloshes over anyway. Mr. Miniver squints up at me. His eyes are light blue, his skin covered in wrinkles and freckles. "Don't tell me you're old enough to be out of school. Who might you be?"

"I *might* be anyone," I answer, setting the mug down, "but I *am* Cady."

"Cady. *The* Cady? Shell's niece?"

How does he know? Has Shell been talking about me—and what's she been saying? Is it *Ugh, I have to go get my poor little niece,* or more like *I've been so worried about my niece and I finally get to meet her?* I swallow and brace myself for another round of *who I look like,* but he holds out his hand. "Good to meet you, Cady. It's nice of you to help out."

I shake it. His hand is thin, the skin papery, but the grip is strong. "It's not like I had a choice, exactly. Not that I mind," I add. Though my feet hurt and I've sweated out about three gallons of water, to my surprise, it beats sitting in a dark room and watching television.

Mr. Miniver tears open a tiny canister of half-and-half and adds it to his coffee. Then another, and another.

"We should have given you cream and let you add the coffee to it," I observe.

Mr. Miniver laughs, a scratchy sound. "Exactly! The coffee gives me a bit of reflux"—he pounds his chest—"and it's decaf, but old habits. You know how it is." He winks. "Say, Claudia, would you box me up an apple crumb? Nancy Mason is laid up and I want to drop it by."

Claudia winks back at him. "Are you into Mrs. Mason?"

"Far too young for me. She's only seventy-three. Just being a good neighbor." He points to his cup. "Ah, Cady. If you please." Somehow he's drunk half the liquid already.

"As you wish." I drop into a bow. It seems kind of British. Mr. Miniver laughs again. I go back to the counter and get the coffeepot.

A few more regulars come in, and Mr. Miniver greets each and introduces me. Then we get two tourist customers, and Mr. Miniver talks to them like they're his friends, too. I've never actually seen anyone act like that—my dad wouldn't normally greet strangers. I think the tourists believe he's Shell's mascot, because of the costume.

Seeing Mr. Miniver act so friendly makes me braver. I clear away people's plates and ask if they want more coffee, and I don't spill once. Well, maybe a little, but I cleaned it up right away. It's not going to be so bad, working here.

CHAPTER 11

I wait in the café for Jay after school, doing the worksheet packet. There isn't that much, because testing's over and we don't do a lot at the end of the year. Just some math and a note that tells me to read twenty minutes every day, with a heart on it from Ms. Walker. I draw a smiley face on the heart and zip through the work.

It did get hot today, with one window unit futilely pumping air and fans blowing it around. There are zero customers after lunch. Who can be in the mood for pie when it's so warm? This is ice-cream weather.

It gives me a nervous feeling to see the pies sitting, mostly whole, on the shelves. They should be getting eaten. How long before pies go bad?

"Mondays are always like that, but Tuesdays are worse," Claudia tells me. "That's why we're closed on Tuesdays. Sometimes people stay in the mountains for a

Monday, but almost never for a Tuesday." Claudia goes in the back.

I sit at a table in the empty restaurant, watching the people outside wandering around. Hardly any are coming up this way—do they even know we're up on this side street? I yawn—I'm so tired from working that I snuck a sip of coffee. Which I immediately wished I hadn't. It was like drinking hot dirty water.

Claudia plops a bundle of letters down in front of me, secured with a rubber band. "Here. Take these to the mailbox."

"I don't know where that is." I push them away from me. I don't want to miss Jay, and besides, it's really hot.

"Corner of Main and Washington, across from the town hall. It's only like a block. Don't be a baby." Claudia marches back to her spot behind the counter.

I grunt. Jay was right about her. But I don't necessarily want to fight with Claudia. I mean, I've already made her brother mad. The whole family could turn against me. I pick up the letters and head outside.

The sun practically scorches my skin off. I squint against the glare bouncing off car windshields and walk down the hill to Main Street, make a left, and start past the stores.

I can't help but look at the top letter. These aren't greeting cards or anything. It's addressed to "ASI Collections Agency." I'm not sure what "collections" means, exactly, but I have the feeling it's some kind of bill. There are three of those and a bunch to other places, like the power company.

I put the rubber band back in place. It felt sneaky to do that, but it's not like this is a government secret, right? While I'm paying attention to the letters, I almost bump into a chalkboard sign on the sidewalk. GRANDMA'S PIES, it says in blue, listing the specials. Besides apple, they've got four other flavors, plus cinnamon ice cream. There's a line of people inside.

Why doesn't Shell have a sign like that? If we could just get a few customers, I bet it'd help a lot. A piece of blue chalk lies next to the sign, and I notice there's a lot of blank space to the right of the specials.

Quickly I pick up the chalk and look around. Nobody's watching. Then I write, "GO TO SHELL'S" with an arrow pointing in the direction of our store. My heart beating fast, I sprint away, not stopping until I reach the mailbox on the other side of the street, and accidentally throw the chalk in there too with the mail.

I start shaking. Why did I do that? I feel as bad as I did that time Dad told me to shoplift a PowerBar, but it had to be done. Sometimes, Dad says, you have to do things you don't want to do to survive. This wasn't illegal. I don't think. It was just chalk. I walk as quickly as I can back to the shop. Nobody from Grandma's comes out to chase me.

María's out front, wiping a table. I glance around—Shell is in the kitchen. I don't want her to know I've looked through the mail, but I do want to know the answer to my question. Jay's mom seems like a safe person to talk to. "María? What's a collections agency?"

María stops wiping, and straightens up with narrowed eyes. "Where did you hear that word?"

Uh-oh. Did I make her mad? I pretend to be interested in picking a crumb off the chair. "I saw it on TV." My neck gets hot, and it's not because I was outside.

"It's a place that collects money from people. For debt they didn't pay on time." She keeps wiping the table, only now she's really attacking it. I swallow. Shell owes money. But that's probably normal for her because she runs a business. I think.

"Hey." Jay's standing behind me, a plate with two pieces of pie and a scoop of vanilla ice cream in his hand. He sits at the table his mom just cleaned.

"If you get crumbs on there, so help me—" María shakes her head and returns to the back.

"Don't worry. I'll wipe it. Sheesh." Jay tucks into his dessert. "She's so crazy about keeping stuff clean."

"Well, you would be too if you knew how much stuff people spilled." Even Mr. Miniver made a little mess. I sit opposite Jay, trying to read his expression. He doesn't seem angry from what happened this morning. But a lot of times mad people don't look mad but secretly are. Me, on the other hand, if I feel mad, I look mad.

He shovels ice cream into his mouth. "Why are you staring at me?"

"I'm not." I close my eyes. My palms get wet. I cross my arms and hide my hands in my armpits. I don't think I've ever apologized for anything on my own before. "I wanted to say I'm sorry. About everything I said and did."

I let out a long breath, and to my amazement, my body feels like I'm being lifted in a balloon. Lighter than I've been all day. What a relief. Still, when I open my eyes, I half expect he'll be gone.

He wipes his mouth with the back of his hand. "No big deal. I've got sisters, remember? We have a fight on every day that ends in *y*." Jay pushes away the suddenly empty plate. He's like Shaggy with that eating. "Have you had any real food today?"

My stomach growls. Now that I've apologized to Jay, I remember my hunger. "No. Just pie." I guess I can't live on dessert alone. "Why?"

"My grandma made empanadas. Let's go get some."

Shell drives us back. "I'll be home around five. Stay out of trouble."

"Okay." I shut the door and look in at her, remembering her earlier promise. "So can we make a pie tonight?"

Shell laughs, dipping her head onto the steering

wheel. Her face relaxes, and that makes me relax, too. "If you like. But I thought you'd be sick of it."

I shrug. Maybe I am, but I also want to use everything in their kitchen. "How about a cake, like Suzanne said?"

"A cake sounds pretty good, actually." Shell lifts her hand in a wave. I wave back. Cake and pie in one day? This is going to be great!

I follow Jay to the right of Shell's house, past the orchard, to a small house. It's one story and sort of looks like a small barn or a shed. But the outsides are covered in the same siding as Shell's and painted the same yellow.

"It's super cute," I say, and I mean it.

Jay snorts. "Yeah. Cute. It's Shell's, like everything else."

I don't understand why he sounds bitter. "That's okay, isn't it?"

"I don't like depending on other people for everything. Do you?" He looks me straight in the eye and I have to admit he's right. I don't. Jay gets me so much it's spooky. We go inside.

A TV blares a show in Spanish. The savory smell of hamburger and pastry fills the air. I sniff. I definitely smell onion and garlic and maybe oregano. What are those other spices? My stomach rumbles.

A little girl about four years old in a hot-pink dress

runs up. "Jay, Jay, Jay!" She holds out her arms and Jay scoops her up and swings her around. "This is Esmeralda, my little sister." Jay sets her down.

Esmeralda peers up at me. "Hi."

"Hello." I don't know what else to say. I hardly ever know how to start talking to other kids. If they make the first move, like Jenna and Jay both did, then it's fine. But if I have to do the talking, I'm worried I'll say something they won't like.

We stand there looking at each other. She's got a heart-shaped face and dark eyes. She reminds me of Jenna, when I met her. I sink to one knee so I'm eye level. "Do you like to read, Esmeralda?"

She nods, suddenly shy.

"Maybe I could read to you sometime." I glance up at Jay to see if that's okay.

He rolls his eyes. "You're going to be sorry. She makes me read the same story two thousand times in a row."

"Well, I've gotta go. Bye!" Esmeralda takes off, her little feet kicking up behind her.

"She's cute," I say.

Jay shrugs. "Sometimes, I guess. Abuelita!" Jay calls. "I'm home. I have a friend and we smell empanadas!"

"There's no need to shout. *Esta casa es pequeña.*" A heavyset woman emerges from the kitchen, wiping her hands on a dish towel. She moves slowly, with a limp, as if her left knee isn't too good. Her hair is short and curly, streaked with gray, but her cheekbones are high like Claudia's and her teeth are as even as María's. She peers at me with distinct disapproval behind her round, pink-framed glasses. "So this is the famous Cady Bennett?"

"Hello, madame." I hold out my hand and give a little bow.

"Madame? Am I French?" She ignores it. "I'm Señora Vasquez."

"Hi."

She continues to stand there examining me, her lips pressed together. "So is this Cady well behaved, Jay?" She sniffs and makes a face. "*Ay,* Cady, won't Shell let you use the shower?"

"Abuelita!" Jay raises his voice. "That's so mean! Don't listen to her." Jay goes into the kitchen. "I'll get us the food."

"Do not tell me what's mean and what's not, Jesús Ignacio Morales. I am telling the truth." Señora Vasquez sits down heavily in an armchair and regards me as if I'm stinking up her whole house.

It's true. I do need to take a shower after sweating all day at the shop. My hair's practically matted to my head. I fight the urge to scratch my scalp. This time I stink because of hard work. Not because I don't have a bathroom.

Jay reappears with two pastries wrapped in napkins.

"Empanadas," he says. They're small pies, shaped like half-moons. "You're okay with beef, right?" He hands me one.

"Yes. Thanks." I bite into it. The ground beef is spicy, with a bit of tomato sauce, but not enough. It's dry, sticking in my throat.

"Sorry about my grandmother." Jay shakes his head. "I don't know what her problem is."

"My problem is disrespectful young men, apparently!" Señora Vasquez turns off the television. In the sudden silence I hear the sound of me chewing. I'm noisy, like a cow. I stop, embarrassed. "We know all about *tu padre*."

Now the empanada turns to dust. "You do?"

She nods. "Your father broke Tía Shell's heart. Moving to Oregon without a word."

What's she talking about? We never lived in Oregon. Maybe my dad had mentioned the idea once. He'd talked about plenty of things like that. Moving to Alaska to get a job on a fishing boat (judging by the TV shows we watched about it, he wouldn't have lasted a half day). Moving to the South, where things cost less. In the end, of course, we stayed here. Where at least we know what things are like.

I'm about to tell her that, when I inhale a crumb and hack until tears squeeze out of my eyes. I double over, my hands on my thighs, coughing.

"Don't stand there. Get her some water." Señora

Vasquez gestures at Jay.

He leads me into the kitchen and gives me a glass of water. I drink it down. At last I stop coughing.

"So you don't like my empanada, huh?" Señora Vasquez says.

"It *is* kind of dry," I say honestly, and at this Señora Vasquez gives a little miffed sound, then snorts what may be a laugh.

CHAPTER 12

We spend the rest of the afternoon with Esmeralda and the dogs, and Jay teaches me how to play Stratego.

I lose both rounds. Somehow with Jay I don't mind.

And he's right—I do read Esmeralda the same book over and over again. It's fine with me. I use British accents and Australian accents and Esmeralda laughs until she literally has to go pee.

Then, when it's almost five, Jay walks me to the orchard's edge. "I'll have to take you to the secret stream," he says. "Sometimes there are even fish there. Not big enough to catch. But in the spring, there are frogs. I'll show you where they lay their eggs."

This sounds like the most amazing thing ever. "Will your grandmother let you? She doesn't seem to like me." I feel a pang. Dad says what other people think about us is none of our business. Easier said than done.

He makes a dismissive gesture. "She's old and cranky because her knee always hurts."

"I don't know what she was talking about. We never moved to Oregon."

Jay shrugs again. "She probably misremembered. But don't worry about her. You going to the shop tomorrow?"

"I don't know." I remember Grandma's Pies, and my stomach flip-flops. Then I think about the collections agencies I saw on the bills. "Jay, is the pie shop doing okay?"

"It's always slow this time of year." Jay's voice sounds so normal that I know he's telling the truth. I smile in relief. "My mom says it's tight, but we're going to be fine. And Claudia wants to move out this summer, so we won't have to, you know, buy food for her."

This makes me remember Claudia's weird fight with María. "Hey. Your sister wanted to go to the city on the bus, but your mom said no."

"So?" Jay examines a tiny apple growing on a branch.

"Claudia's nineteen. I ride the bus all the time, and I'm twelve. So why doesn't your mom want you guys to ride the bus?"

Jay's shoulders stiffen. "Oh. My mom thinks the bus is dirty."

I wonder if it's because homeless people ride the bus. A lot of people complain about that. I don't think there are homeless people in Julian, though. "It's really not bad."

Jay's mouse-quiet for a minute. Then he lets go of the apple, so it springs up on its branch. "If I tell you something, can you not tell anyone?"

I nod. "Of course. I'm an excellent secret keeper." I've had to keep my mouth shut a lot through the years. Keeping stuff from my teachers. Not telling social workers the whole truth.

He scuffs at the dirt, pieces of dead vegetation rising up into the air. "I can't ride the bus because I'm not a citizen."

I think about the citizenship award they give out at school. But that's not what he's talking about. "What is that?"

"I was born in Mexico and my parents brought me here when I was a baby." Jay takes a shaking breath, anger coming off him like heat off a fresh pie. "We're what they call *undocumented*."

It's my turn to kick at the dirt. "I don't know what that means."

"It means I don't have papers to be in this country. Neither do my older sister and my mom and my grandma. It means"—he gives a small, disbelieving laugh—"I'm an illegal alien." He almost spits those words, making air quotes with his fingers, his nose wrinkling. "Haven't you heard people say that? *Aliens*. Like we're not even human." He swallows, his eyes bright. "It means that, I don't know, we're shadow people or something. We can't get Social Security numbers. America's not really my home, but neither is Mexico. I'm in between. Like a ghost."

My stomach turns cold. I don't know what to say. He's shifting his weight back and forth as if he wants to run. *Illegal aliens.* Once, by the beach, I saw a freeway warning sign that was like one of those deer-crossing warning signs, only there was a silhouette of what looked like a family running, the mother figure gripping the hand of an Esmeralda-sized kid whose ponytails flew behind her. My dad said the sign was for the "illegal aliens" who might try to dash across the freeway to get into the United States, so drivers would know to watch for them like they watch for deer. Like they were animals, too, only they were humans. It made me feel sad.

I asked Dad why they needed to come into the country like that instead of just walking over the border, and he explained how the US put a limit on who could be here. So sometimes people traveled through a big desert and even swam part of the ocean to get in. "Their lives must be pretty bad where they come from if they're willing to do all that," Dad told me. We passed a strawberry field, and he pointed at it. "They take all the farm jobs nobody here will do. Cheap labor."

I asked my dad then why we didn't have a way for them to come here to work, and he said he didn't know. I never thought too much more about it, though. Except that Dad told me Grandpa Sanchez came here from Mexico a long time ago. I don't know if he was ever an "illegal alien" or not.

That phrase feels bad, like when people called my dad a "dirty bum."

I imagine what it would be like to wake up every day and pretend to be someone you weren't. I guess I know a little bit about that, but if people found out I was homeless, the worst they'd do is make fun of me or tell me and my dad to move along. But Jay might actually be kicked out of the whole country.

"So we can't ride the bus because sometimes ICE—those are the immigration police—do sweeps and arrest people." Jay looks at the ground.

"But how would they know?" I mean, it's not like I carry ID that says I was born here. Nobody's ever questioned my dad about that.

"Because." Jay points at his arm.

I blink, confused.

He taps it. "This skin color. They look for this skin color." Jay drops his arm.

I hold up my arm. It's a few shades lighter than his, a few shades darker than my father's. I look mostly white. Nobody would stop me. I don't know what to say. It's all so awful. "But—but you guys can become citizens, right? It's not your fault you're here. You were only a baby."

He shakes his head. "There's no way to do it. Not by

going to college or getting married or doing paperwork. Nothing." Jay's jaw twitches. He's ashamed and scared and trying to be brave all at the same time. He focuses on me. "That's why we can't rent anywhere. Go anywhere. That's why we have to depend on Shell for everything. Probably forever."

I feel turned inside out. That might be the worst thing I ever heard. I try to imagine how it would be if I were undocumented. How I'd get around if I couldn't ride the bus. If I knew there was nothing I could do to change it for as long as I lived.

I look at Jay, his chin resting on his chest. He seems so happy, and he's such a hard worker. I wonder how much effort that takes, when it seems like it wouldn't matter whether he tried or not. I feel like he's showing me something real about himself, something he doesn't show other people.

I don't know what to say. Or what I could say.

Jay bends to look into my face. His eyes have turned a very deep brown, almost black, and his brows have a furrow between them. "Seriously, don't tell anyone."

"I won't." I wish I could fix this for him. I can't stand to see him look so miserable. It feels like I should hug him, but I can't quite bring myself to go that far. I give his upper arm a quick squeeze instead. I search for a joke. "Huh. You feel pretty human for an *alien*. And, by the way, if anyone calls you that, they're going to have to answer to me." I hit my chest with my fist, Tarzan style.

Jay wipes his face with his hands, seeming to rub away all the negativity for now. He lets out a quick, relieved chuckle. "I know I wouldn't want to tangle with you."

"Oh yeah?" I grin.

"Yeah. You might throw a whole pie into my face."

"That's right. Maybe that'll be my signature superhero move." We giggle.

Jay hops up and down. "We should totally make that into a comic book."

"Totally. What'll we call it?"

"Pie Girl?" Jay suggests.

"Meh. Doesn't sound strong enough."

"Neither does Ant-Man. And that got made into a movie."

"We'll see." I wave goodbye and he turns around, back to his house.

When I get home, Shell's truck isn't there and the house is dark and cold. Tom mews sadly and the dogs swarm around my legs. "Shell!" I call out anyway. "Anybody home?"

No answer.

I walk through the house, calling, turning on every light I find. "Shell?" It's after five. Shell said she'd be home. Panic rises in my chest. "It's okay," I say aloud to the animals, but it's really to myself. I get back to the kitchen, the animals following, and sit at the table. I draw my knees up to my chest, hugging them, turning myself into a tight little ball. I shiver—the temperature really drops at night here.

I flash back to the last time Dad left me alone. Once, earlier this year, after he got his disability check, we stayed at a motel. He said he was going out to get us dinner. When two hours turned to four, I went looking for him around the motel grounds.

Downstairs, nobody sat in the tattered chairs by the greenish pool. On the curb out front, several people smoked cigarettes. Dad had told me to stay away from everyone. This neighborhood wasn't exactly high-class. Trash flew around the driveway and the noise from the freeway next door thundered. In the manager's office, an older man sat alone watching TV and barely glanced up as I pushed the door open.

"Have you seen a man with, um, glasses?" I tried to come up with a good way to describe Dad. A positive way.

He shook his head, then did a double take. "Your dad?"

I swallowed miserably. "Yeah. I'm sure he's around here someplace." I didn't want this guy freaking out because my dad left me alone. I could handle it—I was a fifth grader. "He went to get dinner."

The man glanced at the clock. "It's ten o'clock. You must be hungry."

I shrugged.

He turned to a shelf behind him and took out five oatmeal packets. "Here. On the house." He squinted at me. "You come back here at midnight if he hasn't shown up. Okay?"

I managed to nod, too torn up to say thanks. I took the packets and ran back to the room. I knew I wouldn't come back. That guy would call the police. I sat up all night, looking out the window, worrying.

When Dad got back after dawn, I was asleep on a dining chair instead of enjoying the bed. "Sorry, Buttercup." Dad rubbed his eyes. "Dang. I'm so tired I fell asleep at the McDonald's lot. Guess that's what happens when you don't sleep for three days." He handed me a bag. "Your mother would be so mad that I'm feeding you this." He sat on one of the beds. "She always said this was trash."

"That doesn't exactly make me want to eat it." Mom had high standards. She would never have let us set foot in that motel. Of course, if she were alive, my dad and I would never have had any problems in the first place.

The food was hot, hash browns and pancakes, my favorite. I didn't think he was telling me everything, but it was pointless to argue. I just ate.

What if Shell is really like Dad? My insides move like hot lava. What if she doesn't come home until tomorrow, either?

Tom jumps on the table. *"Mewarrrr,"* he howls, as if

he's asking why I'm all curled up. I try to think logically. If I'm alone, then I can eat from the garden. Jay will help me. I have everything I need.

Then I spot a yellow Post-it note flapping on the refrigerator door. *Gone to town to do errands & pick up dinner. Back by 6. Shell.*

Relief washes over me. Of course it wouldn't make sense for Shell to leave. And Shell's not going to fall asleep or whatever and not come home tonight. Why did I think that? Because I just met Shell, and for all I know she's exactly the kind of person who'd run off.

I remember the thing about Oregon and realize I don't know anything at all, really.

Tom howls again. He wants his dinner. I feed the animals, and this makes my blood pressure go down the rest of the way.

What can I do to keep busy? "You know what?" I say to the dogs and the cat. "I bet Shell would love some cake."

The thought of baking makes my heart speed up. This is going to make up for me messing up earlier. Shell's going to be so impressed. *Cady,* she'll say, *you're a natural baker. The next Mary Berry!*

And then she'll tell me that my father and I can stay here forever. If we want. She'll help him find a job and everything will be fine.

I look at the clock. Five thirty. I bet I can at least mix

cake batter before she gets home.

Without further ado, I run upstairs to fetch the big cookbook. I open it to where an ancient construction paper flower marks the page. Lady Baltimore Cake. I've wanted to try this forever. It sounds positively elegant and grand. I grab the mixing bowls from the open shelf. I open drawers until I find a whisk and a measuring cup. Thank goodness the recipe's not in grams, like they are on *Bake Off,* where they have to use a measuring scale. Then I search the cupboards until I find baking soda.

Shell doesn't have any shortening, so I decide to use butter instead. I don't know why, but everything in this cookbook has shortening instead of butter. It should probably work the same. I hope.

There's no fancy stand mixer like on *Bake Off,* and I can't even find a hand mixer. I settle on the wire whisk and a wooden spoon.

I take the butter out of the fridge—remembering from the show that it should be soft or it won't mix. Because how can it, when it's solid? Then I look for the eggs. None in the fridge. There are three eggs on the windowsill.

First of all, why aren't the eggs in the fridge? I examine them. One's kind of blue and two are brown. The blue one's also too small. I guess these are what real chicken eggs from farm chickens look like.

The chickens. Of course! They might have eggs. Who

knows if I'm allowed to do this—but Shell had mentioned that the chickens would be one of my chores. I run out to the chicken coop, Jacques and Julia hot on my heels. "Stay," I warn them, before I unlatch the door and go in. The chickens squawk, all excited, flapping and pecking at my feet. "Sorry," I say, and duck into the wooden coop.

There are feathers and droppings all over the place and it's super stinky. Almost as bad as a gas station rest stop, and that's really saying something. At least the smells in here come from chickens and not random strangers.

I look in the nest boxes, pulling out egg after egg. Ten of them. I hope Shell wants them collected. It seems like she would. I lay them in my shirt hem, forming a basket of sorts, and head back inside.

The eggs are dirty, because they came out of a chicken's you-know-where. Ew! I never thought about that before. I wash them carefully with the dish soap, scrubbing and rinsing until they're shiny clean. Then I read the recipe again.

I need a sifter. I think I know what those look like—a canister with a handle. I look in every cupboard but don't see one. I stop and Google "how to sift flour without a sifter" on Shell's laptop. "Use a mesh strainer." Okay, I saw one of those by the pots and pans. That'll work.

First it says to preheat the oven, so I do that. I've never touched an oven before, but I'm good at figuring things out on my own. So I press the buttons until the display says PREHEAT. Easy enough.

I sift the flour through the mesh strainer. I wonder why you have to sift it twice, once by itself and once with the other ingredients. Oh well. I'll have to look into that later.

The butter's hard to cream by hand, but I'm getting it done. Luckily for me I remember what creaming looks like from *Bake Off*.

One of the best parts of the show is how the bakers explain why they're doing things a certain way, like they're giving secret scientific tips. I know why two different bowls are used instead of mixing everything at once. You cream the wet stuff together separately, to whip up air bubbles. Then you add the dry ingredients in, little by little, so the gluten in the wheat doesn't get too developed, which will make the cake tough. The egg whites have to be whipped separately from everything else, because that will add even more air, and then very, very gently folded in. This will give the cake height. Mary Berry would be proud.

I tip the flour bowl into the creamed sugar and butter, but the entire bowl of flour mix falls in at once. Oops. It's super hard to stir. I think it's okay, though.

I begin cracking the eggs and separating the whites, but I'm not good at it, and a bunch of shell fragments fall in. It takes a while to pick them out and I still don't think I got all of them. Hopefully no one will notice. It's hard to separate the eggs, too. It looked easy on the show. Bits of yolk get caught in the whites and I drop a couple of yolks on the floor. The dogs lap them up.

I whip the egg whites with the whisk. They don't fluff up. Two minutes, then three. Muscles I never knew I had, on my wrists and in my armpits, burn. I take a moment to let go of the whisk and flex my bicep. A pitiful muscle pops up. "That's going to change," I tell it. And, since nobody's here, I give it a little peck. *Mwah.* Then I do the same for my other arm.

The work makes me happy, calming my buzzing head. I don't think about Dad or anything else, just the batter and the cake. I'm not worried about Shell. The oven warms the room as it heats. So cozy. The dogs and Tom keep watch over me, though in reality, they probably just want to lick the bowls.

Nothing bad is going to happen.

Finally the eggs look pretty good. I think. They're white now. Good enough, I decide, and fold them gently into the batter.

I want to be someone who can follow directions. Someone Shell will look at and say, "Now, there's someone worthwhile." It surprises me that I want to impress her. I think about what Jay said earlier—that he doesn't like to depend on people. Maybe that's why he works so hard.

Maybe I want to be the kind of person who gives instead of takes, too.

The oven beeps and just says 325, the temperature, instead of PREHEAT. Guess that means it's ready for the cake.

There are still dry spots in my concoction, though. I mix more, and then some more. Finally everything looks nice and combined. It actually looks like a batter.

Tom hops onto the kitchen chair, judging me with his violet eyes. If he could talk, he'd probably tell me I'm doing it all wrong. But Shell's going to love it. It'll make up for the bad pie. She can relax and put her feet up and enjoy some cake instead of helping me.

It's a little after six, but there's still no sign of Shell. I glance out the dark windows, that old fear coming back. *She'll be back soon,* I tell myself. I stick the cake in the oven, careful not to touch the hot rack or sides. Done.

Feeling like I just got first place in a race, I decide to watch TV while the cake's baking.

Shell's remote has about ten million buttons, but somehow I figure out how to make the cable box and TV come on. I find a Food Network show where a lady's making a cake out of olive oil. Olive oil? I don't know if that'll be any good. I rewind and watch the lady pouring olive oil into the batter again. "Be sure to use *good* olive oil," she says with a little smile that might be more of a smirk. What the heck is *good* olive oil? Does anybody use *bad* olive oil?

I hit LIST on the remote to find the recorded shows. I scroll through the *Bake Off* episodes, reading the little descriptions.

Gluten-free. Jenna would like this, too.

I hit play. FIVE SURVIVE, the screen proclaims. WHO WILL WIN?

The two British ladies tell the contestants that this week they have to leave out either dairy, gluten, or wheat in their "bakes." What? How are they going to do this and still make the stuff taste good?

First they have to make bread with some "nontraditional" flour. Chestnut or spelt. I didn't know these existed.

The second challenge, the Technical, is supercomplicated. Of course. It's for some weird recipe nobody's ever heard of, a French gluten-free dessert called "hazelnut da-KWAAZ." Luckily they show the name on screen—"dacquoise."

If I had to make that, I would give up and walk out. But they all tackle it and do a pretty good job. I want to try making this thing, too. I hit pause, run upstairs for my notebook, and rewind it, writing down the word "dacquoise." I'll look up the recipe later. Tom jumps up, settling by my side. "This remote thing is going to come in very handy," I tell him. I fast-forward the show through the commercials. Awesome.

CHAPTER 13

A bit later, Julia's head bobs up. *"Woof!"* Then Jacques goes crazy, barking and whining and running back and forth from the kitchen to the front door. Julia just stares alertly, waiting. Keys jangle. It has to be Shell. My body goes weak with relief.

Shell appears, pizza box first. "Hi, Cady. I'm sorry that took so long. The pizza place had a wait, and then I stopped by the Ranch restaurant to talk about orders . . ." She trails off. "I hope you weren't worried. I guess we should get you a phone so I can contact you."

A phone? That would be pretty cool. "I wasn't worried," I lie. "Did the Ranch order a bunch of pies?" I remember the bills I sent today and my stomach turns.

"No." Shell's voice goes low. "They actually canceled their contract with us. They want to offer cake instead. Twenty pies a week gone." She sighs. "Oh well. Can't please everybody."

That's awful. "Why?"

She doesn't answer, instead sniffing the air. "What's that smell?"

Uh-oh. I was supposed to leave the cake in for twenty-five minutes. I've watched the olive oil lady and almost an entire *Bake Off* episode. They're already on the Showstopper Challenge. That means it's been way longer.

Then I smell it too.

Burning.

"My cake!" I jump up and run into the kitchen.

"Cady!" Shell's right behind me. She opens the oven door, letting out a plume of smoke. The fire alarm screams. She takes out the pans with potholders, tossing them on top of the stove. The Lady Baltimore is Lady Burnt-a-more.

"You used the oven?" Shell's voice rises. "Alone? You could've burned the whole house down." She reaches up and turns off the shrieking alarm.

Shame rushes into my face. I know the proper thing would be to say I'm sorry, but I'm afraid admitting to that would be admitting something more. Like I don't deserve to be here, or I meant to burn the cake. She must think I'm the worst kid in the world. I cross my arms. "I'm twelve. I know how to do all kinds of things."

"I thought you'd know better at twelve. When I was twelve I was working."

When Shell was twelve she had two parents and a sister. I think about my life before. My dad, always there but never really there. Making sure he remembered to pay for everything. Making sure we ate. Yes, I'm twelve, and I can do way more stuff than Shell could ever dream of doing. She's so unfair. Suddenly I'm madder than I've ever been in my whole life, plus a little sick to my stomach. "I'm way mature for my age."

Shell's eyes narrow and her jaw tightens even more. "So you've used an oven before?"

I reluctantly shake my head.

"Do you know how to use a timer? Or a fire extinguisher?" Shell continues. She waves at the dirty bowls (I ended up with three, somehow), the eggshells, the measuring cups, the whisk. "And look at this mess." She presses her fingers into her temples. "It's not a good time for this."

A good time for this? Does she mean making a cake, or me? I stand still, trying to do my deep breathing. "I was going to clean up and put everything back. You weren't going to have to do anything." *I did it for you,* I add in my head.

Shell rolls her eyes. "Sure." She opens the box marked Margherita and throws a piece onto a plate for me. It's mozzarella with basil and tomato. I like pepperoni. "And Cady—Mrs. Moretti, the owner of Grandma's Pies, came to see me." She crooks an eyebrow. "Do you know anything about anyone writing on her sign?"

I pray for a huge earthquake and the ground opening up to eat me whole. "No."

Shell's mouth purses, turns downward. "We can talk about that later. Eat."

The tears that I've been crushing down for three days come to a full boil. "I'm not that hungry," I say in a choked voice. I run out of the room, forgetting my cookbook. I'll get it tomorrow.

CHAPTER 14

I stomp upstairs, my feet making satisfyingly loud *whacks* on each step and on the wooden floor. The walls shake. I'm so mad at myself.

I'm too much trouble. I should have waited for her. I shouldn't have tried to use the oven.

And I definitely should not have written on that other store's board. I bet Mrs. Moretti, whoever she is, was furious and is going to get even with me, like the time I hid Anna-Tyler's lunchbox and then she spilled my food tray on purpose. I punch the wall and all that happens is I hurt my knuckles. I'd feel worse if I dented this innocent house.

Plus there's the fact that Shell's shop is obviously not doing that great. *It's not a good time for this.* Having another mouth to feed probably isn't going to make Shell sleep better.

Shell's going to send me to a foster home. I mean,

I probably would, too. Who wants some kid hanging around trying to burn down your house when your customers are canceling their orders?

I lean my head against the wall and take a couple of deep breaths and accidentally smell my own armpits. I smell like the chicken coop and sweat. No wonder Jay's grandma mentioned it. A bath will make me feel better.

I go into my bedroom and get the fluffy robe and pajamas Suzanne left me. I wish she'd come home. With Suzanne here, I might have a chance. I get the feeling Suzanne's sort of a soft padding between Shell and the rest of the world. But with Shell—I don't know. Now I know why Shell and Señora Vasquez are friends—they're practically twins.

Quickly I open the dresser drawer to check on my food. It's all still there. I might need it sooner than I thought.

Tom meows from the bed. "I need to get clean, dude. I can't cuddle yet." He rubs his face against my hand and I lean down and kiss his head.

The room doesn't feel like "my" room. It's pretty and it's nice, but it's strange, like a motel room. I'm not going to get attached to it. I don't want to miss it when I leave.

The bathroom's down the hall. A pull-down vinyl shade covers the small window, with lacy white curtains over that. There's a pedestal sink and a white tub with brass claw feet. I tap one. It looks like someone cut the feet off a mythical creature, like a griffin, and stuck them on the tub.

There's another bedroom upstairs, but since I'm the only one here, this is basically my own private bathroom. I feel sort of like I'm walking into a library when I go inside—I want to use everything in it, but also keep it clean. I carefully wipe up the hairs from the sink. There's even a toothbrush holder for me and a cup. It looks like something out of a magazine.

Feeling calmer, I turn on the shower and wash myself with the flowery-apple shower gel Suzanne told me was all mine, and the funny poofy sponge. My plan is to clean all the gunk off me, then get in the tub. I don't know the order of what I'm supposed to do.

I stop the shower, sit down, close the drain, and turn on the tub faucet, squirting more soap into the tub to make bubbles. Something I've only seen on TV. It foams up so much I'm afraid that it'll overflow, but it doesn't. I lean back, resting my head on the wall.

Just five nights ago, we were sleeping in the van. Dad parks it under a freeway overpass, someplace where people mostly don't go. Well, I mean, there are homeless people there too. But not regular people.

Mostly everyone left us alone. Sometimes a police officer would shine a light into the van and ask Dad some questions or tell him to move. In those cases, Dad told me to roll over and stay put. I'm big enough to be mistaken for an adult.

On those nights, as Dad snored next to me, I'd stay up all night reading. Either my recipe books or a book from the library or the one book I do own, *From the Mixed-up Files of Mrs. Basil E. Frankweiler.*

Dad bought that one for me at the swap meet for a nickel. "I read that book when I was your age," he'd said, passing his worn hands over the cover.

"Don't you want to get a book for yourself?" We were standing at a vast table of paperbacks.

"Nah." Dad handed me the book. "Grown-ups don't got time to read."

But sometimes I'd see him reading it anyway. I wondered if he was remembering his childhood when he read it.

Dad grew up in Arizona. His parents died when he was almost eighteen and so he began washing dishes in restaurants. He'd moved from place to place before he ended up here and met my mom. What did my mom see in him? I figured he must have done something pretty grand to win her over. Something electrifying, like slaying a dragon. From what he's told me, Mom didn't seem like she was the type of woman to be impressed by anything less.

But then there'd been a run of bad luck, according to Dad, starting when I was about four. First he'd gotten in a bicycle accident—an old man ran a red light and hit him—and he broke his leg badly, pretty much ending his kitchen career because he couldn't stand on his leg for hours. Then my mom got sick, and Dad began praying for her, and he painted the van. One of my earliest memories is of him making me kneel down and pray, pray, pray, as if we could do it hard enough to chase the sickness out of Mom.

"When will we get our own place, Dad?" I used to ask him all the time.

"Sooner than later, I hope," he'd answer. Sometime this year, he'd stopped answering at all. I had to hurry and grow up, be at least sixteen, so I could get a real job and take care of us. Someday I'll be on a cooking show myself. And I'm going to do that whether or not Aunt Shell kicks me out of her house.

I sit in the bath having these thoughts, wondering if Shell will ever let me bake again, or if she'll call Social Services tomorrow and tell them to find me a foster home.

I feel as if I've lost a game I didn't know I wanted to win. I don't want to go.

Then there's a thump at the door and Tom appears, having head-butted his way in. I didn't close it exactly right. *"Mawwwww,"* he scolds, and I meow back, glad for the company.

He jumps up onto the closed toilet lid and peers into

the tub, twitching his orange ears. I wave my fingers underwater, then poke them up through the bubbles, and he cocks his head at them, as if he thinks they're fish. He puts his front paws on the edge of the tub and leans forward, one paw extended.

"Careful," I breathe.

Tom's fat belly wobbles. His paw slips and his front legs fall into the water, backpedaling. I draw my legs away from his scrambling claws just in time. He pulls himself up and out, plopping onto the bath mat, shaking the bubbles off his paws.

I laugh harder than I've laughed in about a millennium. Tom ignores me.

Shell's sitting in my room looking at my photo album, my cookbook beside her. I stride in fast and snatch it away. "That's mine!" Tom scurries under the bed at my loud voice. "I'm not yelling at you, Tom," I say pointedly, staring hard at Shell. "This is private property."

Shell looks as if I've slapped her. "I'm sorry. I wanted to see . . ." She swallows, and I recognize the expression. The *I don't want to cry* face. I know what she wants me to do—pretend I don't see it. That's how I want other people to act for me.

Wanted to see what? I almost ask. Instead I put the photo album in the nightstand. I feel the gap between us widening, and all I want to do is lie under the covers with the blankets over my head. "I'm going to go to sleep now."

"Cady." Shell opens and closes her hands as if grasping for invisible objects. "Let's talk."

I shut my eyes. Here it comes. "Fine. Whatever. I'll pack and you can take me back tomorrow." A bitter taste rises in my throat, and I swallow it back.

"What? No, Cady." Shell puts her hand on me and I open my eyes. "Do you . . . *want* to go back?"

I manage to shake my head once, so small I wouldn't be surprised if she missed it. No.

"Oh my gosh." She squeezes my hand. "I'd never send you away."

I examine Shell's face, warm as her palm. She's telling the truth. Relief flows out of me like Shell turned a faucet on. My breathing evens out. I squish her fingers in return.

"Anyway, can you imagine explaining this to the social workers? 'Yeah, she burned a cake, so she can't live with me.'" Shell pulls me down to sit next to her.

We both chuckle. "They would think you were a monster."

"Precisely. And you know what? The cake's okay. I cut the burned part off. The biggest problem was the oven rack was too high. The cake doesn't look bad. We can frost it and nobody will be able to tell." Shell blows out air. "Cady, the truth is—I'm not used to having a kid around here. I want you to be safe."

I raise an eyebrow at her. "You want me to be safe but you let me go out there with rattlesnakes and whatnot the first day I'm here?"

A wry smile creeps up on her face. "Okay. You got me. But at least you met Jay."

I smile a little, thinking of him. It's not disloyal to Jenna if I make a new friend, is it? He's so different from her, not to mention older, but I think they'd get along fine. "His grandma's kind of mean." I remember what she said about Oregon and wonder if I should ask Shell about it.

Shell shakes her head. "She can be a little crotchety, but she's dependable. And sweet, once you get to know her."

I snort.

Shell moves her shoulders up. "Cady, I didn't mean to yell at you—I was scared. I need to teach you about oven safety. And maybe don't cook alone for a while."

I nod, once. "Maybe." I pinch the bedspread, deciding whether I want to tell her more or if I should stop talking. "I always cooked for me and Dad. Mostly microwave stuff."

Her brows draw together. "I'm sure he appreciated it. What was your favorite thing to make?"

"Spaghetti."

"Spaghetti's one of my favorites, too."

"I made it with ketchup packets and ramen noodles. I'd save the packets from fast-food places and then mix them with a little water to thin it out. And ramen is easy to cook in the microwave." It was the best I could do—convenience stores don't sell pasta. It was cheaper than canned spaghetti. I steal a glance at Shell, remembering the delicious pasta alla Shell. "Do you think that's gross?"

Shell's expression goes from soft to hard and back again. She shakes her head. "It's very creative, Cady." She changes the subject. "Your grandmother liked to make that Lady Baltimore Cake for me and your mom. We'd ask for it on every birthday."

I lift my head. This is new.

Shell picks up the cookbook from where it sits next to her on the bed and takes out the construction paper flower. "This bookmark—your mom made it."

I take the flower. I've had it all this time and I didn't know. I thought this cookbook was the only thing I had of my mom's. Dad wears her wedding band on a chain around his neck. That's it. We moved around so much that Dad sort of lost track of the rest of Mom's stuff. "Dad never said."

"He probably didn't know. Your mom made that in first grade, for our mom's Mother's Day project." Shell takes a deep, shuddering breath. "And this photo here?" She points to the one on the wall, with the two girls in it.

"That's me and your mom, 1984. Before our parents got divorced and Mom moved us into the city."

I examine the photo more carefully. They're actually standing right in front of this farmhouse. Yes, under that layer of baby fat, there's my mother's face. I can see it now. I touch the photo as if I can reach back through time and hold the hand of the little girl who would become my mom. "She was so beautiful." I try to remember her grown-up face. "Do you have any pictures of her when she was a grown-up?" Please do.

"No. I don't." Shell's voice is low. I turn and look at my brand-new aunt. Fat tears hang on her thick lashes and drip off her chin. Without thinking twice, I sit down and put my arm around her, hugging her to me the way I would with Jenna, though Shell's much bigger than I am. This gesture seems to make her cry more, and I wonder if I should let go, but instead she hugs me to her, and it's like warming myself at a fire on a chilly night. We sit there for a while. I don't want to push her away or anything. Well, maybe a tiny bit.

"Mew." Tom swats at Shell's ankle in disapproval. Cats aren't very sympathetic.

Shell reaches out and grabs a tissue, blows her nose. "Your mother was such a riot. Always making jokes no matter what."

I try to hear my mother's laugh in my mind, but I can't. "Did her laugh sound like yours?"

"A little. Hers was higher. More contagious. I think mine sounds more like a rhino blowing his horn."

"It does not. Rhinos can't even blow their horns." I giggle at this, and Tom reappears from under the bed and jumps up between us, purring. I get the photo book out of the drawer and hand it to Shell. "You can look at it as much as you want."

Shell gets up and opens the closet, rifling through a box. "And you look at this one." She hands me a small photo album.

We both flip through the albums slowly. There's a picture of Shell in a US Marines uniform with an American flag behind her. "You were in the Marines?"

Shell nods. "Yup. I enlisted at eighteen. Just for four years, until I figured out I wanted to go to culinary school." She turns the page. "See, it's where I met Suzanne." Sure enough, there's a photo of them standing in front of a giant stove, wearing tall white chef hats.

She opens the album to another page. "These are your grandparents in the late seventies." They're standing in front of the courthouse. My grandmother is young and pretty in this one, wearing a multicolored minidress. My grandfather's wearing a police uniform.

"My grandpa Sanchez was a policeman?" I think of the police who picked me up at the school and wonder if he ever had to do anything like that.

"A good one, too. His picture's hanging in the San

Diego Police Museum." Shell sighs a little bit. "It was hard on him, though. Very stressful. That's why he quit and moved to Julian."

If my grandpa Sanchez could immigrate here and do that, maybe there's hope for Jay and his family. Laws can change, right? My stomach does a hopeful little hop.

I flip through the book again. There are just a few photos of my mom when she was growing up. One from Halloween, with her as Wonder Woman and Shell as a GI Joe. A few from Christmases, opening presents. "How come there aren't more of her?"

"She took them with her when she moved out." Shell closes my photo album and hugs it against her heart. "Cady, I wish I'd known how things were. I would have helped."

I pat Tom. "Dad wouldn't have let you." *He said you never cared about us.* I clamp my mouth shut. "Why did Señora Vasquez think we went to Oregon?"

Shell scratches Tom's rump. "That's what your father told us. About four years ago. You were moving to eastern Oregon and that was that. Never heard another word from him until I got the call to come get you." She seems like she wants to say something else but doesn't.

"But . . ." I falter. "Couldn't you call him, tell him you wanted to keep in touch?"

Shell gives me a tight smile. "I tried, sweetie. I wanted to see you, but he wouldn't let me after your mom died."

Why would he do that? I want to ask. But maybe she doesn't know. Maybe that's something I need to ask my father. I remember our conversation this morning. How he said he'd be coming for me.

I pet Tom's chin. He's drooling. "Shell?" My voice is very small and quiet. "Is my dad really in jail?"

I expect Shell to tell me some story about how she doesn't know and we'll have to wait and see and how it's all for the best, but instead she nods.

Disappointment makes my skeleton crumble. I should have known Dad really wasn't going to come get me. But some tiny part of me thought he'd tell me the truth. I guess the same part that hoped my pie would be fine even though my smart-brain part knew it was messed up. "For how long?"

"I don't know, Cady."

Finally. An adult who's honest with me. For this I'm grateful, even if she's telling me bad news. I think of my dad in jail, sleeping on a bunk. At least he's getting regular food and he'll get treatment. Maybe he won't do all those weird prayers anymore. Maybe.

Maybe they'll teach him how to take care of me again. So many maybes.

My stomach rumbles.

Shell stands. "Enough of this. You need to eat."

I get up. "I quite agree. I could do with a spot of food," I say in my best Mary Berry voice. Shell smiles.

*

After we devour the pizza, Shell makes the Seven-Minute Icing from the old cookbook. She shows me how to do it. "The double boiler is basically a saucepan resting on top of a saucepan filled with water," Shell says. "It's a more gentle heat, so the mix doesn't burn. You use it a lot in candy making."

She unearths the handheld mixer and we take turns standing over the frosting, beating it for the seven minutes. The result is sort of like a melted marshmallow. Definitely nothing like the frosting you get in a can.

Shell opens a cupboard. Neat mason jars line the shelves. "Do you want to put a jam in the middle layer? Pick one."

I scan the types. Pomegranate jelly, apricot jam, strawberry jam. "Can I use a jelly? What's the difference?"

"Jelly's made from juice, jam's from the crushed fruit. But those pomegranate seeds are so small you wouldn't be able to make a jam, unless it was all pip."

"Pip?"

"The seed." Now that she's full of pizza and we had our talk upstairs, Shell's about a million times more relaxed. So am I.

I pick the pomegranate jelly and spread it on top of one of the layers. Then Shell places the other layer on top of that and we frost the whole thing, swooping it in little dabs and waves, like a delicious painting.

"That looks pretty good." I admire our work.

"It does. But Cady . . ." Shell puts down the frosting knife. "We need to talk about Grandma's Pies."

I hang my head. "I wanted to help you."

"I know. However, that was really inappropriate. We don't tear down other businesses to help ours get ahead." She squints at me. "Got it?"

I nod miserably. I don't know the first thing about business, or getting ahead. I guess I was thinking about kids like Anna-Tyler, who *do* seem to get to be popular by being mean to other kids. "Got it."

Shell's mouth twitches. I think that me burning the cake might have actually been a good thing—if I hadn't, she'd probably be yelling at me right now. "Well, we're going to have to think of a way for you to make it up to Mrs. Moretti."

"I'll do whatever you say."

"That's up to you and Mrs. Moretti. You'll talk to her tomorrow." She slices into the cake and puts a triangle on a plate. The red jelly gleams out.

My stomach twists. What if Mrs. Moretti is like Jay's grandmother? It doesn't matter, I guess. I'll have to face her either way. And this cake makes it better. "Okay."

We take our plates to the couch to eat, sinking into the sofa cushions. I take a bite. The pomegranate is a little tart, which is nice because the cake is so sweet.

"You should sell this at the shop."

"That icing is too difficult." Shell bites into the cake, then closes her eyes. "It tastes exactly like your grandmother's."

I wish I could have met her. That she could have made this cake for me, too. "Eating this cake makes me sad and happy at the same time."

Shell nods. "Me too. Bittersweet."

Bittersweet. That's a great word. Lots of things are bittersweet. Including some kinds of chocolate. I clean my plate. "When did she die?"

"Right after your mom and dad got married." Shell holds out her hand for my plate, and I give it to her. "Lung cancer."

My mom died of pneumonia. It happened so fast. One day she went into the hospital for a cough that wouldn't go away, and two weeks later she was gone. The last time I saw her, she was lying in bed with tubes and wires coming out of her. She kissed me and told me I was a good girl. And she kept saying, "I'm sorry, Cady." So I told her it was okay, even though it wasn't, because I didn't want her to feel bad. It wasn't her fault she was sick. "How old was my grandmother?"

"Sixty." She heads into the kitchen with the plates. "She would have loved you, Cady."

I think about the recipes she marked. I'm pretty sure I would have loved her, too.

CHAPTER 15

Right after breakfast the next morning, Shell takes me to my possible doom. Grandma's Pies. While Shell's is closed today, Grandma's is open seven days a week. I guess things would be messed up if all the pie shops took Tuesday off, though.

Mrs. Moretti is a tiny woman with dark brown hair and light tan skin. She doesn't look like a grandma—she's maybe a few years older than Shell. I look at the floor as Shell introduces me.

"Hi, Cady." Mrs. Moretti shakes my hand firmly.

Shell puts her hand on my shoulder and I know what she expects me to do. "I'm sorry I wrote on your sign," I say woodenly. I look around her busy pie shop. She's got twice as many pies as Shell's in the window and more in the back. Three times as many tables. A full food menu, too. I think she could spare a few of her customers. "It's just that—"

"No excuses, Cady," Shell says. "It waters down the apology."

Shell's right. Truthfully, I wanted her customers to come to Shell's, just like I do right now, and that wasn't how to get them. With difficulty I raise my head and look into Mrs. Moretti's eyes. They have deep laugh lines around them and a very kind expression, and I realize she's probably a perfectly nice person. "I'm really sorry. I shouldn't have done that." And I mean it this time. I feel better as soon as the words come out, the same as when I apologized to Jay. Does everyone who messes up and apologizes feel like this?

Mrs. Moretti touches my arm. "Thank you. Apology accepted." She glances at Shell. "I think my windows could use a cleaning."

Shell nods. "Sounds like a plan."

I spend the next hour or so cleaning Mrs. Moretti's windows with a squeegee and a bucket of suds. Outside the jewelry shop next door, a tied-up rottweiler lies panting. He looks up at me and whines.

"Are you okay, boy?" I let him sniff my knuckles, then scratch his head. He looks sadly across the street. "It's a hot day."

I pick a pie pan out of Mrs. Moretti's trash, wash it out, and fill it with water for the dog. He slobbers it all up, splashing all over the sidewalk. I pet his huge head. I'm really getting used to dogs.

"I was just about to do that. Thanks." A man about Shell's age comes out. "I don't know where the owner went—they're not in my store."

"Oh." I keep washing the windows. The man looks a little familiar, but I shouldn't talk to strangers. Dad's told me a billion times.

"I'm Grant Anderson. Gable's father." He smiles. "Gable told me about you. He says you're hilarious."

"That's because I am," I say in a serious tone, just to make him laugh. It works. He's got dark hair and the same kind of features as Gable, just with a little more flesh and wrinkles. "You look like him. Except older. And with no earrings."

He laughs. "Not anymore." He shows me his earlobes—full of holes. "But I sell them."

"Oh." I touch mine. "I don't have pierced ears." I've always wanted them. Pretty much every girl at my school has earrings. But Dad wouldn't let me. He was afraid they'd get infected because we couldn't keep them clean. And also, who knows how expensive it'd be.

"Well. If you wash my windows too, and your aunt lets you, I could pierce them as a trade."

"Deal." I stick out my hand. I guess this morning didn't spell my doom after all.

For the next week, I go to the bakery every day with Shell. I like working alongside María, who plays a Spanish-speaking music station, singing along as we prepare the pies. It's what I imagined a home to be like. Shell tacks a piece of paper up on the wall so I can tally how many crusts I make. It gets tedious after the third crust, and my shoulders ache and my hands hurt. María watches me but only offers help if I ask. Which I try not to.

"What if I become expert level before one thousand?" I ask Shell.

"You won't."

"But I *could,*" I argue. "My crusts are two hundred percent better than they were the first day."

"Doesn't matter." Shell is immovable. "One thousand."

Other than that, I slice up Granny Smiths and Galas and prepare the fillings. I'm not used to using a knife, so I cut my fingers a bunch of times and have to wear blue rubber coverings over my Band-Aids. But it's never life-threatening. And it's what the *Bake Off* contestants wear.

On the Saturday before Memorial Day, I have Band-Aids on three different fingers. Shell comes in the back and watches me peeling the apples. She smiles a little.

"What?" I work the peeler around a Granny Smith. We're actually kind of busy today because of the holiday, and I want to make as many pies as I can.

Shell points to my hurt fingers. "You're not a complainer."

I shake my head, pleased that she noticed. "No point." I grumble plenty in my head. Then I tell myself, *Just get on with it,* as Dad would say. Plus, nobody whines on *Bake Off* if they get hurt.

"María." Shell narrows her eyes and does a big, dramatic head nod. "It's time. Show Cady how to use the machines."

María demonstrates a large contraption bolted to the side of a counter. The apple goes on a spike and then you push a button, and the machine does all the work, peeling it, pushing out the core, and slicing it into neat pieces. "That's all there is to it. Just don't stick your fingers in."

And then—we move on to the pie crust machine! I stand in front of it like it's a treasure and I'm a pirate.

"I feel like I should, I don't know, bow down." I bend deeply at the waist. "Greetings, King Pie Crust Machine."

María laughs and imitates me. "Yes. We must pay our respects." She shows me how to curtsy. "Just in case you ever really do meet a king."

Then she shows me how to use the pie crust machine. This is going to be a hundred times easier now. I'll have a thousand pies done in no time.

I wonder if we'll have the customers to eat them. But things are going so well with Shell, I don't want to say anything that'll upset her. I keep my mouth shut and my hands busy.

JUNE

83 Pies Down

917 to Go

CHAPTER 16

The first Tuesday in June, Shell takes me to an indoor mall in Escondido and we pick out a bunch of stuff for me at Old Navy. Underwear. T-shirts. Jeans. I think of Dad's words. *We don't need your charity.* He'd want me to tell her no. But I don't want to. Because guess what? I need clothes. Dad hasn't bought me any in forever. I've grown—I hadn't realized how short my pants were.

Shell points out the sale signs and lectures me about how to calculate percentages. Then she makes me do it. "If this shirt is thirty dollars—well, twenty-nine ninety-nine, but we're rounding up, and it's twenty percent off, how much will we pay?"

I purse my lips, doing the math. "Twenty-four?"

Shell holds up her hand. I slap her palm.

Then, of course, Shell makes me calculate the price of every single thing we look at. "This is making my brain hurt," I complain.

"It'll get stronger," she says. "It's a muscle. You have to use it."

Shell picks out a jacket that has a zip-out lining from a clearance rack. "Nights and mornings are always cool," she says. "You'll need it no matter how long you stay. Not that I don't want you to stay," she adds when she sees my face. "You'll stay for as long as you need."

But what if that's forever? I swallow hard, unable to decide if that's good or bad.

"Plus." She points to the sign: 80% OFF. It's only twenty dollars right now.

I grin. "Four bucks? That's a bargain!" We smile like we just shared a secret.

I try on blue jeans and find a pair that fit, but as we walk to the register I spot colored ones. Pink and teal and regular blue. I've never had jeans like these. They're so pretty. I run my hand over the material. The model in the picture smiles, wearing pink ones with a flowery shirt. "Do you like those?" Shell says.

"These are fine." I hold up the blue ones in my hand. We're already headed to the checkout. I don't want Shell to get annoyed and impatient.

But she gets annoyed and impatient anyway. "If you want the colored ones, just say so."

I shake my head. I'm going to stick with what I said. The colored ones cost more, and I don't want Shell to hate me for making her spend too much.

Shell sighs and picks out colored jeans in my size. "It's okay to change your mind, Cady. Go try these on."

Finally, we're in line, and I'm looking at the earrings they have on display along the way. "I could get you a pair," Shell says. "They're half off."

"My ears aren't pierced." I lift my hair to show her.

"Huh." Shell frowns. "That's funny. Your mom had them done when you were a baby. In our family, in our culture, actually, that's really common."

A sharp imaginary jab pokes my stomach. That's another thing I didn't know. I tell her about Gable's dad and his offer. Shell purses her lips. "I'm not sure. We should ask your dad."

"But you're my guardian, right? And besides, they were pierced before, so what does it matter?" I don't want to wait for the next time we talk to Dad. And I'm also afraid he'll say no. Just his usual, automatic no.

"It's a permanent change to your body." Shell sighs and seems to be talking to herself. "We'll ask him next time we talk."

While Shell's busy paying, I look out of the store across the mall corridor, to the pretzel place. Those pretzels smell so good, like salt and sugar. I head straight toward the girl handing out samples before she goes back inside.

"Cady, you should ask if it's okay before you go running off." Shell rushes to catch up with me. "I looked behind me and you were gone!" Her eyes are big.

I only went twenty feet. Dad didn't make me ask permission for samples. Or for a lot of things. I stop in my tracks. "Shell. May. I. Please. Get. A. Pretzel. Sample?" I sound like a resentful robot.

"Sure. See how easy that was?" Shell hands me the bag of clothes. "Carry your own gear."

So many rules. I'm not sure that I like them all. I make a face at my aunt and clomp over to the pretzel place.

CHAPTER 17

A few days later, Jay takes me to see the stream. He has me sit on the back of his bike, giving me his helmet. I'm pretty sure this is highly dangerous and probably illegal, but when I tell Jay this, he shrugs. "This is Julian. We're old school."

We ride to the state park's main entrance, where the ranger waves us through. Then he locks up the bike and we begin the next part of our journey, hiking through a field with waist-high grass. The dirt gets into my tennis shoes, which have netting on the toes. "This grass is so dry."

"Yeah. It burns every once in a while." Jay crushes a blade. "It needs to. That's how some of the wildflowers get their seeds out. If they don't burn, they'll die out forever. Isn't that funny?"

The wind kicks up, searing my nostrils. I shiver a little anyway. I don't like the idea of fire—who would? But there's always something to deal with, no matter where you go. In California, there are earthquakes and wildfires. In Florida, there are hurricanes and alligators. In Kansas, there are tornadoes.

"There aren't that many year-round streams, but this is one of them. And you won't find it on any map." Suddenly Jay veers off the trail and into the underbrush. "Try not to break any branches." Jay holds the brush so they don't thwack me in the face. "Technically you're not supposed to go off trail."

This makes me mighty nervous. "I don't want to get into trouble." That'd be all I need. Getting booted out of a state park like some hooligan.

"Don't worry." Jay holds a particularly thorny palm branch for me. "The ranger lets me dig out the non-native plants. Like this Mexican palm." He taps the huge thick fan-shaped branch with spikes protruding from the sides. "So it's like a good deed, really."

"How do I know which ones are native, and which ones aren't?"

"It's not that hard. I'll show you the worst ones." Jay holds up his hand. "Watch out for the poison oak." He points down. "'Leaves of three, let it be.' It's got this oil on it that'll give you a bad rash."

I examine it. There are three leaves coming out of a branch. The bushes spread all over the place. "Why don't they get rid of all of it?"

"It's native, and besides, we're in nature. You can't get rid of all possibly dangerous things." He grins. "If there was no risk, it would be no fun."

I laugh at this. I remember what Ms. Walker said about ecosystems. Things exist for a purpose. Bees might sting, but we need them to pollinate crops. Sharks keep down seal populations. "What good does poison oak do?"

"Squirrels eat the berries." Jay shrugs. "I don't know what else."

I pretend to have a heart attack, clutching my chest. "Something Jay Morales doesn't know?"

He snorts out a laugh. "I know, right?"

We keep on hiking. Before long I hear the trickle of water nearby and the deep croaking of frogs. Jay leads me down a bank that gets squishier and muddier, and suddenly there's an honest-to-goodness stream, trickling over rocks. It's pretty small, but it's a real proper stream. The closest I've been to something like this is a concrete drainage ditch (where sometimes I actually did hear frogs). And also the San Diego River, which always has some trash in it, plus very tall, thick reeds hiding its edges. There are homeless camps by the river, but Dad wouldn't let us go there.

The frogs stop making noise as soon as we get near the water. "They don't want humans catching them," Jay tells me. "Sit down."

We rest on some flat rocks by the water. It looks like a museum painting again, with the sunlight glinting through the trees onto the water. It's so quiet. No car noises or other people—nothing but the moving stream, birds, and the leaves rustling in the breeze. "This is so cool." That word seems kind of inadequate to describe it all. I sneak a peek at Jay, wondering why he would want to hang out with me. Why exactly he thinks we're friends. He's so much more confident than I am.

Jay looks around, then grabs a plant with a feathery green top, crushing the top in his fist. "Smell that."

I do. "Smells like black licorice."

He nods. "Fennel. It's not supposed to be growing here, so the ranger wants it gone." He takes a Swiss Army knife kind of thing out of his backpack and flips it open to a knife. I gasp, but all he does is use the blade to pry up under the plant. It sort of looks like a fatter, whiter chunk of celery. "Ta-da! You can sauté it or bake it. It's kind of sweet, but not *too* sweet." He presents it to me with a flourish.

I sniff the stem, which also has that black licorice scent. "What does it taste like?"

"Like a harder apple that's crossed with celery?" Jay shrugs. "Fennel is fennel. I don't know how to explain it."

I wipe the dirt off the bulb with my shirt, thinking of *Bake Off* and how they use "unexpected ingredients" all the time.

Jay leans over. "If you ever forage, the first rule is to make sure you don't do it where the Park Service sprays weed killer. They only spray in the picnic areas to get rid of the poison oak. The second rule is to show the ranger everything we pick.

"Fennel has yellow flowers and these feathery leaves." He points to another tall plant with white flowers. "That one looks similar, but it's poison hemlock. It doesn't smell good, though, so they're easy to tell apart."

"Who taught you all this?"

"The ranger. And Shell. Sometimes she takes us hiking."

"Shell?" A jealous pang hits me. "I thought she was too busy."

"You've only known her a few weeks." Jay looks a little sad, too. "Yeah, she does work a lot. She didn't use to be like that. Neither did my mom. Even Claudia used to be nicer."

I think about Claudia and her alleged non-boyfriend, Gable. "She seems kind of . . . out of place."

"My mom's trying to get her to go to college, but all she wants to do is hang out with that guy." Jay frowns, digging out another bulb. "I'm going to college, though. I'm going to be a game developer."

This surprises me. "I thought you'd want to do something outside. Like be a park ranger." I have no evidence for this, except for what I've observed about Jay. He seems like he's as important to the land as one of Shell's trees.

He gives me a fierce look. "I want to do something to support my family. Like create an app that makes a million dollars."

I understand that. If I made that much money, my dad wouldn't have any more trouble. I think. But then I see all these magazines with stories about celebrities with all kinds of money who are addicted to bad things. Maybe how much money you have doesn't matter when it comes to things like that. Maybe you're the same on the inside, no matter what you have.

I don't know if that thought is the greatest one I've ever had or the worst.

"What do you want to be, Cady?" Jay works on digging up another bulb.

I've thought about that one. I want to be a chef. But until I got to Shell's, I had no idea how I was going to do it. "I want to take over Shell's Pie one day," I answer without thinking. "How about that?"

Jay raises his eyebrows. "We'd better make it succeed, then."

Yeah. "I don't think we sold enough yesterday." I picture Shell's worried face. No wonder she never has any fun anymore. I don't know how I could help, though. It's not like my mad table-wiping skills are going to make people come buy her pie. And writing on the competition's sign wasn't the answer.

Jay grabs my shoulder. "Don't move." He points across the creek.

I turn my head and follow his finger. A group of deer slowly make their way down to the water through the bushes. I hold my breath. There's a female. A smaller female follows, and then two babies on long, slightly wobbly legs. They're gray brown, tinged with a hint of cream on the tips of their fur. I really want to pet one. Obviously I know I shouldn't even try.

The lead cocks her head and looks right at us, though neither of us has moved. It's like she read my mind and said, *Uh-oh, that girl wants to touch me!* She pivots and so do the others, all of them bounding back through the brush.

I let out my breath. "That was awesome!"

Jay's eyes shine. "I've never been that close before."

"Will they come back?" I want to look at them again.

"After we leave." He checks his watch. "Oops. It's getting late." We run for home.

CHAPTER 18

The following evening, Shell teaches me how to make a lattice crust. We set the ingredients out on the big, square butcher-block island in the middle of the kitchen. "In the old cookbook, almost all the recipes say to use shortening, not butter," I tell Shell.

"That's because that cookbook's from the 1950s. Shortening was popular then because it keeps forever, unlike butter. Plus they did a *lot* of marketing for it. Did you know shortening's melting point is higher than your body's, so it leaves a waxy taste on your tongue?" Shell leans forward on the kitchen island, her powerful arms crossed in front of her. I can tell she's enjoying giving this lecture. "Now, a lot of people use butter and shortening, but I like the all-butter crust. It's flakier and rises higher. However, it doesn't let you do real fancy things with the edges—it won't hold its shape so much."

"So if I wanted to do a fancy pie with cutouts of crust leaves on top, that wouldn't work?" My mind's whirring.

"Correcto-mundo!" Shell grins and I'm pleased with myself for getting it. This is way better than, say, math class, where I rarely get it.

"I think they always use all butter on *The Great British Bake Off.*" I don't remember ever seeing a can of shortening on the show, but I could be wrong. I haven't seen every episode. "Why is it called *The Great British Baking Show* here and *Bake Off* in England?"

"I guess they thought Americans wouldn't know what a 'bake off' was."

I shake my head. "We might not have them, but I can *infer* what a bake off is." Ms. Walker talks about that—if we run across a word we don't know, we can *infer* its meaning by reading the rest of the sentence. Why would it be hard for grown-ups to do?

My stomach hollows as I think of Ms. Walker and what I've been missing. During the last two weeks, they're having parties and picnics to celebrate the end of elementary school. It feels like I've lived three lifetimes since I've been gone, but it's only been about a month.

Shell and I stand in the kitchen talking about *The Great British Bake Off* as our hands work on the pie crust. She gets a piece of cloth out of the freezer and places it on the counter. "This is a pie canvas," she says. "To keep it from sticking when we roll it out."

I wrap the dough in plastic and put it in the refrigerator to rest—I've learned my lesson. Shell regards me with a thoughtful look. "Did you like hiking with Jay?"

"It was pretty good. We saw deer."

"Very cool! You know, I've got a couple of books you might like." Shell goes into the living room, to the packed, sagging-shelf bookcase near the TV. She picks out a couple of thin volumes. "Local bird guidebook." She puts it in my hand. "And local scat guidebook."

"Scat?" I open it. It's all about how to identify animals based on their poop. Like if it's got hair, then it's probably a predator's, like a coyote's. Totally gross and kind of awesome, too. My mouth tugs upward. "Thanks."

Shell scratches her head. "Yup."

We get back to pie making, which is easier than this kind of talking. She takes a small knife out of a drawer. "A paring knife. Let's peel."

She shows me how to use this to peel the skin off the apple. The trick is to move the apple more than the knife. "You just have to apply a little pressure." Shell peels the apple in one long curly strip.

"Wow." I eat the crunchy peel. I'm a little bit scared of the knife, to be honest. I start mine carefully and go really slow.

Shell studies me. "You're taking too much of the apple with the skin. But you'll learn."

I put down the knife and the apple and stretch my

aching fingers. "Don't you ever put anything else in with the apples?"

"You could. Cherries. Pears. Whatever. As long as it's not too watery."

Huh. I think of *Bake Off* again and run to the fridge. "What about fennel?" I get the bulb.

"Fennel?" Shell's brow crinkles. "That'd be more like a savory pie. Do you even know what it tastes like?"

I shake my head.

So Shell and I take a break from the pie and chop up the fennel. She shows me how to sauté it in a pan with a little butter. "Throw some apple slices in there."

"You can sauté apples?"

"Sure. They're great with pork chops."

I'm learning so much. I throw in some Granny Smith slices, and then some Gala. Shell adds some cinnamon, then pauses. "Have you ever tried this?" She takes out a little jar and holds it to my nose. "Cardamom."

I inhale deeply. It's a little like nutmeg and a little like cinnamon but is its own thing. Just like fennel is its own thing. And I've seen it on *Bake Off*. Paul Hollywood always, I mean *always,* worries it'll taste "medicinal."

"So that's what cardamom smells like," I say. "Can we use it?"

She hands it to me. "Just a little, like a quarter teaspoon, or it'll taste—"

"Medicinal," I supply.

Shell laughs. “I just love that you love *Bake Off,* too.”

It smells heavenly. We stand in silence, me pushing the wooden spoon around the pan, making sure things cook evenly. The apples and fennel sizzle, then bubble, giving off a sweet smell. I’m just about the calmest I’ve ever been. I could do this forever. I smile at Shell and she smiles back and ruffles my hair. Warmth explodes in my chest.

After everything is softened, Shell pours it all onto a plate. We each take a bite. I like the fennel and the apple combo. Like Jay said, it’s not too sweet, and it kind of gives the apple a hint of the licorice.

“Not bad,” Shell says, “but it needs something to marry them together.” She goes to the pantry and takes out a box of raisins. “Are you opposed to these?”

“Why would I be?” Opposed is a strong word to use against raisins.

“Some people don’t like them, but I love them in baked goods. It gives a lot of—depth.”

“Now you sound like Paul Hollywood.” I smirk at her.

“Hey now.” She has a deep laugh, from her belly, and I giggle. I wish I’d known her since I was little. If I had, I might be an entirely different person now. That’s crazy to think about. Like in some other universe there’s an alternate Cady who’s been baking pies with Aunt Shell forever, who’s never slept in a van or a foster home. Who would I be then? The thought’s exciting but also scary, because this Cady is all I know.

She tosses the raisins with the still-warm mixture and we try it again. I have a bite with raisin, fennel, and apple all together.

I'm in love.

Shell gives me a thumbs-up. "All right, Doctor. I think our patient's alive."

We chop up more fennel and mix it with apples and raisins and spices. Shell says we don't need to sauté it; it'll cook inside the pie. "This might take more than one try," Shell warns. "We might be forced to eat multiple pies."

"Tragedy." I grin.

Shell shows me how to cut the crust with a rolling pastry cutter, measuring it into strips three-quarters of an inch wide, then weaving them together like a basket. Over, under. Over, under. It's sort of like braiding hair and it's easier than I thought it'd be. "It looks so complicated when it's done," I say.

"Well, a lot of things look complicated when they're done, and they are complicated—but you have to remember every single project gets broken down into a bunch of smaller steps. So nothing is really that complicated after all."

I think about this. Everything is complicated, yet nothing really is. "You sound like Master Oogway in *Kung Fu Panda*."

She bows. "I accept your compliment." Shell cracks an egg over a small bowl, then beats it with a fork. We use a milk wash on our crust at work. "The egg wash will give it a deeper gold, shinier color than the finish we get from the milk." She adds a little water to thin it, then lets me brush it over the lattice.

We've just put together the whole pie when Shell's phone chimes. "Who could that be at this hour?" Shell glances at the caller ID. Her brows lift and she steps out of the room.

"I don't know if now is a good time," she says in a low voice. I mix the fennel some more, my skin prickling. Who is she talking to? Is it a bill collector, coming for the pie shop? I move over a little bit so I can hear. Tom jumps on the table and meows.

"You can't be up here with the pie." I put him on the floor.

This excites the dogs, who bark as Tom lands between them. He leaps up to the windowsill and glares at me.

"Cady?" Shell pokes her head in from the living room. "Cady, your dad's on the phone."

"Dad?" I repeat kind of blankly, my brain unable to process this. Then, a second later, it kicks in. Dad. My father. Dad, who is in jail. I haven't talked to him in weeks, since he called when I first got here.

It's hard to admit it, but now I can't imagine not standing in this kitchen baking stuff, not petting the animals every morning. Not getting to see everyone every day.

Swallowing hard, I wipe my hands on a towel and walk slowly forward, my limbs stiff. I want to do several things all at once. Run upstairs and cry into my pillow. Yell at my dad. And cry and tell him how badly I miss him.

Shell hits mute. "You don't have to talk to him, Cady. But he sounds pretty good."

So much has happened to me since they took me away, but he's been in there, alone, waiting like time stopped.

My throat opens again and I reach for the phone. Shell unmutes it.

"Buttercup?" Dad's voice sounds crackly. "Are you there?"

Shell busies herself in the kitchen, washing a mixing bowl. I nod, forgetting he can't see me. "I'm here, Dad. How are you?" I don't know what else to say.

"I'm not bad, Buttercup. Not bad at all. How are you?"

"Okay." This time he's actually asking about me, but somehow I think it'll make him feel worse if I tell him about the fun I'm having. As if I'm better off without him. Then he won't have a reason to get better.

"Just okay?" His voice is sharp. "Is she taking you to church?"

I sigh. "Dad, you never took me to church, either. But Shell is treating me better than okay. Don't worry." I change the subject. "How is it in there?"

"I go to church here. There's a chapel." Dad's voice quavers. "And they have me in a program. With doctors and medical treatments. I really think it's going to take this time. I'll get out and everything will go back to normal."

I'm quiet. What's normal? Living in the van or at a motel? I look around the comfortable house, at the dogs snoring on the floor. What if I don't want my "normal" back?

I sit heavily down at the table, put my head on it. What about a job? I want to ask him. Where will we live? Would Shell let us stay here, and would Dad be okay with that? I keep quiet, though, because that will make him sad.

"Buttercup?" Dad sounds pleading. "I need to hear your voice. Talk to me, Buttercup. Tell me something. Anything."

I'm sick of him calling me Buttercup. "My name's Cady. Or did you forget?" Suddenly I'm angry. I'm so angry that I can't talk anymore. Why do I always have to comfort him? It's not fair. He should comfort me. I'm a kid.

"Buttercup?" Dad's voice reminds me of a stretched-out piece of gum. "I'm your father. Don't you have any respect for me?"

I look at Aunt Shell. *Help.* Shell takes the phone away. To my surprise, she puts her hand on my back, as if she's shielding me. "I'm sorry. She's overwhelmed."

"Overwhelmed?" I hear my father say. "It's up to me when to say my daughter's overwhelmed, Michelle. Don't be trying to come in between me and my daughter like you did me and my wife!"

Shell's face turns red and she steps out of the room again. But her voice is calm. "I'm not getting into this with you."

How dare he call and tell us what to do? It's his fault he's there. It's even his fault I'm here. I don't want to go back to that. My mom wouldn't want me to, either.

Why couldn't my dad hold it together after my mom died? That's what he was supposed to do. Or why wouldn't he come ask Shell for help?

I don't want to overhear anything else. Quickly I open the pantry and get a box of Pop-Tarts and three more granola bars. I run upstairs and put those in my drawer, too. I look over my food. I'm collecting a pretty good stash. I might have to use two drawers soon, or maybe the closet.

"Cady!" Shell calls me.

"Are you off the phone?" I yell.

"Yeah."

So I run back down, and Shell's picking up the oven mitts. "Okay, kiddo. It's getting late. Let's get this pie into the oven before we turn into pumpkins."

I wait for her to tell me what Dad said, or to ask me

endless questions about how I'm doing, how I feel, the way adults usually do at times like these. But Shell doesn't, to my relief. Instead we throw ourselves into the pie baking and cleanup. "Don't forget to add this one on your pie count!" Shell gives me a high five.

Maybe action can help with feelings as much as words can, sometimes.

CHAPTER 19

Jay and I walk up and down Main Street on our Grand Pie Tour, weaving through the tourists taking selfies. It's a Saturday and the weather's almost one hundred degrees, but most of the stores have awnings built over the sidewalks for protection.

Downtown Julian looks sort of like pictures I've seen of Old West ghost towns, with faded wooden buildings, except of course it's not a ghost town and therefore not creepy. Just old-fashioned looking. Up the side streets above the hill, small Victorian houses and bungalows peek out among trees. Some of the houses are painted in brighter colors, purples and greens, and have a lot of fancy trim on them—in curls and diamond cutouts and all sorts of other shapes.

"First I gotta show you the important stuff." Jay gestures. "The town hall is there. Public bathrooms are behind it, in case anyone asks. They cost a quarter."

"Got it." I point to a steepled building on a hill. "Is that a church?"

"No. It's the historical museum. It used to be the schoolhouse. But never mind that. It's candy time." Jay leads me into a place that has two sets of stairs and doors and three signs above: MINER'S DINER, SODA FOUNTAIN, JULIAN DRUGSTORE. We enter on the right and walk all the way through a souvenir store crammed with trinkets and cards. A room to the side leads to a grill—I smell the delicious grease of hamburgers and fries. "Are you sure this is the right place?"

"Do you think I haven't lived here for practically my whole life?" Jay retorts.

Finally, he leads me to a set of stairs. The doorway's framed in logs and a wood-burned placard reads CANDY MINE. Hand-painted wooden signs above the stairs say LOW BEAM and DANGER, DUCK YOUR HEAD. "Behold," Jay says dramatically as a large basement room opens up in front of us.

I gasp. Every possible kind of candy I ever could have imagined seems to be here. Metal buckets are filled with individually wrapped pieces of candy. Then there are packaged candies, old-time candies like Necco Wafers, buttons, hard candy sticks, Red Hots.

I run to a bucket and pick up a handful of wrapped peppermints. I want to eat every piece in this place. And I want to fill up a bucket and put it with the food stash I started on the first day. I wonder how long candy keeps.

"The stuff in the buckets is sold by weight, so it's easy to spend a bunch," Jay warns.

I put down the mints, circling the room at least five times, deciding. Jay gets a box of Nerds. "All this candy and you're getting regular old Nerds?"

"It's my favorite."

He's got a point. I like them, too. I get a box for later and a few pieces of assorted hard candies, and we take them upstairs to the clerk, a man with curly black hair who wears glasses. "Is that *all*?" The clerk sniffs kind of snobbily. Jay just shrugs, but shame pricks at my skin. The clerk pushes a handful of wrapped taffy across the counter. "You can take some of these," he says as if he's doing us a really huge favor.

"We don't need your charity," I say stiffly, and the clerk freezes and seems to shrink. I sound just like Dad and I immediately wish I hadn't said it. At least, not like that.

"Who's this?" he says.

"Cady Madeline Bennett." I have my hands in my pockets. "Who are you?"

"Adam Shaw." He folds his arms over his chest. "What's the matter with your friend, Jay?"

I look over at Jay, expecting him to back me up, but his cheeks are red and he's frowning. "She's new." Jay takes his change and turns and leaves the store, shoulders hunched.

I struggle to catch up. "What's the matter?"

"He just wanted to give us some candy, Cady. It's not charity." Jay shakes Nerds into his mouth. "You made him feel bad."

"*I* made him feel bad? He was acting like we didn't deserve to be in there because we were only getting Nerds." I'm mad too. Jay should see this.

Jay shakes his head. "He always gives us taffy. He gives all the local kids taffy. It's just what he does. Because he knows us. He didn't mean anything except that I usually buy a lot more."

I slow down almost to a stop. I haven't had anyone know me like that, except my teachers. I remember the canned food drives at school, watching tins of pineapple in heavy syrup and baked beans getting put into the collection bins and knowing that I'd probably be one of the people eating them later. Anna-Tyler dancing in with a whole flat of tomato soup cans from Costco, saying, "I bet this will make the homeless people so happy!" And every time, it was like they were kicking me in my pride. At some point, I started believing almost everyone was just like Anna-Tyler. "I didn't know."

"Well. Just don't assume people are out to get you all the time. Most of us aren't." Jay stops and turns around. I stand there. "You coming or not? Those pies aren't going to eat themselves."

I nod, glad Jay's helping me. I keep messing stuff up with people like I'm some weird monkey who's trying to do math. I can't get it right.

*

"We'll start with the most famous pie place," Jay says as we step out into the blazing sun. The Julian Pie Company. "They have a factory, and sell frozen pies all over the place." We step down onto a mossy brick patio and go inside. Jay orders us apple pie slices, no sugar added. "This is my favorite."

I take out the money Shell gave me, but Jay waves it away. "My mom's treat."

"No, this is from Shell." I don't want to depend on Jay, especially after I messed up, and besides, Jay's mom doesn't have a ton of extra.

Jay pays instead of answering. "You get the next one."

Well. Jay's mom must like me. I'll have to thank her.

We sit at a wrought iron table and cut into the pie with plastic forks. It's different from Shell's. "They use shortening in the crust," Jay says. "It's crisper."

I eat the pie. "It's yummy, but I like Shell's better."

Jay asks to see the ingredients list and we study it. Yup, butter and shortening. "Interesting." Jay strokes an invisible beard like a wise man.

I pretend to have a beard too. "Very, very interesting."

Next we visit a pie shop that has a selling window opening right onto the sidewalk, catching a lot of the tourists as they wander by. People stand in a line down the street. Then we go into one that's up a little alley. "Let's try the pecan here," Jay says. "Just for fun."

An older man sits on the stoop, his bald head hidden by a cowboy hat, playing "Where the Streets Have No Name." He belts out the words with his whole heart and lungs, like he's in a stadium instead of in front of two kids. U2's my dad's favorite band. I remember his phone call from the other night—Dad really would like it here, I bet.

I take one of Shell's dollars and put it into his guitar case. To my surprise, Jay starts dancing, swaying and moving his body to the beat. My face goes hot. I can't believe he's dancing in public.

"Come on, Cady." Jay gestures to me. "Just move with it."

For a second, I really want to join him. Jay hops around like he doesn't care people are watching. But then my face heats up. "I'm good." I run a few steps down the street. I wish I didn't care what people thought about me, but that's not going to happen anytime soon.

Jay leads me across the street after that, to Grandma's Pies, which also has a long line. It's making me sad that these other places have so much business while at Shell's we barely get a dozen people all day. "How long have you been waiting?" I ask the man in front of me.

"About a half hour."

"That's nothing. On weekends people wait for an hour just to order, then another half hour for food," Jay says. "For this place, we should come back when they first open. Beat the line. Come on." He leads me to a bakery behind town hall. It's small, with corrugated steel covering the walls. This place has bread and lots of other pastries as well as pies. They sell something called "chocolate bombs," and I open my mouth as I look at them. Drool-worthy. "We'll try one of those another day," Jay says.

The little bakery has a patio for extra seating. Most places do, but not Shell's. I wonder if that makes a difference.

We're kind of stuffed, so we take our pie slices in to-go boxes and leave the shop. As we head up the street, Jay gestures. A wooden sign with a finger pointing to Shell's. But there's so much other stuff to look at, I didn't notice it, and this isn't the main road. "That sign is pretty much useless."

The answer to what could help Shell's seems like it's on the tip of my tongue, like the title of a book I've forgotten. It *feels* like I should know. I stomp a foot in frustration. "There's got to be more we could do. We just haven't thought of it yet."

"Maybe." Jay sounds doubtful.

We decide to check out the schoolhouse, walking up the steep hill to it. Jay jumps over the steps onto the porch and disappears inside.

I climb the wooden steps more slowly, full of pie and

candy. There's a large open space with displays around the perimeter, a video playing on a monitor in the wall, and old school desks in the middle.

A sweet-looking older lady comes out of the back room, with steel-gray hair curled close to her head and dark brown skin. She's wearing regular clothes, a blouse and elastic-waisted pants, unlike Mr. Miniver in his pioneer dress. "Jay! Who's this?" She squints at me through her glasses, as if squinting will help her recognize me.

"Hi, Mrs. Showalter." Jay hugs her. "This is my friend Cady. She moved here last month."

Moved here? Like it's permanent. My stomach does a flip-flop and I can't tell if I'm excited or nervous at the thought. Maybe both. "I'm staying with my aunt Shell."

"It's nice to meet you." Mrs. Showalter makes a move to hug me, but I stick out my hand so she shakes it instead.

The ceiling is at least twenty feet high, but the room itself is fairly small. I can't believe all the kids used to crowd into this one room. Mrs. Showalter explains that they made the high ceilings so the hot air would rise in the summer. "But it did get cold in the winter." She points out a stove.

We check out the history of Julian in photographs. "Julian was founded by freed slaves and former Confederates after the Civil War," Mrs. Showalter says. "People who had no place in the world came here to start new lives." She shows us a photo of the Bailey brothers and their cousins, the Julian brothers, the ex–Confederate soldiers who came to California in 1869.

A freed slave found the first gold in 1870. Fred Coleman happened to be riding by a stream when he saw some gold glinting. That's how the Julian gold rush started. But, Mrs. Showalter explains, in most California gold rush towns, once the gold ran out, everybody left. Here, people stayed and made a community.

"Did they get along?" I ask. "I mean, the Confederates were fighting to keep slaves, so how could they all work together?"

Mrs. Showalter bounces on her heels. "Great question, Cady! I don't know the answer to that. But look." She points to a picture of a building that reads HOTEL ROBINSON and a picture of a couple seated on its steps. "Albert and Margaret Robinson opened the first hotel here. Mr. Robinson had been a slave. Mrs. Robinson was renowned for her cooking and hospitality. In fact, it's called the Julian Hotel now." Mrs. Showalter taps the trees in the photo. "Those cedar and locust trees the Robinsons planted are still there, too."

I recognize the modern photo. We passed it on Main Street.

Jay's eyes light up. "Oh my gosh. That's amazing! He went from being a slave to a hotel owner."

Mrs. Showalter nods. "We also know that Julian didn't

have a sheriff. When you've been swinging a pickax all day in the mine, you don't need one."

"Because they were too tired to fight?" Jay asks.

"Or because they were all strong and nobody would win," I say.

"Maybe a little of both." Mrs. Showalter smiles. "Maybe hard work, done together, has a way of equalizing things. Everyone had to help each other."

"We should go visit a mine too," Jay says to me. "The tunnels are pretty cool."

I look at the photos of the Julian brothers and Mr. and Mrs. Robinson. I wonder how they felt when they arrived. They must have been scared, but hopeful. Did they ever want to give up? Did they think this was their real home right away, or did they plan on moving on? How could they forget everything in their pasts to become successful?

Did they feel at all like I do right now?

"Come on," Jay says. "I'm hungry for lunch."

I cover my midsection with my hand. "You're joking. Even I'm full."

"Pie never counts." Jay dashes out the door. I have no choice but to catch up.

CHAPTER 20

That evening, as we close up the shop, Shell says we're not going home. "There's a meeting at the town hall I have to go to. Come on."

"What kind of meeting?" Every meeting I've been to, not that I've been to many, was extremely boring.

"Planning." Shell notes my look of disgust. "People bring food," she adds with a smile. She knows that'll get me.

"In that case." I pull on my jacket and wait at the door.

She puts the pies we didn't sell that day into the back of her little sedan. I actually prefer the truck, but Shell says it's not always practical to drive.

When we get there, there are already a couple dozen people sitting in folding chairs and eating snacks. Shell puts her pies down on a table with a bunch of other food, everything from deviled eggs to chips to one lone casserole covered in cheese, still piping hot. There are also chips, red Jell-O, salad (not the bitter kind, I'm glad to see), and glazed chicken wings.

My stomach gurgles. Shell nudges me toward the stack of paper plates at one end of the table. "Go ahead."

Pretty soon I'm carrying two paper plates full of food. I know it's rude, but you never know when you might get to eat again. Dad would tell me to cut it out, like he did when we went to Thanksgiving at the shelter downtown and I kept asking the volunteers for two scoops of everything. But Dad's not here, and he's not going to be, and I don't care what he thinks anymore, anyway.

I sit down in the front row with my bounty, balancing the plates on my knees. Shell's up front, fiddling with the mic. She must be the sound person. She sees my plates and her eyebrows go up, but she just gives me a wry smile. "Get enough there, kiddo?"

I shovel mac and cheese into my face and nod. I've never had mac and cheese that wasn't boxed, and it takes me a minute to get used to these textures, plus the bits of onion in it. But it's good, even though it isn't the same.

Then Shell leans into the mic. "Good evening. Thanks for coming. I'd like to bring this meeting to order." Her voice is confident, full of authority, and she grips the sides of the podium. I bet she could pick the whole thing up and throw it if she wants.

I didn't know she's the meeting runner. I look around as people get back in their seats, all going quiet like Shell's the president. Our school never got this quiet for the principal.

Then Shell looks at me. "Cady, can you please lead us in the Pledge of Allegiance?"

I almost choke on my mac and cheese. I nod mutely, putting my plates on the chair as I get up. I'm trying to remember how to do it, because I've never led it before. Come to think of it, I haven't led anything. A great big ocean-sized swell of nervousness washes over me.

The flag's in the corner behind Shell, so I angle my body to face it. "Place your right hand over your heart. Ready. Begin."

My knees sag a bit. I did it. As we say it, I notice the older man next to me isn't participating but sits with his head bowed, his hands clasped. I wonder if Shell will say something to him, because most of our teachers made everybody participate—but nobody says anything.

"Please be seated," Shell says grandly, and everyone sits. She turns on a projector and a picture of a convenience store comes on the screen. "As you know, tonight we will discuss and vote on the Quickie Break market, part of a nationwide chain that would like to put a store in Julian."

"No!" some lady behind us yells.

Shell's brows knit only a little. "Please do not talk out

of turn. We have the developers here tonight to tell us about it."

Two men in suits get up and talk. The store will bring more jobs. Blah blah blah. I eat some more.

The man next to me leans over to whisper, "How's the mac and cheese? Mrs. Moretti made it." He's pretty ancient, probably older than Mr. Miniver.

I give him a thumbs-up. Then I look at his cane and realize it's probably hard for him to get food. "Want me to get you a plate?"

His eyes light up, but he shakes his head. "No, that's okay."

I leap up anyway, scurrying to the table, and plate some food for him. I decide to add some salad, just in case, and then I grab a few napkins and a fork and return.

"Thank you, my dear." His gnarled hands reach for the plate, and I help him steady it.

Finally the men are done talking and Shell tells people they can ask questions. And boy, do they ever.

"All you big-time corporations are going to want to move in," a lady says. It sounds like the same person who yelled earlier. "Then we'll be nothing more than a mall."

"That's right!" the man next to me says. "It's a slippery slope. Let's keep our town locally owned!"

Everyone applauds. The two visiting men have frozen

smiles on their faces. I almost feel bad for them, but not a hundred percent.

Then someone else stands. "Personally, I think the increase in jobs will make up for everything else. Plus, I'd like to get some cheaper foods in here. Everything's so expensive."

"We do live on a dang mountain," the lady pipes up again. "What did you expect?"

Shell stands and the place goes quiet again. It's crazy how she can do that. She really needs to come to school. "I have my reservations too. On the one hand, competition is a good thing. And as we get more tourists, maybe we could use another store like this."

The crowd murmurs now.

"But on the other, Julian has a certain character. It's our duty to be stewards of the town, for future generations. Like my niece, Cady, here." Shell points at me just as I'm eating a piece of cornbread, the crumbs all over my cheeks, and I feel myself flush. "So I'm going to recommend a vote of no."

The project fails in a vote. I hold up my hand for the "nays" even though I'm a kid and I'm not sure if my vote counts. It's fun to participate.

After the meeting, Shell comes over and gestures to the man sitting next to me. "Cady, this is Mac Spencer. The oldest man in Julian."

"People call me Mac and Cheese," he says in a raspy tone. "That's why I like it so much."

I hold out my hand. "Nice to meet you, Mr. Spencer."

"Mac. Please. Mr. Spencer's my father." He chuckles.

"Tell Cady how old you are, Mac." Shell nods, watching my face.

"One hundred and two," Mac says proudly.

"Really?" I can't believe it. "And you're still moving around?"

"Sort of." Mac uses his cane to get up. He's pretty much bent in half. "Thanks, Shell, for another great meeting. You make me sleep well at night."

Shell flushes pink, then changes the subject. "There's a ton of food left. Take some home."

"That won't be necessary." Mac waves his hand.

But Shell grabs one of the aluminum foil chafing dishes that's half-full of mac and cheese, then scoops up wings and some other food into the clear end. She crimps down the lid. "I'll take this to your son's car."

Mac takes Shell's hand and squeezes it. "Thank you."

"My pleasure." Shell leans down. "I'm going to come check on you and your son next week. You need anything in the meantime, you call me."

"Will do." Mac wipes at his eyes.

A younger man—meaning about eighty—appears and helps Mac out of the town hall. Someone grabs the aluminum foil chafing pan and carries it out for them.

Shell watches them leave and shakes her head. "I worry about them living alone. His son can hardly take care of himself. But Mac says he'll only leave his home feet-first." She shrugs. "I guess I understand that."

"He seems kind of stubborn," I observe. "Kind of like you."

Shell lets out a laugh. "Takes one to know one, missy." She play punches me in the shoulder and I giggle. "Was that as boring as you thought it'd be?"

"It was okay." I put my shoulders back. A satisfied kind of feeling wells up. I'm proud of my aunt. Everybody seems to respect her. She's always helping people. I'm not used to all this niceness, but it's good. "I still have to hit the dessert table."

CHAPTER 21

I clean the counters and tables all over again. It's two o'clock the day after the community meeting, and not a single person has been in since Mr. Miniver left at eleven. Not one. I keep stepping outside and looking down the street to make sure we didn't time warp into another dimension where no customers exist.

I dust the windowsills. I scrub the baseboards. I basically clean every nook and cranny until the place sparkles. The air conditioner groans and spits coldness into the silence.

Shell comes out of the back and observes the empty chairs. Her jaw twitches. "Nobody since the last time you checked," I say.

She gives a terse nod. This can't be good. Not at all. "This came for you." She hands me a letter. "Who's it from?"

I recognize Jenna's shaky writing—just for my name.

The rest her mom obviously wrote. "My reading buddy, Jenna." I rip it open, pieces of envelope flying down like confetti. It's typed, because Jenna's handwriting's pretty illegible.

Dear Cady,

Yay! Your aunt sounds nice. I miss you though. My new reading buddy is Ryan. The bread didn't get in my mouth, so I'm okay.

Love,

Jenna

I smile, picturing her sitting at the computer, slowly pecking out the letters, and suddenly not seeing her gives me a homesick kind of feeling.

Just to have something to do, I take the little bit of trash we have to the Dumpster in the alley. I've never seen anyone go into the Realtor's office, so there's nothing up here but us, basically. We need something that people will walk up a hill for. Something they can't get anywhere else. Like that one shop has those chocolate bombs. What about the Lady Baltimore Cake? But that icing's too hard to make in bulk, I bet. I'll have to come up with a better idea.

I toss the bag over the edge, watching it to make sure nothing extra falls out.

CHAPTER 22

Jay shows up at the bakery a little later. "Hey. Thought you might like to play ball instead of working."

Working? Is what I do really work? I don't think so. It's more like playing. I mean, it is work, but I don't mind. But Shell says, "That's a good idea, Cady. Go play with Jay."

Jay gives me another baseball mitt, worn and soft as a pillow, and we walk along the road through downtown, past the yellow Julian Hotel, under the trees that Mr. Robinson planted, all the way through the downtown area, passing the gas station that marks the entrance. Beyond this are some fields, and in the distance, large buildings. "Is that the school?"

"Yup. The one in the middle."

"Fantastic. At least my heart and lungs will be superhealthy if I keep living here, with all this walking."

"You can meet my friends."

I flash back to my old school. What if his friends are like those kids? What if they're mean or don't like me, or—this is the worst—treat me like I'm wearing a magic invisibility cloak? My feet slow down on their own until I'm dragging my toes through the dirt. It should be okay. Nobody knows about my dad's van. Nobody will think I'm a freak.

But what if they do?

"What's up?" Jay turns to me.

"The sky." I don't want to admit what I'm thinking about. I know Jay will tell me it'll be fine. What else can he say? He can't control how other people act.

"Ha ha." Jay picks up the pace. "Come on. I see them."

"I'm really bad at baseball." There's a rock in my shoe. I lean against a fence post and take it off, shaking my shoe, slipping it back on.

"I'm not a star, either." Jay tosses me the ball and I scramble to pick it up. "My dad taught me a couple of tricks, though." He holds his mitt to demonstrate and I try to copy him. "Hold your hand down like this if you're going to catch it low. Up, if it's high. And watch the ball."

"Did you do a lot of stuff with your dad?" My dad didn't play catch with me. I try to think about what he did teach me. Let's see. He helped me with my math a lot. And I sure needed it. I hope Shell or Suzanne's good at math.

"Not too much. He got sent back to Mexico right before

Esmeralda was born," he says in a matter-of-fact voice.

"Oh." My throat seems to close up. Got sent back isn't good. "Is he going to come back?"

"Probably not. He moves around a lot. We haven't heard from him in a while." Jay looks at some invisible object in the distance, his jaw set. For a second he doesn't look like a boy anymore, but like a glimmer of his future grown-up self. He sniffs, and when he speaks again, he doesn't look at me.

I never thought I'd think this, but I might be kind of lucky. At least I know I'll see my dad someday, even if I don't want him to come back until he's totally better. At least I don't have to be afraid of being kicked out of the country, even if Shell's Pie closes forever.

And just by chance, my grandfather somehow happened to live in a time when he could come to the US. Who would I be if he hadn't? I turn Jay's situation over and over in my head like a Rubik's Cube I can't solve. It's just not fair. "You're going to make that app and you'll make so much money that they'll let you stay."

"Yeah." He runs his hands through his hair so it poofs, like it did the first day I met him.

"Come on. I'll race you there. On your mark . . . get set . . ."

I take off before he finishes *set,* giggling. I already know he's going to win, but I'm not going to make it easy.

*

A couple of hours later, after a bunch of scoreless games, Jay says he's supposed to meet his mom at the shop. We say goodbye to the kids and head back.

It was like Jay said it'd be. A big group of boys and girls who all said hi to me and acted . . . totally normal. All we did was play ball. Nobody had to talk about anything except how excited they were that school was over. They told me about the upcoming youth group trip to the beach and about how we were all going to love middle school.

No stinky Cady Bennett comments. It's a summer miracle.

Jay and I discuss baseball as we walk up to the shop. Through the pie shop window, María stands at the register, counting the money. The door sign says CLOSED, though it's only four and we stay open until five.

Shell's at a table with papers in front of her. "If we can hold out till fall, it'll be okay."

Jay stops me, putting a finger to his lips in the *shush* sign. We press ourselves against the wall by the open windows, so they can't see us but we can hear them.

"But everyone who wants money won't hold out until fall," María says. "We might lose the business."

"Don't I know it."

María's voice rises. "What will you do? What will my family do?"

Shell hesitates before she responds, and what she

says, barely loud enough to hear, makes me feel cold from the inside of my scalp down to my toenails. "I don't know."

Jay and I stand quiet. I think I forgot how to breathe. Then he thumps the baseball against the wall, startling me. The women stop talking. "Cady, I sure am hungry."

"Me too," I say, louder than I need to. I step inside. María and Shell both raise their heads. "Hello! We had a fine time. A grand time. I learned how to hit a ball."

"And her arm's not too bad. Though her aim could use some work."

"Hey. I only threw it over you once."

"Twice."

Shell wipes her eyes quickly, a gesture so fast I think I imagined it, and then she plasters a smile over her face. *I know everything,* I want to tell her. *You don't have to pretend.* But I don't want Shell to be upset, so I pretend I'm still in the dark about the shop, and everybody sits around pretending everything is just fine. "You guys ready for a ride home?"

All we can do is nod.

CHAPTER 23

A week later, Suzanne and Shell drive me back into the city, to my elementary school. Though I haven't been gone for too long, everything looks alien. The houses seem too packed in, like you could reach out your bathroom window and steal a roll of toilet paper from your neighbor's house.

Shell parks her car on the street and we get out. "This is a nice neighborhood," Suzanne exclaims. "Wow."

I hear the surprise in her voice. I nod. "Dad put me in the best school he could. If you're transient you check that on the form, so you can go to whatever school you want." They look confused. "'Transient' means homeless."

Suzanne and Shell exchange a glance, then Suzanne reaches for my hand and squeezes it. "That shows he cares about you," she says.

I kick a pebble out of my way. If he really cared about

me, wouldn't he be the one walking me into school right now instead of sitting in jail? Couldn't he have made himself get better or asked Shell for help instead of telling her we moved away?

"Cady!" Jenna's running toward us from the school. She flings her arms around me. "You look beautiful! I missed you so much."

I'm wearing a long turquoise cotton dress, with capped sleeves and a tie belt, and I think I look fairly magnificent—taller and straighter and powerful, somehow. Suzanne said the color brings out my majestic olive skin tone, and she lent me a turquoise necklace, too. I have new gold sandals on my feet and Suzanne painted my toenails a bright turquoise to match.

"Thanks, Jenna. I missed you, too." She's bigger than I remember. Less skinny. That's a good thing—whenever she gets too thin, that means she's been sick. I pick her up and swing her around, even though I'll get yelled at if anybody sees. "You look pretty."

I put her down. "This is Jenna," I tell my aunts.

"Jenna, so nice to meet you." Suzanne holds out her hand, but Jenna throws her arms around her.

"It's nice to meet you too," Jenna says, her voice muffled. She lifts her head up.

Shell blinks. "Um, that's great."

Jenna's teacher calls her back to the lunch arbor, where the younger kids are having snacks. I pry Jenna's arms off Suzanne, and Jenna waves at Shell. People generally don't try to hug Shell, and I guess Jenna's no different.

"See you later!" Jenna whips around and runs off.

"Walk!" some adult cries.

Shell and Suzanne watch her go. "That's the reading buddy who wrote to you?" Shell says. "She's small for her age."

"She's got celiac disease." I tell them a little bit about it.

"Well, she's very energetic anyway," Shell notes.

I explain how easily Jenna gets sick, but we've arrived at the promotion ceremony. Ahead of us, on the lower sports field, chairs are set up for the promotion, and some adults are popping up tent covers. The fifth graders are on the upper field, waiting to make their grand entrance below.

"Cady, go up with your class." Suzanne points.

Suddenly I don't want to. "I'd rather stay here with you."

"No." Shell gently steers me toward the ramp leading up to the other field. "You go. Or else there's no point."

I know Shell's right. Slowly I walk up to the upper field. Everyone's excited and making a ton of noise, dressed in their best clothes and roaming around.

Then Anna-Tyler spots me. "Cady!" she shrieks, and runs over to me and hugs me as if I rose from the dead.

"Everybody, it's Cady!" The rest of the class crowds over, all talking at once. I don't know what to think of this. What's that quote—absence makes the heart grow fonder.

"All right, class. Give Cady some room." It's Ms. Walker, her curly brown bob bouncing as she moves. She's wearing the long blue dress she always wears for special events, printed with pink flowers. Her "parent meet-and-greet" outfit, she calls it. The other kids go back to what they were doing.

I smile up at Ms. Walker, suddenly shy. "How's it going without me?"

"Things are a lot more boring." Ms. Walker holds her hand in a fist. That's like a hug, because adults aren't allowed to hug kids at this school, so they do the fist bump instead. "I'm so happy you got to come." Her deep blue eyes grow an even darker blue, until they're the color of deep ocean. "We've missed you."

I look straight at Ms. Walker. When I walked into her class at the beginning of the year, I had a hard time meeting her eyes. It kind of hurt physically to do it. She used to remind me to try, lifting my chin up gently. I can barely remember being like that now. It doesn't hurt anymore.

I've changed a lot.

I think of all the ways she helped me, all the things I remember from her class. "Thank you," I whisper, so quietly I'm not sure she can hear me above the din, but she gives me another fist bump and nods.

Ms. Walker grabs my shoulders and bends her knees so she's at my height. "I want you to know that I'm always here for you. Even if you need something in high school or college. Got it?"

I nod. I believe her.

She pats my shoulder. "Good. And I expect high school *and* college graduation announcements. So don't forget about me."

I wipe at my eyes and have to look at the ground. "I couldn't."

We stop at the top of the ramp, in height order. Since I'm basically a giant, this means I'm last. Ms. Walker, her hair flying in the wind, holds up her hands as if she's a conductor. "Wait for the music."

The music starts. "Somewhere over the Rainbow," a Hawaiian version. Down below parents are snapping photos with big cameras and phones. I stop at the top, and for a second automatically search for my dad.

Instead I see Suzanne waiting at the bottom of the ramp, muscled into the very front row of parents with her camera. Like she's been coming to these kid things for years.

She sends me a thumbs-up and I send one back. I glance toward the audience. Shell waves at me from where she's saved them seats. They're here. Both of them. I let out a breath. I hadn't realized I felt so nervous. But I don't have time to think about it, because the kids are moving. I follow them down.

Afterward, we take pictures. Suzanne asks the one person she shouldn't—Anna-Tyler's mother. She's an older version of Anna-Tyler, dressed in a pretty pastel-blue skirt and blouse and a purse with some designer logo stamped all over it.

I get right next to Shell and Suzanne and try to smile happily, but it's hard because Anna-Tyler and a few of her friends watch, whispering to each other. "That's a nice dress, Cady," Anna-Tyler says as her mom hands the camera back to Suzanne.

I for real can't tell if she's being sarcastic. "Thanks."

"You must be glad to get some real clothes." She smiles at me. The other girls titter. I should ignore her, or tell her to be quiet, but a wave of shame washes over me and I want to hide under one of these chairs.

Shell notices, though, and she steps between me and Anna-Tyler. "What's with the mean-girls routine?" Her voice goes an octave lower. "That wasn't a very kind thing to say."

Whoa. Who knew Aunt Shell was so savage? I kind of like it. "No, it wasn't. You hurt my feelings." I stick out my chin toward Anna-Tyler. She does her *whatever* head roll.

Now Anna-Tyler's mom gets defensive. She puts her hand on her hip. "Oh, you know. Kids will be kids. It toughens them up for the real world."

Shell and I snort at the same time. Like I don't have experience in the real world. "Listen here," Shell says, her voice getting loud. "If you want to raise—" People stop and stare.

Suzanne slides her arm through Shell's and interrupts with her trademark Suzanne tenderness. "You know what they say. The energy you put out is the energy you receive. Good luck with all that negativity." She pulls Shell away toward the front of the school, leaving Anna-Tyler and company to huff and puff with nothing to blow down. "We'd better get going."

"You didn't let me say what I wanted," Shell complains.

"And what was that?" Suzanne rolls her eyes at me with a smile, but I want to hear it too.

"I was going to say, 'If you want to raise a pack of trolls, I guess that's up to you.'" Shell narrows her eyes. "Either that or I was going to have to challenge that mother to a duel."

For the first time, I feel sorry for Anna-Tyler. It must be hard to go around looking for bad things to point out about people. It doesn't leave you time to do anything else. "Anna-Tyler needs to get a hobby," I say. "I bet baking would calm her down."

Suzanne's laugh tinkles like crystal chandelier chimes. "I bet it would."

I link my arm through Shell's other side. Instead of shame, I'm proud. Proud of both my aunts. Shell for being so passionate, and Suzanne for being so sweet.

Nobody's ever stood up for me like that. My heart swells like the Grinch's. I lean my head against Shell's arm, and she puts it around me.

I close my eyes and let Shell lead me out of the school.

As we step out through the gate, Jenna runs up. "Wait, wait!" She's sniffling like crazy. "Do you really have to go?"

"I do." I put my hand on her head. "Wow, you're getting tall. Pretty soon you'll be taller than me."

"Maybe I'll be ten feet tall!" Jenna giggles. "I'll be the Big Friendly Giant!"

I hug her. If I had a sister, I'd want her to be like Jenna. Maybe that's why she was my reading buddy, because I didn't get a little sister of my own.

"Anyway." She steps back, looks up at me. "I have something for you." She holds up a small brown bag with handles. "I hope you like it," she says, suddenly shy.

"Of course I will." Jenna could literally pick a leaf off the ground and call it a gift and I would love it.

"Honey." Suzanne touches me gently on the arm. "I'm sorry, we have to go." She smiles at Jenna. "Maybe

Jenna could come visit you sometime."

Jenna nods vigorously. So do I.

As we walk to the car, Shell turns to me. "We took lots of pictures for your dad. He'll be sorry he missed it."

I don't want to think about him and start being sad. I pull the handle.

"He cares a lot." Shell says this so quietly I almost miss it, as I'm shutting the door.

I wonder if she's thinking of the day my dad will come get me. Another bad thought pops into my head. It'd be better for Shell if I weren't around, especially with her shop troubles. I'm one more thing to worry about.

Suzanne slips in and turns to me. "That was a lovely ceremony, Cady. I'm glad we got to share it."

I hesitate. On one hand, I wish Dad could have been here to see the promotion. On the other, it was a lot different to have Suzanne and Shell—different in a good way. I wish they could all be here together. I jerk my head in a quick nod. "Yeah." That's the best I can do as far as emotion sharing right now.

I pull out several things from Jenna's gift bag. A package of stationery with dancing teddy bears and kittens across the top and matching envelopes. A stamp booklet. And—there's a bookstore gift card. "Ohhhh," I say involuntarily.

"Oh, my!" Suzanne sees the card. "Would you like to

stop there on the way home?"

Would I? Do I have two eyes? I nod, and though I think I should try not to be too happy, I can't help it. I hug the gift card to my chest. I've never had a brand-new book.

I wish I had something to give to Jenna, too.

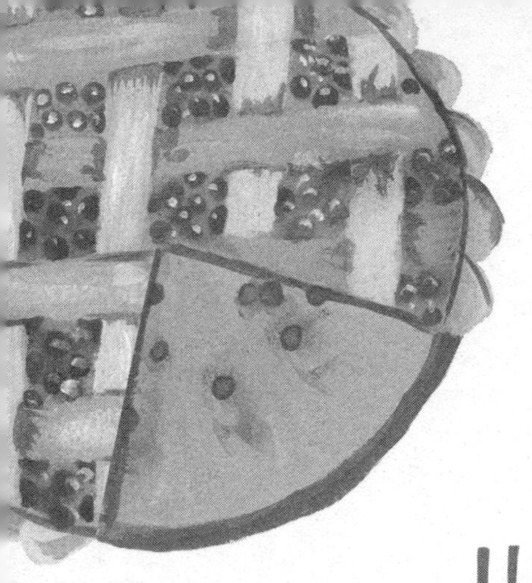

JULY

385 Pies Down

615 to Go

CHAPTER 24

My pie crusts ramp up from *meh* to *okay* to *good*. By mid-July, my pastry is finally pretty much perfect. I've got a lot more tally marks on my sheet now, rows and rows of them.

The machine rolls the crusts out smoothly, and I drape them over a tin as gracefully as a lady curtsying in a hoop skirt. It's a long way from when I knocked that pie onto the floor. With every crust I make, I feel like I'm stamping an invisible sign on it that says CADY SEAL OF APPROVAL.

But the customer situation isn't getting any better. Shell spends a lot of time out doing errands—María says she's trying to get other restaurants to take our pie.

"You should be like the Julian Pie Company and open a factory so you can sell pie everywhere," I say to Shell one morning while we eat cereal—Honey Nut Cheerios for me and Shell and plain granola for Suzanne.

"We'd need a factory first." Shell rubs her eyes.

Suzanne pours them both more coffee. "You never know, Shell. Dream big."

"Ugh. I can't take this much optimism so early in the morning." Shell sips her coffee.

Suzanne rolls her eyes at me. Suzanne and I have our secret language of facial expressions about Shell. It feels like I'm one of the popular kids or something, even though there are only three people in this group.

Shell's expression goes dour. "I wish you guys would stop laughing at me all the time."

Guilt wraps itself around me like a too-small sweater. I stare at my empty cereal bowl. Suzanne puts her hand on Shell's shoulder. "Oh, honey, we're not making fun. We like what a sourpuss you are." I can tell Suzanne's not serious, but I already know Shell can't. I stiffen.

Shell gets up, her entire body tense. "You're always telling me I don't consider your feelings, Suzanne. Maybe you should consider my feelings for once." She stalks out.

Suzanne's face is so stricken that I grab her hand. "I guess I went too far. Shell just can't be teased these days." She squeezes my hand, then goes after Shell.

It seems like Shell's looking for a reason to be mad. But maybe we do make too much fun of her. I don't mind her expressions. She's just so stone-faced that we could never tell she minded.

I guess maybe people who don't show their feelings might still have them.

*

I spend a good part of every morning talking with Mr. Miniver. He's eighty-two and still gets up to volunteer at the museum almost daily, and of course comes here for pie. "If you don't do things, you waste away," he tells me.

Mr. Miniver sort of reminds me of a combination of Mary Berry and Paul Hollywood, so of course I like him. Mr. Miniver looks like Paul Hollywood will look in thirty years, plus he often tells people exactly what he thinks. But he's sweet and kind, too, like Mary Berry. He's also the one who knows everything about everyone in town. He draws me a map of the whole village, including where all the families live, where the bed-and-breakfasts and hotels and restaurants are, and tells me all kinds of details, like who got married, who used to be married, and who he thinks should be married. He introduces me to everyone he knows—people who come into Shell's, people who come into the museum when I go visit him there. Now when I walk through downtown, I always see at least three people I know. And they always say hello to me and ask how I am and ask how Shell's doing. Even Mrs. Moretti from Grandma's Pies waves.

I was always used to being invisible. Most people wouldn't even look at me and Dad as they walked by. In school, being invisible was better than getting bullied. It's the weirdest thing ever, to have everyone in Julian notice me, but I think I like it.

Gable's dad has told me twice that his ear-piercing

offer is still good, but I haven't reminded Shell to ask my dad. She'll make me talk to him, and I don't want to.

A man in a plaid shirt and jeans walks by this morning and Mr. Miniver lowers his voice. "There's Kirk Nelson. Now, if you ask me, he'd be a better match for Claudia. He's going to inherit his dad's winery."

"I don't like Kirk Nelson," Claudia says from behind the counter, where she's doodling on a pad. Mr. Miniver's the only one here right now. "He picks his nose. And I don't need you telling me what to do, thank you."

Mr. Miniver raises his bushy white brows. "I'm just saying you could broaden your horizons. Though when I was your age, I'd never listen to what an old geezer had to say, either."

I giggle and refill his decaf. "Did you ever bake, Mr. Miniver?"

"Oh, yes. Not professionally, but when my wife was alive, she and I used to whip up dozens of treats for the holidays. I don't anymore—my middle grandson can't eat gluten, so his mother is the one who makes our treats."

"Really?" I almost drop the coffeepot. "My best friend in San Diego has celiac."

Mr. Miniver whips out his phone and shows me a picture of a little brown-haired boy. "This is Emory. He's got Crohn's disease. That means that his body's decided food is an invader. Gluten makes him flare." He gestures around the shop. "Needless to say, I don't bring him here. Too much he can't eat. But he'll come up for Christmas. In fact, I'll invite you to our big Christmas Eve party."

Christmas. My heart leaps like a bounding deer, and I'm not sure if I'm super happy or super frightened. My emotions are funny like that—sometimes I can't tell what they are, as if they're a foreign language. Will I be here in December? That's five whole months away. "Will it snow?"

He smiles. "Sometimes we get lucky with a white Christmas. You should see the crowds. Something about people in our old-fashioned costumes, wandering around in the snow, makes it seem real festive."

Snow. I've never seen snow. I try to imagine the town blanketed with white, fluffy stuff. I can't actually picture what snow is. The only thing I can picture is that white blanket stuff stores use for fake snow displays. It's cold. Is it soft? I have no idea. "I can't wait," I blurt out, and then my stomach hurts. I'm wishing I could stay for Christmas. Without my dad. How bad would that make him feel? I would feel terrible if I knew my dad was wishing he could be somewhere for Christmas without me.

"Christmas party?" Claudia returns from the back, her mood shifting to normal. "How come I've never been? Don't you like me?"

"You used to come with your family when you were younger," Mr. Miniver replies smoothly, "but you've been busy the past four years or so."

The corners of her mouth turn down, and she opens it like she's ready to argue. Then she sighs and flips her sketchbook closed. "I'm going on break." She flounces out, throwing her apron on the counter. She's cranky because Gable hasn't been back for a week. He's moving to the city for college.

I move her sketchbook to the side so I won't spill coffee on it. It falls open to a picture of Gable in colored pencil, sitting on his motorcycle. I flip through it. There are tons of Gable drawings. Gable looking dreamy. Gable drawing a picture of Claudia. I laugh at that.

And then there's me.

I touch the pencil, smearing it a bit. Me, with a coffeepot in my hand, my hair in a net with tendrils escaping. I don't know what I expected Claudia to make me look like, but here I'm strong. My Bennett chin juts out. I'm squinting like I'm considering throwing the coffeepot at someone.

Claudia's kind of made me look like a superhero.

I hold up the book to show Mr. Miniver. "Impressive. That girl needs to go to college." Mr. Miniver takes another sip of coffee. "Get at least an associate's degree."

"She's only nineteen," I say, because that's what I've heard Shell say when María says the same thing: "My daughter needs to get out and do something." Shell says, "Give her time. She's young. Only nineteen." Nineteen seems pretty old, but I know it's not. I also know that by nineteen Shell had already enlisted in the military, so I'm not sure why she's so gentle on Claudia.

Claudia pops back and grabs her sketchpad out of my hand. "But why bother? I can go to college all I want, but I'll never get to be a citizen," she mutters, returning to the back.

Mr. Miniver takes a breath. "It is an unfortunate situation."

"Is it true?" I remember what Jay said about his dad. "It's not Jay or Claudia's fault that they're here, though."

Mr. Miniver leans back. "Their parents came here because there was nothing for them in Mexico. No way to make a living. Lots of violence. I don't really blame them. Things are never as black and white as we want them to be." He cups his mug. "Sometimes there are no good choices, and we can only do our best."

We're quiet for a moment. If Jay and his family got deported, I don't know what I'd do. They're like my family too now. If the thought scares me, think of how Jay feels. My chest contracts. "I hate that Jay has to wake up every single morning worried about getting kicked out of the only place he's ever known." My voice rings through the shop.

Mr. Miniver looks at me kindly. "Me too. But we all must learn to live with uncertainty, Cady." We're quiet for a moment, and I know he's thinking about his wife.

He clears his throat. "Anyway, it won't *hurt* Claudia to go to college. You'd be surprised at how fast time passes. One minute you're nineteen." He snaps his freckled fingers. "The next you're an eighty-two-year-old widower. She's like Han Solo frozen in carbonite in here!"

"You like the old *Star Wars* movies?" I ask. My dad loves those.

Mr. Miniver clutches the collar of his pioneer-man clothes. "Do I like *Star Wars*? My dear girl, I took my children to see that in the theaters no fewer than six times. And they only wanted to see it twice."

I grin. "I haven't seen the whole thing. Only parts of it when it was on TV." I never knew ahead of time when it'd be on.

"I'll bring you the DVD." Mr. Miniver raises his mug of coffee to me. I see a cobweb forming under the window and wipe it clean—in the mountains, cobwebs can appear in seconds. In the month I've been here, this shop has come to feel like mine. I'm the one who makes sure the windowsills are dusted, who gets out the broom and dustpan after a little kid's been here. Not because Shell will be mad if I don't, but because the pie shop is mine. Or sort of mine. Anyway, it feels right, and that's what matters.

CHAPTER 25

"Hey! Where is everybody?" Shell shouts from the front of the pie shop. It's Sunday at noon, and it should be busy, but it's been so slow that María and I went to work in the back. She sticks her head in the kitchen. "Why are you sitting around? Did you forget about the three dozen pies for the football fund-raiser? It's tonight!"

I rush to tie on an apron. I'd just been hanging out with María, who was showing me a chicken pot pie recipe in an issue of *Martha Stewart Living*. It's not like we want to sit around. The front case is full of pies, with nobody to eat them. Both María and I are trying to keep busy, but I can tell she's as worried as I am by how she keeps jiggling her foot when we sit.

"I haven't started them." María doesn't move from her perch on the stool.

"Why not?" Shell puts her hands on her hips.

"Every year, you donate the pies. Are you donating

them this year?" Her tone's almost accusing, like Shell said she was going to steal puppies from small children.

"Of course." Shell washes up.

María sighs through her nose.

"I have to, María. I do it every year." Shell sounds defensive.

"This year you shouldn't," María says flatly. "This year, they should pay."

"It's a community event."

María slams her hand on the counter. "We can't afford it!"

I freeze where I am. I've never seen María lose her temper. She looks like she's breathing steam.

"María." Shell turns and takes a deep breath. "I promised. I can't not do it. It'll look bad."

María shakes her head. "Put aside your pride. Be realistic."

"It's fine. I promise." The bell tinkles at the front door, and Shell goes out front.

María picks up a broom and begins attacking the floor, though it's pretty clean. "Is everything okay?" My voice shakes. I want her to tell me it is.

María nods silently. "*Lo siento.* Don't worry about it, Cady."

"But I can't help worrying." I start crying. María falling apart means things are really bad. I think about my food store in the bedroom. I'd better add more in case all of us end up without a home.

María drops the broom and holds out her arms. "It'll be fine, Cady."

"How do you know?" I step back. I can't be hugged right now. I bite my lip and the tears stop.

"I don't, really. But what good will it do me to worry? I can't control what happens." She picks up the broom and sweeps the few crumbs into a dustpan.

I don't know how María can put such a brave face on. But I'll do what Aunt Shell says. I get out more flour and start measuring.

"Hey." María opens the fridge and takes out a plastic grocery bag. "Jay brought more fennel. Do you want to make a few of your new special for the football people?"

"Sure." It does get boring making the same flavors over and over again. María must be sick of apples. We wash the fennel and get everything ready.

The high school is next to the middle school. In fact, all the schools are clustered together, with the high school taking up the most land because of the sports fields. The library's there, too. You could spend your whole life in this five-mile radius and have everything you needed.

I help Shell set up the pies on the dessert table in one corner of the gymnasium. Besides the pies, there are doughnuts and cake. None of those chocolate bombs, though, I'm disappointed to see.

The football players and cheerleaders are serving spaghetti and meatballs and garlic bread. The gym is filled with people joking and eating at round tables decorated with maroon and white, the school colors. A banner that says JULIAN EAGLES hangs down. My stomach growls.

Shell kind of pushes me toward the line. "I gather you're hungry."

"You gathered correctly." My mouth waters. I watch Shell give the money collector a twenty-dollar bill for admission and chew my lip anxiously. Can we even afford to eat at this fund-raiser? But Shell told me to trust her, so I guess that's all I can do.

We sit at a table with a couple who are around Shell's age and that guy I saw walking around that Mr. Miniver wanted Claudia to date. Kirk something or other.

"These are the Culvers," Shell says about the people who are her age. "They live near us. They have the white horse."

"Oh! Nice to meet you." Jay and I pet the white horse all the time.

"Miss Daisy," Mrs. Culver says with a smile. "She's the white one."

Kirk spends the entire meal talking to Mr. Culver about soil, which I guess could be interesting for some people but would definitely put Claudia to sleep. He seems super bland compared to Gable, like American cheese compared to extra-sharp cheddar, so I can't really blame her. But then again, some people prefer American cheese.

A lady comes up to Shell. "We've missed you at knitting club!" she says.

"Oh. Hi, Vicky. I've been really busy." Shell pats her mouth with a napkin and they catch up. That happens a couple more times, with a man saying he hasn't seen Shell at the library, and another saying they missed her at some other meeting.

I can't help compare Shell to Dad. Dad never took me to one of these things. Other people don't come up to him and tell him they miss him.

I wonder if he wishes they would. Or if he could ever get to where it could happen.

A group of five football players run over to our table like a herd of buffalo. "What kind of pie is this?" the biggest one asks Shell, holding out his plate.

Shell raises a brow at me. "It should be apple."

"Oh. It's apple fennel raisin." A nervous shock shakes my whole body. What if he doesn't like it? What if the football players riot because they hate raisins?

Shell nods. "Apple fennel raisin," she repeats.

He scrapes the plate clean and gives us a thumbs-up. "Seconds!"

"Better hurry!" one of his teammates yells. There's a minor skirmish at the table as they try to get the last pieces. María and I only made three.

Shell turns to me with a small smile. "Well. Looks like you have a hit."

"You're not mad, are you?" I give her my best Jacques-eyes.

She ruffles my hair. "How could I ever be mad at you when you're so clearly imitating my dogs?" Then she leans forward. "It's okay because María helped you, but I've got health standards to uphold. So don't think you can make random pies for the public any old time. Deal?" She holds up a pinky.

I loop it with mine. "Deal."

Other than my daily duties and hanging out with Mr. Miniver, I spend most of my time in a corner of the pie shop kitchen, trying out new flavors. Shell told me I could pick whatever I liked out of the garden. "The best way to learn how to cook is to do it," she said.

So Suzanne and I have been making dinner when she's home. Roasted chicken with lemon and thyme. Pasta sauce with fresh tomatoes, basil, and garlic. I chewed on a basil leaf, enjoying the herby flavor, if herby is a word. "Am I allowed to use this in a dessert?"

"There's no rule against using herbs in pies," Suzanne told me. "There are no hard and fast rules about anything. That's why your fennel pie worked."

First I write down my ideas in my notebook. Sometimes I watch *The Bake Off* and get super-crazy ideas.

On one show, the baker named Nadiya made cheesecake in soda flavors, so I thought of making a pie that had root beer flavor. Then I realized I didn't really know how to do that. I look at these ideas later and wonder what I was thinking. "That's brainstorming," Suzanne said when I showed her my notebook. "You write every single idea down, and if it works, great. If it doesn't, no worries."

So now I've got pages and pages of pie ideas I'm not going to use, but also a lot I still want to try. Shell lets me get whatever I like out of her garden, and Suzanne buys me extra ingredients when I need them. Suzanne says I have a penchant for sweet and savory combinations, meaning I like those the best.

What I do is imagine the ingredients first. I write the possible combinations in my notebook and narrow them down. Then I talk to Shell or Suzanne about them. Shell says simpler is better. After that, I gather the ingredients. I Google recipes to see if the pie already exists (even if it does, Shell says it's fine to tweak what's there). Last, I try making the pie.

Some of them are total duds. I tried to make a chocolate pie with a crushed pecan crust—I didn't make the pudding right, the chocolate oozed out, and the crust fell apart. Shell said I'd overheated the chocolate and made me try it again. That time it held, but it was so bitter I spit it out. Turns out I didn't add enough sugar. Then

Shell said we'd try chocolate again later because we ran out, and chocolate's expensive.

So this morning, I look through my notebook and decide which recipe I'm going to try. Strawberry pie. Pretty simple. First I have to finish my chores, though. I head outside, Jacques and Julia following like they always do. Even though I didn't like dogs a couple of months ago, now I feel sort of weird when I go outside without them. Like I forgot my shoes or something.

I feed the chickens and the pets and clean all their poop up from all their places. I also collect all the eggs from the chickens and place them in the kitchen. Shell told me fresh chicken eggs don't have to be refrigerated for a few weeks, but they do have to be washed. After all, they come out of the chicken's you-know-where. This part is kind of gross. But I like fresh eggs, so oh well.

Finally, I get to pick my pie ingredients out of the garden, beginning with the fruit. Shell had said that strawberry can be a little tricky. "You have to taste them, then add the right amount of sugar," she'd told me. "So you might need more or less than the recipe says."

"How much more or less?" I'd asked.

"It depends on what they taste like," she'd said.

Well, that advice wasn't helpful.

Shell had also suggested rhubarb. Rhubarb and strawberry, she'd said, is classic. "But the rhubarb leaves are poisonous."

"How poisonous?" I'd asked.

"Deadly."

I definitely don't want any rhubarb leaves. I look at the planting box where Shell said the rhubarb was growing, next to the beans sprouting up their poles. She said it looks like pink celery. I look over the plants and don't see anything like it.

"Is it this one?" I touch a big green leaf. The stalk looks a little reddish, maybe. Mostly green, though. "I'm not sure."

Jacques barks at me. "Should I not do it?" I ask him. "Well, then. Maybe it'll be a plain old strawberry pie." I'll ask Shell later where the rhubarb is.

I wonder what my dad eats in jail. Do they have a garden? It would be nice if they did. I imagine Dad outside, digging in black soft earth with his hands and a shovel. I hope Dad is happy. Well, maybe he can't be happy, but at least not sad. Without all those big peaks and valleys of his moods. That's what I'd like him to be.

Dad likes to garden. He used to save paper cups and put dirt and seeds in them and keep them in the van. Usually they didn't get very big—they probably needed more light—but once we grew a pretty large tomato plant. Once it outgrew the cup, we transferred it into an old orange bucket, and it actually gave us five tomatoes. They were small and orange, not red, but they were tomatoes all the same. "The bounty of the earth, Cady!"

Dad had chuckled as he'd picked them.

Thinking about him is like when I get a cut on my finger and it's almost healed, but it still hurts. Especially if you push hard. It makes me go through everything I wish he'd done. All the things I wish could be happening. I should write him a letter, ask him about the ear piercing.

He's still my dad.

I count the berries I have in my cardboard box. About two dozen. It's more than enough. I eat a berry and toss the stem onto the compost heap in the far corner of the yard, which steams with layers of chicken manure and vegetables. I'll have to turn that later so the fresh top layer gets a chance to decompose. Then we use the dirt on our garden.

Shell had told me to pick basil and oregano for a marinara sauce, so I head over to the herb bed and pick those next. Basil's easy to identify. It has tender green leaves a little bit like lettuce, but small. Oregano has smaller leaves and I always get it mixed up with thyme, but thyme's woodier.

I take another juicy bite of strawberry as I head back into the house, wiping my chin where it's dripped. The smell of basil's still on my fingers. I inhale. The scent of both of them mixed together makes my mouth water.

I stop short. The dogs stop too and look up at me expectantly.

"Strawberry basil," I say to the dogs. "That's what I'll do."

"Ruff!" Julia wags her tail.

"I'm so glad you agree, love," I say in my British accent. "It shall be a right proper pie. No soggy bottoms to be found."

Inside, I get out my stationery and smooth it on top of the kitchen table, thinking of what I can say.

Dear Dad,

Hi. It's Cady, your daughter. I'm still doing fine. Don't worry, Shell doesn't take me to church.

Dad, I want to know something. How come you weren't stronger, like Shell and Mom?

I cross that out and crumple it up. I can't write that to him. "Now I've wasted a perfectly good piece of stationery," I say to the dogs. They don't look up from their naps this time, so I can't pretend they're talking.

I start again.

I hope you're doing okay. I hope they give you pie in there.

Sincerely,
Cady

P.S. BTW, I'm getting my ears re-pierced. I'll assume you're fine with that, since Mom wanted them that way. And I do, too.

It's the best I can do. I fold the paper up and stick it into an envelope. Then I neatly write the address Shell gave me. *Inmate #423042.* That's Dad. So odd to have a dad who's a number, even if it's only temporary.

"Cady." Shell almost gives me a heart attack by appearing at the bottom of the stairs.

"What are you doing home?"

"I came to get you, but you were outside." Shell's carrying a laundry basket, but there are no clothes in it. Instead, she's got all my food. My cheeks fire up when I see how much I've collected. It looks like I could open a small grocery store.

She sets the basket on the table. "Cady, why do you have all this in your bedroom?"

Her tone is very gentle, especially for Shell, and this throws me off more than anything. I shrug, staring at nothing. "Don't know."

Shell sits across from me. "You don't have to hoard food, Cady. It's okay. We're going to feed you."

Now my breath catches in my throat, and I glare at her. Dad's probably not coming back for me for a long time, but there's something else now, too. "How do I know that? I know the pie shop's in trouble."

Shell looks stricken. "I'm not going to lose the pie shop."

"Jay and I heard you and María talking. I know about the debt collectors." I bite my lip really hard.

Shell puts her hand on my arm. "Cady, don't hurt your lip."

I stop that. "So what if you lose everything and we don't have anything to eat? At least I'll have some food. I'll even share it."

Shell's head dips down to the table. Then she lifts it. I'm afraid she'll be crying, but her eyes just look hollow. "I'm not going to stop you from keeping the food if it makes you feel better. Just nothing that will attract bugs. Okay?"

I nod mutely.

"But I will always take care of you, Cady. You have my word." Shell stands up.

I pick up the basket and head upstairs, trying my hardest to feel better. I've got her word, but so did a lot of other people, like those people she promised she'd pay.

I don't know. Maybe Shell's word is only as good as Dad's. Bitterness rises in my throat. I set the basket in the corner. There's no reason to hide it anymore.

In the afternoon, I go to the pie shop with my box of strawberries and basil. Shell raises her eyebrows at this. "I wouldn't put basil into something sweet." She says "basil" like I said I wanted to use dog food.

"Your name isn't Cady Madeline Bennett, either." I shrug. "Besides, Suzanne says it could work."

Shell's lips twitch. "Don't use too much. Maybe like a dozen leaves."

Some recipes say "a few" and some say "twelve." I decide on eight. I make this one with a lattice pie top like Shell taught me. The lattice top has the added bonus of letting steam escape. No holes needed like you have to make with other pies.

When it's done, I take it out to the front. Suzanne's home from the boat and sitting with María and Shell, talking in low voices at a corner table. Mr. Miniver and a couple of other locals sit nearby. Jay's working on a laptop.

"Cady! Come see the game I made. It's pretty awesome." Jay waves to me.

"In a second." I put the pie on the counter and begin cutting it for everyone to try. This is my favorite part, and the worst part. Favorite because of course I want everyone to love it. Also the worst because it's terrible if the filling runs out, or if there's a soggy bottom, or if anyone hates it. Last week I made a blueberry-mint that Jay actually spit out. "Toothpaste!" he declared, then saw my probably horrified-looking face. "Sorry, Cady."

This time, I take a bite of it myself first. The brightness of the berries and the basil combine perfectly. The basil tastes . . . green. But that could be me. Shell says that palates are subjective, meaning everyone's palate has a different opinion. That's why some people like chocolate best and some people like vanilla. However, if watching *The Great British Bake Off* has taught me anything, it's that there are still some things that you *can* judge. Like, if you make a chocolate tart, the chocolate shouldn't be grainy or runny, or too bitter or too sweet. If you make a fruit pie, it shouldn't be grossly sugary or mouth-puckeringly sour. So there are still rules everyone follows.

I cover the pie pieces in whipped cream and carry three plates to the table for Shell, balancing one on my forearm like Claudia taught me.

Suzanne leans across the table, looking more intense than I've ever seen her. "Shell, I'm telling you, my boss would put up the money. He loves your pies and he always offers them on the boat. Everyone who charters the yacht loves it."

"I'm not getting involved with a partner. It's too messy. He wants twenty percent."

"Twenty percent of something is better than a hundred percent of *nothing*!" Suzanne fires back. I haven't seen Suzanne mad before. "It's logical."

Shell massages her temples. "Sheesh, Suzanne. Give it a rest."

Now's maybe not the best time, but oh well. I'm here.

"Voilà." I put the pie down with a flourish. The three women look up at me, their foreheads creased with worry. They're having an Important Adult Conversation. I can tell they wish I'd stayed in the kitchen. "Everything okay, Aunt Shell?" My stomach twists a bit as I remember that big stack of bills and what Jay told me and the conversation Jay and I overheard.

Jay catches my eye and shakes his head. I give him one of the plates.

"Everything's fine, Cady," Shell says a bit too firmly. Suzanne leans back. "Now, tell us about this pie."

"Strawberry basil."

Suzanne takes a bite. Immediately I know from her expression she likes it. "My goodness. You wouldn't expect those to work together because basil's not nearly as sweet as strawberry. But it tastes so . . ."

"Fresh," María supplies, pie oozing from the corner of her mouth. She wipes it.

I stand there watching Jay spoon bites into his mouth. "What do you think?"

He points to his nearly empty plate.

"I was wrong." Shell's face relaxes. "The basil was a good idea."

"I'm not even the first one to think of it," I say modestly.

"Well, I wouldn't mind trying some of that," Mr. Miniver pipes up. "My goodness, a new flavor! How exciting." The other people in the café look interested, too. All two of them. My stomach flips in worry.

"Cady, cut the pie up and put it into those little Dixie cups," Shell says. "Let everyone try."

My heart racing, I do so. This is the first pie Shell has let me give out to anyone. She's never even suggested it before.

Claudia helps me cut up the rest of the pie and put it into little paper cups. "Oh! I have an idea." I jump up and down. "Shell, can I go outside and give them to people?"

Shell nods. "I don't see how that could hurt."

"Not at this point, especially," María adds darkly. Suzanne nudges her.

Without waiting another instant, I head out the door and down the hill, past the dusty parking lot to the main street. "Wait!" Jay runs after me, holding the sidewalk sign normally in front of the store. "Let me help you."

We stand on the street. "Sample?" I ask everyone. "Would you like a sample?"

A group of hipster-looking kids who look like they could be friends with Claudia gather around. "Strawberry basil?" A man with a huge fluffy beard smacks his lips. "I haven't seen that anywhere."

"We're trying a new flavor. The strawberries are organic," I add. They seem like the type of people who'd like that. They all take a cup, and in another minute, we're out of samples.

Suzanne appears. "How's it going?"

I show her my empty tray. "How do you think?"

She claps. "That's great!" Then she taps her chin with an index finger. "Well, Miss Cady, if we can't convince Shell to expand, maybe we can convince her to add a new flavor."

Jay wrinkles his brow. "I don't know. She's pretty stubborn about those two kinds."

"I know. Trust me, I know." Suzanne kind of barks out a laugh. "But I've been working on changing her mind for, oh, four years now."

The fluffy-bearded guy walks up. "Can I get a whole pie to take home? My mom loves strawberries."

I give him a thumbs-up. "You will, soon." Jay and I run back to the store, laughing like two maniacs. We probably scared the customers away. Oh well.

CHAPTER 26

Señora Vasquez sits in front of the TV, her head lolled to the side, a snore escaping her parted lips. From a shelf, a radio plays the same Mexican music station María listens to. A small, doll-sized cap attached to a pink ball of yarn lies in her lap. Jay says crocheting's her main hobby, due to her knee.

I try to enter quietly. Shell told me that I had to stay here today while she took María and the kids into town for a doctor's appointment. No matter how much I pleaded to be left alone.

"You could both use the company," Shell had said, and she'd said it in her *no more arguments* tone, so I gave up.

"Don't people knock these days?" Señora Vasquez doesn't open her eyes or move her head. "Well, don't stand there letting the flies in."

I hop in and shut the door. "Um, hi." What am I supposed to do here all day? Maybe I could offer to clean the house, which would be better than watching her crochet. And that way I could sort of hide from her. It's pretty clean, though, so it probably wouldn't take long. "What are you making?"

She opens her eyes. "A preemie hat. I send them to the hospital."

"Oh." That actually doesn't seem like something a mean person would do, and I relax a bit. Maybe she could teach me, but I don't exactly think Señora would be the most enthusiastic teacher.

She lifts her eyebrows at me as her fingers turn the hat circle. "I hear you almost burned the house down."

I blanch. I didn't think Shell had told anyone. "That was *weeks* ago. And we still ate the cake."

"And that you threw a pie *a mi nieto*." Her lips twitch.

"That's one hundred percent not true!" Who's telling her about this stuff? I've never had so many people interested in my business. There was only ever my dad. Of course, I never had the chance to push pies off tables before, so it didn't much matter. Is this how it's going to be from now on—everything I do getting discussed by a whole crowd?

"I'm not saying I never wanted to throw a pie at him myself. He can be somewhat of a know-it-all." She smooths down the cap.

"Jay's not a know-it-all. He does know everything he talks about," I say hotly, even though that's why I got so mad at him that time. "What am I supposed to do here all day?"

She blinks. "Whatever you want, as long as you don't hurt yourself."

Then I'm going to see the cows. I open the back door. "Be back later."

"Where are you going?" she calls. "I need to supervise you."

I put my hand on the doorknob, puffing through my nose. A sharp reply wants to burst out. Then I get a better idea. I give her my most regal, chin-pointy look. "I know that your knee hurts, my dear Señora Vasquez, and I am sorry for that. But I would most appreciate it if you could stop hurling insults in my direction!" I make sure to say *appreciate* with a *c* like an *s*, like Mary Berry might say.

Señora Vasquez looks surprised, and for a second I'm afraid she's going to throw her crochet needle at me like a spear. But then her eyes sparkle, and she begins coughing. She leans over, her face turning deep brick red. Uh-oh. She's choking.

I rush over to her and pound her back. "Do you need water?"

She holds up a hand and raises her head, still making the choking noise. I realize it's not choking at all. It's laughter. It's so rusty it sounds like the cough of a dying smokestack.

When she finally stops, she has to take off her glasses and wipe the tears out of her eyes. “There’s that feistiness I heard about. I was beginning to think the stories were all lies.”

I sit back on my heels, astounded. “Stories?”

“Jay talks about you all the time.” She pushes her glasses up on her face. “I don’t get out much. I have to get my entertainment where I can. Now. Do you want to clean out the shed or make a *tres leches* cake?”

I grin. “I bet you can guess.”

CHAPTER 27

I inhale the scents of sugar and flour and cinnamon as we mix up the batter. The egg whites are the hardest part; like the Lady Baltimore Cake, you have to whip them separately. Between my chores and all this baking, my arms are most definitely getting ripped. In fact, my whole body feels stronger. I notice that it's easier to stand up straight, and I'm not getting tired like I did last month.

"This is the main reason I don't make this cake very much. I don't have a mixer. It's too hard to beat the egg whites stiff by hand." Señora Vasquez watches. "Hey, you're pretty good."

"I try," I say modestly. I lift the whisk out to see if it makes a peak again. It does. "It's ready."

"That's not a stiff peak. When it's really stiff, it can't fall over." Sure enough, my peaks are melting. "Stiff means *stiff*." Señora Vasquez gestures at me. "Keep going."

I guess when I made the other cake, they weren't as stiff as they should have been. It still tasted pretty good, though.

My favorite part is combining everything. How it mixes and becomes something new. I add the milk mixture and the flour to the egg whites a little bit at a time, stirring each time with an old-looking wooden spoon.

In the kitchen, I stop thinking about anything else. There's just me and the cake batter, the hiss of the gas as Señora Vasquez heats her teapot, the TV softly chattering in the background. Señora Vasquez is more relaxed, too. She seems to enjoy directing me as she watches and dunks her teabag up and down in the hot water. "Do you want some tea?" She pushes the box toward me. Chamomile. I sniff. It smells like grass and flowers and a little bit of lemon.

"Yes, please." I haven't had tea before. She pours hot water into another mug and puts the teabag in it.

I carefully tip the bowl over the pan, scraping the batter out, then set it in the oven. Señora Vasquez hands me a plastic bear filled with honey. "You don't have to have your tea sweet, but I do."

"No harm in trying it." I give the bear a good squeeze into my tea, watching the golden liquid settle into the bottom, then stirring it up with a spoon. Finally I blow and take a sip. It tastes like it smells, kind of a soothing thing. I add more honey. I guess I like it sweet, too.

As we sip our tea, Señora Vasquez tells me about the time her late husband crashed their car into a tree. "He was messing with the radio." She shakes her head at the memory. "I was so angry at him. Do you know how hard it was to save up money for a car?" She glances sidelong at me. "And yes, he should have been paying better attention. But blame and anger don't get you very far."

"Everybody makes mistakes," I say almost automatically. That's what every teacher has been telling me since the beginning of time.

"Hmmm," Señora Vasquez says. "Once I could get past that, we could move on."

The refrigerator rattles and whirs like an old lawn mower. Señora Vasquez ambles over and hits its side. "The ice maker keeps trying to make ice, but it's disconnected."

Then we hear the sound of a car driving up to the house and both of us glance out the window. The Jeep turns around in the dirt driveway, sending up a cloud of dust and hiding the driver. "Who could that be? I don't trust Jeep drivers—no doors. They can hop out, rob someone, and drive away." Señora Vasquez wipes her hands on her apron. "If he wants to rob us, I hope he takes that full trash bag, too." She picks up a cast-iron frying pan and holds it as if she's going to hit someone on the head, bracing herself on the kitchen counter.

Someone climbs slowly out of the car. A white-haired

man. "That's Mr. Miniver! Mr. Miniver!" I almost collapse with relief. It's like we expected a robber and got Santa Claus instead.

"That old fool got a Jeep?" Señora Vasquez puts the pan down with a clatter. "Driving around like some young *caballero* up to no good. What could he possibly be thinking?"

Mr. Miniver hobbles up the steps, clutching the handrailing. He's bearing a white plastic grocery bag. "Dolores?" he calls. "Cady?"

I run to the door and hold it open. "What are you doing here?"

"I knew you were babysitting and thought you could use some lunch." He holds up the bag. "Hello, Dolores."

"Stanley. Do you think I'm too old to watch Cady and cook at the same time?" Señora Vasquez glares at him.

"I thought she was babysitting you," Mr. Miniver says with a grin.

"Hmph," Señora Vasquez grunts. I giggle.

Mr. Miniver glances around. "Well, it's almost lunchtime and all I see is a tres leches cake being made. While I'm a fan, that's definitely not a meal."

Señora Vasquez relents. "Oh, fine. Sit down."

"That's as close to a thank-you as I'll get," he remarks to me.

"Thank you!" I open the bag. He's brought us fried chicken and potato salad from a restaurant in town. I eat four pieces, and then Mr. Miniver says I can have his wing and Señora Vasquez gives me an extra drumstick.

I eat, half listening as the two gossip about everyone in the village. "So the Smith girl is marrying that marine after all?" Señora Vasquez shakes her head. "I always tell Claudia not to get married until she's thirty. I doubt she'll listen."

"She's not going to get married. Claudia says that she and Gable are artists and artists belong to no one," I chime in.

Mr. Miniver and Señora Vasquez look at each other, trying to keep straight faces. Then they burst into laughter.

"What?" Claudia was super serious when she said that.

"I got married when I was eighteen and it was a good job I did. My wife straightened me out." Mr. Miniver scoops more potato salad onto his plate. It's really good, with sour cream and bacon in it.

"Who wants to straighten someone out?" Señora Vasquez scoffs. "We want someone pre–straightened out. A real man."

"A man won't be straightened out unless he wants to be." Mr. Miniver isn't insulted. In fact, he looks amused.

I wonder if my dad had his act together when my parents got married or if my mom thought she could "straighten him out" too. And if he was willing. Because my mom was the strong, healthy one in that relationship.

I decide I'll never get married. That way I don't have to worry about anyone but me.

"Did you guys know my mom very well?" I ask, interrupting their conversation.

Señora Vasquez wipes her fingers on a napkin. "Not too well, but I remember once, before you were born, there was a potluck at Shell's and she made Korean tacos. Your father loved Korean barbecue. She would take Korean barbecued meat and make tacos out of it." She smiles. "It was very unusual at the time. My daughter was horrified. 'Mama! Did you see what she did to tacos? They're not authentic anymore.' But I didn't care because they were delicious."

"I knew her when she was a little thing. She and Shell played with my daughters." Mr. Miniver smiles at me. "She loved riding her bike. She was daring, your mother. She even got my girls into it. I set up a ramp for them in the backyard. My wife was not too pleased about that. Especially not when my Stacy broke her arm." He chuckles. "If there was any thrill to be found, your mother was the one to find it."

"A bike, huh?" I can't imagine riding a bike, much less doing stunts. My mother grew up here. Mr. Miniver knew her. A bolt of excitement pulls me ruler straight. Suddenly Mom seems more real and alive than she ever was before, when she only existed in the memories of me and my father. Instead of only two people knowing her, now there are many. And they seem to love her almost as much as I did.

I lean forward. "Tell me everything you remember about her."

After the tres leches cake comes out of the oven, we have to let it cool for a while. Then we poke holes in it with a skewer and pour the mixed sweetened condensed milk and regular milk over the bare cake. "It soaks it up like a sponge," Señora says.

Mr. Miniver rubs his hands together. "My favorite."

I take a bite. It's creamy and sweet, the wetness and the dry crumb all combining perfectly. But it's so rich I can only have a little piece. Mr. Miniver doesn't seem to have this problem, because he eats a giant slice. We eat quietly, concentrating on the cake.

Señora Vasquez looks pleased. "It's always good when people shut up while they eat. That means they love the food!"

I lift my fork. "To Señora Vasquez!"

"Three cheers!" Mr. Miniver lifts his fork, too.

The refrigerator rattles again, and Mr. Miniver cocks his head. "Whatever that is sounds like it's about to break." He gets up.

"It's fine," Señora Vasquez says. "It's been like that for years."

"It's the ice maker. I can disconnect it completely."

Mr. Miniver opens the freezer door. "Cady, go out to my truck and open the glove box. Inside there's a leather case, with my Leatherman multi-tool." Mr. Miniver winks. "Do you know what my job used to be? Professional problem solver, aka engineer."

When I get back, Mr. Miniver has the refrigerator pulled away from the wall and Señora Vasquez is saying, "But the store right next door is empty. Shell could expand and then start selling to retail stores, too. There's not enough business here."

Mr. Miniver flips open a little screwdriver thing from the tool. "Now, that is an investment I'd be willing to make." His head disappears behind the appliance. "You have to spend money to make money."

My stomach somersaults. "Does she know you'd do it?" She must not. Otherwise she'd let him help, wouldn't she?

Mr. Miniver gestures at Señora Vasquez. "No, but I bet she will in about two minutes with this one on the case."

"Oh, you." Señora Vasquez rolls her eyes. "I'll tell her, but she'll resist. She's too stubborn."

"Like someone else I know." Mr. Miniver laughs.

She snorts. "Besides, the landlord's asking too much. She needs to negotiate."

They continue their discussion. I lean back in my chair, enjoying how they talk back and forth. How the kitchen smells so good with the chicken and the cake. How much they care about my aunt, and about me.

I've never known any grandparents, but Señora Vasquez and Mr. Miniver seem like they're a pretty close substitute. Señora Vasquez puts our cake dishes in the sink and turns on the water.

I get up. "Sit down. I've got this." I take over. For the first time since I overheard María and Shell, I'm hopeful. Maybe there's still a chance for the shop, if Shell will let us all help her.

CHAPTER 28

Later, when I get home, both Suzanne and Shell are waiting for me. "You got a postcard from Jenna." Shell hands it to me.

Yes! I run upstairs to read it.

"Come right back down," Suzanne calls. "I got us Chinese food."

"Okay," I shout back. I examine the postcard. It takes me a minute to figure it out. Jenna's still not that great at spelling. I wasn't either in second grade.

> *Hope your having an awsome summer. I accidentlly had somethng bad at the fair. I'm in the hospitl. There's nothng to do hear & the food is bad. I miss you.*

Poor Jenna. I hope she's all right by now. If only there was something I could do to cheer her up. I can't afford flowers and I don't want to ask Shell for help with that, knowing how tight we are on money, so instead, I write her a letter.

Dear Jenna,

I bet by the time you get this, you'll be at home. Feel better. Jacques, Julia, and Tom say hi.

Love,

Cady

I draw her a picture of us reading a book, with Tom on her lap, rubbing his face on the pages, and Jacques and Julia on their stomachs, listening.

It will have to do for now.

I take the letter downstairs. Shell and Suzanne are on the couch, watching *The Bake Off* with the sound off. "Haven't you already seen all the episodes?" I plop into the chair and put the letter into the little basket on the coffee table for mail. Suzanne's got the boxes of food arranged on the coffee table.

She spoons white rice into a bowl, then puts orange chicken on top of it and hands it to me. "Chopsticks or fork?"

"Chopsticks." I'm not great at them, but if I never use them, how will I ever learn? I rip open the package and imitate Suzanne as she scrapes them against each other, removing the splinters.

"When I rewatch the show, I always see something I missed the first time," Shell says.

Suzanne takes off her long hoop earrings. "Ah. These are too heavy."

That reminds me. "I wrote to my dad and told him I was getting my ears pierced. So can one of you take me to Gable's dad?" Jacques's nose sticks up over the coffee table, the nostrils sniffing. I pick up my food quickly. He's kind of a thief.

Shell frowns. "Shoot. I forgot about that. We should wait for your dad to say it's okay."

"No. I *told* him I was doing it." I lift my chin, watching a baker cry over his bread. "I don't care what he thinks. Every time I talk to him, he only talks about himself." I let out all the thoughts I've been keeping inside me. I eat a piece of orange chicken but don't taste it. "And it's his fault we're homeless. Only my mother was a real parent. Why should I have to get *his* permission to do anything?"

They exchange a look, communicating something—I'm not sure what.

A list of all the ways Dad let me down scrolls through my head like one of those super-long register receipts. All these years wasted. I could have known Shell and Suzanne for my entire life, but I didn't. "The worst thing is this." I wave my hand around. "He *kept* me from you. My mom would have wanted me to know you. To live here." My voice gets louder and I pound my fists into my knees.

Shell angles toward me. "There's something else you need to know."

Uh-oh. From their expressions, this can't be good. My body goes on high alert, like it's ready to run. I cross my arms tight across my chest. "Okay."

"Are you sure, Shell?" Suzanne says.

"Cady's mature and intelligent. She needs to have all the facts." Shell nods toward me, and I nod back, a fleecy sensation enveloping my body, blanket-like. Shell thinks I'm intelligent.

"Yes. I want to know." Whatever it is, I can handle it. My life story's like a book with random scenes and plot pieces cut out of it. How can I make sense of it without filling those holes?

"You remember how I told you I didn't know why your dad said you were going to Oregon?" Shell's voice quavers. Suzanne rubs her knee, and Shell regains control. "Here's how it was."

Suzanne scoots over. "Cady, why don't you come sit with us?"

I mechanically stand and squeeze in next to Suzanne. Her spot is like a burner set on low. I settle in. "Go on," I say to Shell. "I want to hear it." I give them my best brave smile. "Remember, I'm tough. I'm a Sanchez."

"Yes," Shell says softly. She clears her throat. "Cady, I

know you think your mom was perfect and it's your dad who had all the problems."

I nod. "Pretty much. We would have been fine if it wasn't for him." That last part makes me feel guilty, but it's true. I look at my lap.

Shell shakes her head. "But your mom had her own issues. Way before you came along."

My body goes ice-cold. "What kind of issues?" I feel like I'm standing outside this scene, watching it happen. Like I'm not really here.

"Drugs." Shell takes in a breath. "We tried helping her."

"But you can't make an adult do anything," Suzanne adds, rubbing my shoulder. Her touch reminds me that I'm still in the room. That my aunts are here.

"Anyway, she did come home for a while when she was pregnant. She cleaned up for you. But she went back to your dad before you were born. She said they were both clean." Shell's lips quiver. "After a while, she stopped communicating. She'd answer the phone maybe on holidays or her birthday, but that was it."

"We tried to see you as much as we could when you were a baby," Suzanne adds. "They seemed functional enough. You seemed healthy. But she and your dad were unfriendly. Sometimes they'd pretend not to be home." Suzanne squashes me against her like she can crush the pain out of me.

Shell's mouth twists. "Then, when you were about three, she told us to leave her alone for good. She didn't want her baby to have two aunts. We thought that was the only reason she didn't want us around. Now I think it was an excuse." She shakes her head. "We didn't even know your mom was sick until—it was too late."

I stare hard at the coffee table, willing my heart to explode, because that's how bad it hurts right now. "I thought . . ." I can barely speak.

"After your mother died, we spoke to your dad every once in a while. We wanted to know you were okay. I tried to visit, but the address he gave was no good." Shell rubs her eyes. "I guess he told us you were moving to Oregon so we'd stop bothering him."

I move away from Suzanne. My side is coated with sweat and every muscle I have tenses. "No. That's not right. My dad was okay until she died. He loved her so much he couldn't help going downhill." I try to stop my lips from trembling. "She was the glue!"

Shell stares at the floor. Suzanne tries to put her arm around me, but I don't want any touching right now. I'm shaking, my fury smoldering. "But really, it was because both of them were bad."

My father had lied. Right to my face, over and over, for years. He only cares about himself and making him and my mother look good, like they had no part in anything. Like everything was someone else's fault, when they had been the ones pushing everyone away. "Did they ever love me?" My voice cracks. I kick the basket of letters, sending them flying. Julia runs over and sniffs them. Jacques retreats to hide by Shell.

"I'm not mad at you, Jacques," I tell him, but he looks away. That makes me feel worse.

"Of course they loved you. Remember your mother got better for you!" Suzanne says. "They loved you, but they—"

"No, Suzanne," Shell interrupts. "Cady is allowed to feel how she feels." She stretches out her arms and grabs my hands, which I let her do because my emotions are about to blow me off the couch. "You had a rougher life than any kid deserved. There were lots of things your parents could have done differently to put you first. But their judgment wasn't exactly high functioning." She rubs my hands with her thumbs, the pressure calming me. "And maybe we should've done more. Gotten custody somehow. I don't know."

"She should've gotten help," I blurt out. "That's what a normal person would do. Right?"

Suzanne's eyes well. "Cady, we don't know what was going on in her head. But I know your parents didn't intend to become addicts. Who would? But once they started, it was hard to stop. And when your mom died, your father got worse, too."

"And the mental illness with all the religious

mania—alcohol and drugs don't help." Shell takes a deep, shaky breath.

Why? Why? Why? my brain yells. Why weren't my parents stronger? Why didn't they get help? Everything has to have a reason, doesn't it?

It's so unfair.

I'd felt so guilty when I got taken away. It was never my fault. *I'm* the kid. They were supposed to protect me.

The judges are tasting the Showstoppers now. I turn up the volume to fill the silence. What would I give to be in that tent, crunching into those monsters and houses made of gingerbread, instead of right here? Someone's Godzilla-like cookie falls over, and everyone jumps, including me.

Suzanne rubs my back and I let her. We watch the show silently for a minute. "I wish it could've been different," I say at last in a teeny-tiny voice.

I think about my dad sitting alone and reading my letter, and a hollow spot opens inside me. But then the taste of resentment as strong as those salad greens comes into my mouth. "I still want to get my ears done," I say in a low voice. "I don't care what he thinks."

Suzanne and Shell look at each other again. Shell nods. "Okay," Suzanne says. "I'll take you this weekend."

CHAPTER 29

I'm down for the rest of the week. I go to the pie shop every day, but I don't feel like baking anymore. "Do I have to go to work?" I ask Shell on Thursday morning.

"Of course not." Shell inhales. "Feed the chickens. Do your chores. Maybe visit with Señora Vasquez."

I shrug halfheartedly. "Okay."

As soon as Shell leaves, I add more food to my laundry basket. It's overflowing. But this time I don't feel any relief when I do it. I don't feel anything at all.

I don't care if Dad ever gets me. I don't think I want him to.

I go back downstairs and turn on cartoons, only getting up to feed the animals and to make myself food. Other than that, I stay on the couch all day. When Jay knocks at the door in the afternoon, I don't answer.

I just want to keep my mind turned off for a while.

*

On Saturday, Shell specifically asks me to go to the shop. "I don't want to," I say.

"I need your help with something. Please." Shell never asks like this, so out of surprise, I agree.

When we get there, Mr. Miniver, Claudia, María, and Jay all greet me like I've been away at war. I say hi to them and follow Shell, who's barreling into the back room. She opens the walk-in refrigerator to reveal a stack of plastic flats. Strawberries. Lots of them. "Well, Miss Cady. Looks like the public has voted and we've gotten a new flavor."

For the first time since I learned about my mom, I smile and get the excited, floaty feeling I usually get when I think about pie. "Really?"

Shell nods. "For the first time in my history, I am offering a third option. All because of you." She holds up her hand and I give it a good hard smack. "Well done," she says in a British Mary Berry voice, and I almost cry, I'm so happy.

"Thanks, Shell. I won't let you down." I go put on my apron and wash my hands. This is going to take my help. My heart pounds as I think of all the pie we're going to make. And I remember what Mr. Miniver said. "Did you talk to Mr. Miniver, Shell?"

She nods. "It's not the worst idea, but I'm not ready. I told him I'd think it over."

Think it over is one step closer. I'm excited.

María grabs Shell's arm. "Shell. Cady's got the right idea. Remember the football fund-raiser? We should do the apple fennel raisin pie, too." María gestures with her hands as if she's pointing at a sign. "Made with local ingredients. That could be how we stand out."

"We could get more fennel!" Jay pumps his fist.

Shell's forehead furrows. "I don't know. We're going to need a lot. And what if you accidentally get some that's been sprayed?"

"The ranger told me all the safe places," Jay says.

Shell throws her hands up to the sky. "You win. You've worn me down!"

"We need advertising." I turn to Claudia, who's behind the counter. "Claudia can draw something up."

She shakes her head. "I could ask Gable."

I shake my head back at her. "Why don't you want to try?"

"Come on, *mi hija,*" María says. "Just a little flyer."

"What would it even be?"

I look around. Apples? Every other pie shop has pictures of apples. A picture of pie? Too obvious. Then I see Mr. Miniver in his pioneer getup. I point. "Put him in it. He's pretty much our mascot anyway."

"Hey," Mr. Miniver says. "I resemble that."

Jay sticks his face in front of Claudia's. "Or use me. I'm the most adorable one here!"

"I don't want to scare the customers." Claudia turns

away, her long hair only partly hiding a little smile. "I'll see what I can come up with."

Suzanne takes me to Gable's dad's shop in the afternoon. "You ready for this?" He gestures to the back room, where there's nothing but a dentist-like chair that leans back.

Suzanne grips my shoulders. "She is."

But as soon as I see the chair, I want to leave. I think of Dad again, and the tone in my note. I didn't ask him, I *told* him.

It's like me getting my ears pierced means I don't care about him at all as a father anymore. That I'll do what I want and not care about his opinion. And why shouldn't it be like that, after what Shell and Suzanne told me?

But something stops me. Maybe he wanted to protect my memory of Mom. If I knew she was like him, then I would have had nothing at all to hold on to during those hard years. I would have felt like even more of a nothing.

Somehow it seems important that I hear from him first.

"I changed my mind," I say to Suzanne quietly.

"Sure," she says, to my relief. In fact, she smiles really big at me.

"You're not mad?"

"No. I'm happy you're finally comfortable enough to

change your mind with us." She hugs me to her. Gable's dad watches us with his brows raised, no doubt thinking we're kind of weird.

I'm okay with that.

CHAPTER 30

The following week, I get ready for a field trip with Jay's youth group. Jay goes to the local Catholic church every Sunday. Which is definitely not where Dad would want me going. He doesn't trust Catholics. Or Baptists, or Lutherans or Episcopalians or Evangelicals. Jay assures me that there are lots of kids who aren't church members going.

The beach! It's been forever since I've been there. Dad used to take me sometimes, but I didn't have a real swimsuit so I just paddled my feet.

Shell let me pick out a brand-new bathing suit before this trip. The one I chose is a turquoise one-piece with matching board shorts. Shell added a rash guard, which basically is a T-shirt made out of swimsuit material. "This will protect you from the sun," Shell told me. "Along with a hat and lots of sunblock." She got me a hat, too, with flaps on the sides and hanging down the back.

It's a clear, hot day. I can't wait to get to the water. I try on the hat. I look like Goofy. Everyone's going to laugh at me. I leave the hat in my bedroom and head downstairs.

Shell puts two twenty-dollar bills into my palm. "For the fee and lunch."

I turn the money over in my hand. "I could stay home." Forty dollars could buy a lot of strawberries.

Shell sees that look. "Cady. We're fine. Don't worry." She stares at my head. "Go get your hat."

"Fine." I run upstairs and grab the hat. Inside, I'm pleased. Shell cares about whether or not I get sunburned. I fly back down. "Happy?"

"Very." She squeezes a huge glob of sunscreen into her hand. "Let me get your back."

Most of the middle school comes, along with the youth group leader, Miss Mia, and some parent chaperones. We go to Belmont Park at Mission Beach, where a big wooden roller coaster stands guard above buildings full of games and rides and, of course, the ocean. I have a wristband for minigolf, something called Sky Ropes, and bumper cars. Then we go into a souvenir shop and Jay buys a tiny snow globe for Esmeralda, who's too young for the trip, and I buy a poster of a San Diego beach sunset.

It feels like a different planet from Julian, with the

wetter air. It smells different too—like sunblock and popcorn, but also like salt air. The sun beats down hot on my skin and I'm glad I have the hat.

Before lunch, the group of us sit on the wall that separates the wide concrete boardwalk from the beach, watching the various kinds of people—people in running gear, on skateboards, tourists with cameras, teenagers, parents with strollers—go by. People in every age group, color, shape, and size.

My dad and I used to come here and sit on the wall and people-watch, too. We'd dip our feet in the water, use the cold outdoor showers to rinse off as best we could. I'd always get a sunburn. Today a man dressed in a tattered olive-green trench coat sits on the wall, drinking from a Big Gulp cup and reading a raggedy paperback. Another cup sits at his feet. Dozens of people walk by and don't seem to notice him.

My arm hair stands up. That could be Dad, I realize. Almost invisible. Alone. The series of problems—my parents' issues, then Mom's death, then him getting worse, then losing his job and falling behind on rent—maybe if just one of those things hadn't happened, we would have been okay. But once we lost our place, he was never able to save up enough to lease a new one.

Dad always said we were digging ourselves out of a quicksand hole. What we'd needed was a rope.

The man stands up and scratches his rib cage, all

without letting go of the book or the Big Gulp cup.

"Ew," a girl sitting next to me says. "Do you think he has fleas?"

My breath goes all shaky. Should I tell them about me? Should I not? I stand up from the wall and face the group. I want them to like me, but I can't sit here all quiet. If they don't like what I'm about to say, then I don't want to be friends with any of them. "They're here because there are showers and bathrooms," I say. "Do you know they keep the public bathrooms downtown locked?"

The whole group goes quiet, staring at me.

"I mean, it's not like being homeless is exactly fun. You don't know what's happened to him." I stare at the sidewalk, halfway hoping it'll open up and swallow me. I ignore that sensation.

"Cady's right," Miss Mia says at last. "We should practice kindness in our words and actions." She smiles. "Come on, let's go swimming." She shepherds the group back to the water.

"Sheesh," the girl who made the comment whispers to me. "You're a little sensitive."

Jay leans over so his face is right next to the girl's. "She's just not a jerk," he whispers back.

I walk over to the man, Jay following. As I get closer I smell the man's odor—the clothes that haven't been washed, alcohol, body. Like Dad at his worst. Now that

I've been living with Shell the smell seems overwhelming.

Jay grabs my arm. "Don't talk to him. He could be dangerous."

I shake away. "I can tell he's not. He's not talking to himself. He's reading." I stand in front of the man. "Hi."

He squints. Sand's caked in the wrinkles of his face and most of his teeth are brown or missing. He looks surprised. "Hi," he croaks, as if he's not used to speaking.

I want to talk to him like a regular human. The way I'd want someone to speak to me. "Is that a good book?"

He nods, turns it over. *The Lord of the Rings: The Fellowship of the Ring.* "My favorite."

I can smell the alcohol mixed into his soda. Again my heart aches, thinking of my father. "When was the last time you ate?"

He shrugs. "Not very hungry anymore."

I've got twenty-four dollars left after the trip fee and poster. I hold out the cash. "Here." I won't be able to eat lunch, but I'll survive.

His eyes dart from me to Jay to the money, then he makes some noise in his throat, clutches it to his chest, and shuffles off.

I wonder if he ever had a family. A kid. Someone who misses him.

A police officer rides up on a bike. "Was he bothering

you?" Her voice sounds deep with concern. "Did you give him money? You shouldn't." She looks at Jay, then at me. "Are you guys okay?"

We both nod. I'm not afraid, because she's just making sure we're fine. She smiles at us in a friendly way. "Are your parents around here someplace?"

Jay stiffens. I hear his breathing go funny.

Then I remember. He's told me that sometimes, if a police officer suspects someone's undocumented, they call up immigration right then and there. In fact, one time his mom's purse got stolen, and she didn't report it, in case she got deported. Even when they really need help, it's too dangerous to take it.

But I'm with Jay today. In my new swimsuit and dorky sun hat, I look like a kid who "belongs" here. That shouldn't be true, but that's how it is. I speak up fast. "We're here with a church group." I point toward them. "We're fine, thank you."

"Okay." The police officer rides off. "You kids be careful. Not everyone's nice around here. Stick with your group!"

Jay relaxes. "I thought we were goners."

"That lady was nice. Mostly, police want to help you." I think of my grandfather, whose picture is in the police museum.

"Yeah," Jay says unconvinced. Then he shakes himself all over, like Jacques shaking water off his fur.

"Come on. Let's split a Dole Whip."

I'm too glad to get back to having fun. My mouth begins watering, imagining the cold pineapple sugar. "Sheer perfection," I answer in my Mary Berry British voice.

AUGUST

735 Pies Down

265 to Go

CHAPTER 31

At the end of the first week that we've had new flavors, Suzanne and I are making breakfast. Bacon and eggs. She uses long chopsticks to move the bacon in the pan. I try, but I'm not good enough at holding them yet.

"Hey." Shell comes into the room so suddenly that Tom jumps out of his post on the kitchen chair. "These two new pies outsold our two regular flavors!" She peers at me and Suzanne over her reading glasses.

"Well, high-five!" Suzanne jumps up and down. I give her a super–high five, so hard she pretends to fall over. "Girl, we need to get you in the boxing ring."

I flex. "I know, right?"

Suzanne holds up her hand for Shell. "Up high!"

Shell does a super-soft slap. "Let's just see how it goes." She exhales a big sigh. "We're not out of the woods yet. Not by far." She shuffles off.

Something's wrong with Shell. I don't know what it is,

but she's just got to be cheered up soon.

Suzanne looks at me and shrugs. "Well, Cady. Want to work on your room today?"

We're going to paint the walls my favorite color, green. Mr. Miniver actually got me the paint, matching it to a pair of the jeans I got at Old Navy—a soft mint. Now Suzanne and I cover the furniture and floors with rolls of heavy clear plastic. She and I push the dresser into the center of the room and open the window. "We don't want to die in here from the fumes," Suzanne says with a grin.

Next, she shows me how to mix up the paint with a stick and pour it into a long tray, then how to dip the roller brush in it so there are no drips. She demonstrates how to use the roller on the wall, going in sort of a V shape, then hands it to me. "You do the walls and I'll get the edges." She holds up an angled brush and climbs onto a stepladder.

Cautiously I try it myself. My roller's too full of paint so it drips, but I quickly roll it over those, too. It's hard to go over the little gaps between the panels, and Suzanne says it'll take two coats. "Then you can put up your sunset poster, and maybe we can get that big chair out of the other bedroom for you. I don't know if you've seen it—it's currently being a quilt holder." Suzanne snorts. "What do you think?" Suzanne's high up on the ladder, straining to reach the parts by the ceiling.

I pause. "Um, Suzanne, is that safe?"

"Sure it is." She's up on the part where it says DO NOT USE AS STEP. I put down the roller and steady the ladder with my hand. "Cady, I'm fine."

"Get down from there." Shell's striding in, pushing up her sleeves. "Let me do that."

"I'm perfectly capable." Suzanne's arm looks like it might pop out of her socket as she tries to extend the brush.

"You're capable, you're just too short." Shell holds out her hand, and Suzanne takes it and climbs down. "You get the part by the floor."

Suzanne salutes her. "Yes, ma'am. You can take the girl out of the Marines, but you can't take the Marines out of the girl."

I'm just relieved Shell shook off her crabbiness enough to help. We paint quietly for a while, until Suzanne says we need music and takes out her phone.

"Play some old Johnny Cash," Shell says. "We've got to introduce Cady to him." Suzanne puts on "Ring of Fire" and Shell sings along off-key. "How do you like that?"

I squint. "I might like it better without, um, the accompaniment."

Shell laughs. "Fine. I know singing's not my strong suit."

So that's how we spend the morning, painting my

room with Johnny Cash and some other random old music I don't know. *My* room. At noon, Shell has to go to the shop, but she promises to clean out the rest of the closet later so I'll have it all, and then Suzanne and I go to the extra room and take the pile of quilts off the chair. It's covered in a rose-printed white-and-pink fabric. "Shell isn't a big fan of flowery stuff. It was from my old place." Suzanne runs her hand over it. "It's so comfy, I could never bear to get rid of it. Even if it is just a quilt holder."

"It's perfect." I throw myself into the chair sideways, so my legs hang over the arm, my insides tingling. The chair kind of swallows me up. I can't wait to curl up in here with my recipes and books and Tom.

"Let's see, I've got a reading lamp in the garage we can use, too. And you can have a couple of these." She takes out a small patchwork quilt and a crocheted pink blanket and throws them on top of me. "Comfy?"

"Yeah," I say from under the blankets. Suddenly I get tears in my eyes.

Suzanne touches my arm. "You okay?"

I nod. I don't know how to explain why I'm crying over a chair and paint. But I've never had a place with a door I can shut. A place just for me. "I'm happy, is all." I throw the blankets off. "And a little hot."

Suzanne sinks down and hugs me tight, not saying a word. For once, Shell would say. That makes me smile.

*

Within a week, three more local restaurants place orders for the new flavors. Shell's been going in super-early with María to help make crusts, and even Claudia's been pitching in.

"The strawberry basil is so refreshing!" I heard one lady say.

"That makes sense," Suzanne said when I told her. "Strawberries mean summer, and that's what people are in the mood for."

So my notebook ideas are about all the fruits that are in season right now. Peaches, nectarines, and plums. Strawberries and blackberries and cherries. I think we should have more new flavors.

I tell Suzanne my idea as she drops me and Jay off at the shop one afternoon. "It's too soon to introduce another one." She slings her big purse over her shoulder as she shuts the car door. Suzanne's so petite that almost every purse looks enormous. "But what if we switched out the two new pie flavors every month? We have our regulars, then the two new ones, to keep people guessing."

"So I can come up with the September pie flavors right now?" I ask.

"Exactly." Suzanne pops open her trunk and hands me a box to carry.

"Which flavors say *September* to you?" I ask Jay.

"Apple," he says promptly.

"That's not helpful." I shake my head at him. "We already make that."

"Pumpkin."

"We need to save pumpkin for Thanksgiving," Suzanne says.

I think hard. What's sort of like pumpkin, that says fall? Something that's not apple. "How about carrot?"

"Carrots?" Jay shudders. "No vegetables in pie."

I stick my tongue out at him. "I bet if I didn't tell you it had carrots, you'd eat it." I step off the sidewalk as a family walks by us, pushing a double stroller. The good thing is, there are still plenty of people in the mountains today. Maybe everyone hoped it'd be cooler here. "How about carrot with some fruit?"

"Oooh. Nectarine?" Suzanne suggests. "That could be good. We'll get some today and you can try it."

Inside the shop, there's one person in line, but about a dozen sitting at the tables, chowing down. That's almost two pies' worth. This is good for ten thirty in the morning.

"You want to go to the Candy Mine later?" Jay asks me. "I want some more Nerds."

I still feel bad about how I reacted to that Adam guy. I pick up a boxed strawberry basil pie. "Let's go right now."

Adam's sitting at his station, reading a comic book. I march in ahead of Jay and put the white box down in front of him. “Here. Compliments of the house.”

He pushes it back, pursing his lips. “We get our pies from Grandma’s.”

Ouch. I’m not sure what to say now, or do, but Jay steps in.

“Come on,” Jay says. “Don’t stay mad. It was a misunderstanding.”

Adam finally looks up. I lean forward. “I’m sorry I, like, freaked out a little bit the other day. Will you please accept this scrummy pie as a token of my apology?”

He squints. “What’s scrummy?”

I shrug. “I don’t know. It’s British. Like scrumptious, I guess.”

Adam’s mouth turns up. He pushes a few taffies toward us. “Trade?”

“Sure.” I pop a peppermint one into my mouth and grin. Making things right feels pretty good.

When we get back, Suzanne calls a team meeting in the kitchen. Shell’s taking pies out of the oven. She looks up but doesn’t say anything as everyone else gathers around. My stomach turns all over again.

Suzanne props a large flat object, wrapped in a black trash bag, on a table. “Shell, come here.”

“I’m a bit busy,” Shell says.

“Well, you can see from there.” Suzanne chooses not to acknowledge Shell’s grumpiness. She grins at Claudia. “This is something the shop’s needed for a while.

A little update. Claudia, will you do the honors?" She makes a gesture like she's pulling off the cover.

Claudia tears off the trash bag.

It's a sign. A cartoon Mr. Miniver holding a pie, printed in red on white. In the cartoon his cheeks are plump and his eyes are somehow twinkling. Sort of like a beardless Santa. The words SHELL'S WORLD-FAMOUS PIES are written in a half-circle shape underneath.

It's Claudia's drawing, blown up to three and a half feet tall.

Claudia's mouth drops open and her eyes widen into platters.

"This is for the inside of the store. I'm also having one made for the outside." Suzanne's practically jumping up and down. "And that's not all." She opens the box Jay had. Inside there are napkins printed with the same logo.

María hugs Claudia. "Such a great job, *mi hija*! I'm so proud of you."

"Cartoon Mr. Miniver is cute," I say. "He looks like one of those dough ornaments that little kids make."

Jay snaps his fingers. "Yeah, he does."

We all look at Shell, whose mouth is so upside down and eyebrows so furrowed she literally looks like the angry-face emoji. "You're very talented, Claudia." She turns and checks the oven, even though she already took the pies out and it's empty.

My stomach feels like it did on the way up those winding mountain roads.

Nobody says anything. Claudia's smile fades. María pats her daughter on the shoulder, then tugs her and Jay gently to the front. I don't know if I'm supposed to follow them or stay. I don't move.

"What's the problem, Shell?" Suzanne draws her shoulders back. "I got a good deal and I paid for them. Don't worry."

Shell's jaw muscles work and twitch. "Thank you, Suzanne." Obviously she's not all that grateful. "But you should have saved your money."

Why doesn't Shell see how these signs will help? Does she want the store to fail? Why is she still so grumpy? I open my mouth to tell Shell to be happy about what Suzanne gave her, but I close it again. It won't help.

"Oh, and I called about leasing the space next door. I think we could do very well with our new flavors. Shipping them to stores in the city." Suzanne's tone is determinedly cheerful. "I thought you were on board."

Shell seems to sag down into herself. "I only ever said I would think about it." She rubs her temples.

"But—"

"I already called every store in San Diego County. Nobody's interested. They've got enough pie. They don't think new flavors will work outside a local shop. Frankly, I think I agree." Shell shakes her head. "That's just how it is. We're stuck with what we have."

Suzanne turns to me. "Go put these napkins out front, please."

Neither of them says another word, which makes me more worried than ever. I slink out to the front, my stomach folding in on itself.

The next morning, I wake up to the sound of Shell and Suzanne arguing downstairs. Jacques and Julia clack into my room, their tails between their legs, like they're to blame. Jacques sticks his head under my bed as far as he can but he doesn't quite fit. I reach down and stroke his smooth fur. "It's okay." Julia flops under my window, sighing as if she's exasperated. I try not to listen, but their voices carry straight up to me like they're yelling into an intercom.

"I gave you my share of the mortgage and bills!" Suzanne says. "What happened? You said you would take care of it."

"If I didn't pay off the suppliers, we would have closed. When the pie shop made money this month, I was going to pay the mortgage."

"I knew we shouldn't have taken out a second mortgage." Suzanne sounds like she's going to choke. "The late fees double or triple our costs."

"It's what I had to do." Shell pounds the table with each word. "If I hadn't, the shop would have gone under two months ago. We can ask for an extension."

"Oh, they're not going to wait any more than they have to. They can make a ton of money off this house if they resell it." Suzanne sounds like she's got stones in her mouth. "How late is the mortgage?"

Shell doesn't answer. In that silence, it's as if a dark cloud, heavy as lead, covers the house. I swallow and pet Jacques harder.

"How late?" Suzanne demands again.

"Four months," Shell says reluctantly.

"Four months?" Suzanne sounds hysterical. "That means they can foreclose. They're going to take it back. Why didn't you tell me everything?"

"I didn't want you to worry. It wouldn't have made a difference. Neither of us had the money."

Suzanne's crying for real this time. "This is going to take a huge amount of cash, Shell!"

"We can do it," Shell says, and I recognize this strange note of fake confidence. The same as when Dad says, *Everything's going to be fine.* It's a lie and it makes tears spring to my eye. "I'll work out a payment plan. It'll be fine."

So much for her word.

It's the *house* too, not just the pie shop. The place where we live, that belonged to my grandparents. We're going to lose absolutely everything.

And what about Jay and his family? How could Shell

let this happen? Julia comes over to lick the tears off my face.

The front door slams. Suzanne's car starts and takes off, wheels churning up gravel.

I go downstairs, Jacques and Julia following. To my surprise, María's here, sitting next to Shell at the kitchen table. "Is everything okay?" I will them to tell me the truth.

María looks pale. "No, *mi hija*. I'm afraid not."

Shell puts her hands over her face. The backs of her hands are red and calloused. "I won't let anything bad happen to you, Cady. Or to María or her family."

That's like promising ice won't melt when it's a hundred degrees. Nobody can keep a pledge like that.

María shakes her head. "You told me what the risks were. I said to do it."

I lean against the counter. So María knew and not Suzanne? I wonder if that's another reason Suzanne's so mad. Shell should have told Suzanne. "Are we losing the house? I want to know if we are."

"Of course not." Shell sounds fake. It's not a good look for her.

I cross my arms and glare. Shell looks like she's getting ready be upset, too. The muscles in her jaw twitch.

"It's not a worry for a child," María intervenes. "Especially not after what you've been through."

I'm a kid, but I know when stuff is going on. Why do

they expect me to pretend it's all okay? "I can handle it. Remember?" I stare at Shell. "I can handle *truth*."

"I know you can, sweetie. I just wish you didn't *have* to." Shell's eyes fill with tears.

My heart turns to jelly. Poor Shell. This time I walk over and put my arms around her.

CHAPTER 32

Shortly after we open, a little girl comes into the pie shop. She's all by herself, wearing jeans with holes in the knees and a coat although it's pretty warm today. "May I help you?"

She twists one dirty-looking pigtail around in her hand. "Do you have gluten-free pie?" Her voice is particularly high and clear, like Jenna's.

I feel a sad jolt. If Jenna came here, she wouldn't be able to eat anything, either. "Sorry, we don't."

Her face falls a little, but not much, like she's used to hearing this. "Okay."

I'm a little afraid for her. She looks about six. Who lets their six-year-old go to town to buy pie? "Where are your parents?" I say it as if I'm ancient, like I'm thirty years old myself.

"They're in a shop." She shrugs. "They're coming."

That's good. "Can you have vanilla ice cream?"

She nods and hops up to a table.

I put a scoop in a bowl and hold up the can of whipped cream. She nods again. I put on a gigantic squirt and set it in front of her.

She produces a five-dollar bill from her pocket. Crisp and new. “Here you go. Keep the change.”

“It’s on the house.” Shell won’t mind. She’s been complaining about needing to get rid of the ice cream before it gets freezer burn.

She narrows her eyes, then shrugs. She sits there eating her ice cream, and her parents come in. Her dad has long hair poking out from under a floppy fedora. He wears about ten bracelets and silver rings on every finger. Her mom’s got on a long flowery dress and her sandaled feet are dirty from Julian’s paths. She wears a big diamond ring. “Any luck here, Sammy?”

Sammy shakes her head but points at her ice cream. Her parents order two slices of apple. The little girl comes up and puts the five dollars into the tip jar. “Thank you.”

I lean against the counter. “So does your daughter have celiac?”

The man blinks as if surprised. “No. Why?”

“I don’t like eating gluten,” the girl says. “It makes me poop funny.”

The woman giggles while the man looks embarrassed. “Honey, that’s private information.”

"It's true, though. Her tummy hurts, and she gets stopped up and bloated for a week," the woman says matter-of-factly. "Doctor's orders. No wheat. We couldn't find any gluten-free pie in town, though."

"Do you have gluten-free pie where you live?" My mind whirs.

"In a few places around Los Angeles. But it's hard to find. A lot of gluten-free bakers make sweet breads and cake, but hardly anyone does pie. And I know several people who are intolerant."

"Bakeries have to have a space just for making truly safe gluten-free stuff," the man says. "You can't use the same equipment. So not many do it."

That's what Jenna needs, too, so she doesn't get sick. "Huh. Very interesting." I almost touch my invisible beard, until I remember I'm not with Jay and these people will think I'm a weirdo. This girl reminds me so much of Jenna that it makes my sides ache.

I walk over to where Mr. Miniver's sipping his coffee and reading the paper. "Mr. Miniver. Did you hear all that?"

"What?" Mr. Miniver asks, but he winks.

I slide into the seat across from him. I know that I don't have to tell him about the big trouble we're in or about this morning's fight. María would have told her mother, and Señora tells Mr. Miniver everything.

"What if we used the shop next door to make a gluten-free space?" I whisper. "And sold it all over the place where people want it? Do you think that would make us enough money?"

Mr. Miniver looks off into the distance. "Possibly. Possibly. Do you know what we need?"

I shake my head.

He slams his hand on the table. "Hard numbers."

Mr. Miniver says if we sell these gluten-free pies only in our shop, the cost of adding the space won't be worth it. But if we can get other stores to sell the pies, then it would be.

He opens a browser on his phone. "Make a list of all the grocery stores in the Southern California region. Call them. Ask if they would carry gluten-free pie. That way, we know exactly how much we should be able to sell," he explains.

The thought of having to talk to people on the phone makes me nervous. "Can't I email them?"

"Voices are better," he says firmly. "You want the personal touch. But you can write down what you'll say."

"What if they hang up on me?"

"What if they do?" Mr. Miniver shrugs. "Will lightning strike you dead?"

"Probably not," I mutter. "But I might die of embarrassment."

"Only three people in the world have ever died of embarrassment," Mr. Miniver says gravely. I look at him, surprised. He chuckles. "Okay, none that I know of."

*

I dial the first store. Mr. Miniver helped me write a script. While the phone rings, I pretend that I'm Suzanne. Confident and cheerful. "Hello, this is Cady Bennett from Shell's Pie up in Julian. Is your manager available?" I ask.

Sometimes people say no. Usually they put me through, though. And nobody questions if I'm a kid. By the end of the week, I've called ninety-eight stores. The area actually has hundreds, but that's too many to call. Besides, if it's a big chain of stores, some main office decides what they're going to carry. So I mostly call smaller stores. Thirty stores say they might be interested, if the pies were good and reasonably priced. Some say they'd do it if they were frozen. Mr. Miniver says we'd need to use some kind of special facility to do that. We don't count those stores. All in all, we have a pretty good case.

Mr. Miniver shows me the plans he's drawn up. He's spent the week doing research and pricing out all the things we would need to put in the new space. "I'll be the money guy. But you know what we need that only you can provide?"

I shake my head.

"A good-tasting gluten-free pie." He winks.

Mr. Miniver calls a meeting with Suzanne and Jay and me to discuss our plans. He takes us to the Rongbranch

Restaurant off of Main Street, which serves a lot of steaks and burgers and has an Old West theme. Not surprisingly, it smells like beef in here.

Suzanne slides into the booth next to Mr. Miniver. Jay and I sit across from them. "Get the burger," Jay advises as I look over the menu. "With extra cheese."

My stomach agrees. We all order. Then Suzanne puts her elbows on the table. "Thank you for taking us out, Mr. Miniver. But why all the secrecy? Why couldn't we meet at the shop?"

"Cady and I have a business proposition." Mr. Miniver laces his hands together and I imitate him. Jay wiggles his eyebrows up and down.

"Oh, no. Shell's not going to hear of it." Suzanne shakes her head sadly. "Besides, I'm afraid the ship has already sailed. The new flavors *might* help us break even in three months, if we didn't have an overdue mortgage and bills. I don't know what else we could do to save the place. Even a cash infusion would only help out for a little while."

Mr. Miniver nudges me. "That's where my plan comes in," I say. I take out the floor plan Mr. Miniver's drawn up, along with the business proposal we wrote. "Voilà." I put it on the log table with flair.

"Gluten-free pie?" She skims the plans. "Because of Jenna."

"Not just because of Jenna," I correct her. "Remember, lots of people can't tolerate gluten anymore." I tell her about the family that came in and the numbers I looked up. Eighteen million people have non-celiac gluten sensitivity, and six million have celiac. More people avoid it for other reasons.

Then I flip the page and show her the numbers. Cost of the pie kitchen remodel and rent. Ingredients. Truck, gas, driver. Sale price of the pie. Stores that want to buy the pie. I thought it would be a confusing jumble of numbers, but Mr. Miniver showed me how to put them into columns, and Jay helped enter them and double-checked the math.

"If we sent pies to all these stores, conservatively, we would be making money by month three." Mr. Miniver points. "Plus, as far as I know, nobody else in town is on the gluten-free bandwagon."

"That's right." Jay nods so dramatically that his chin hits his chest. "Shell's will lead the way!"

"Hmmm," Suzanne says. But there's a new sparkle about her.

"Once again, I'm offering to front the necessary funds," Mr. Miniver says. "In return for a fifteen percent stake."

I hop up and down on my seat. This is exciting. It's just like that TV show *Shark Tank,* where inventors present ideas to investors. Except Mr. Miniver's both the investor and the inventor, so maybe not.

I hold my breath, waiting for Suzanne's response.

"Ooh, is that our food?" Jay breaks the silence as a server walks by.

I shush him. This is too important.

Suzanne raises her eyes from the table. "We would need an excellent gluten-free crust," she says. "It has to be palatable to the average person."

"You mean tasty, right?" I say.

She nods. "Very tasty."

I nod back. "I'm on it. I just need the flour to practice."

"Well. If you can get that piece of the puzzle, then . . ." She slaps her hand on the table. "I'm in."

"Yes!" I put my hand over hers, Jay slaps his over mine, and Mr. Miniver places his hand over Jay's. Like a team. Team Pie.

The following Tuesday, Shell and I are at home while Suzanne's working. It's super warm again and there's no air-conditioning at the house. Shell says in the old days, it didn't use to get so hot. By old days she means the 1980s.

I'm testing my gluten-free pie recipe today, but my butter's melting. Summer's not the best pie-making time. Jacques and Julia and Tom all watch me prepare the crust, the dogs drooling slightly at the smell of the butter. "If these don't taste good, you might get a treat for dinner," I say to the dogs.

I read through three different recipes, deciding to

combine them and try it out. One wants egg, one wants lemon juice, one wants something called xanthan gum, which I don't have. This is hard. What does lemon juice do? I don't know. I sigh and write the new recipe in the notebook. If it doesn't work, I'll try another.

Suzanne bought me a bunch of gluten-free all-purpose flour. Today I plan to make three pies with this recipe. Shell says you have to do that, to make sure you can get the same result every time. Baking is sort of like doing science.

These won't be Jenna-safe pies, but right now I'm only worried about taste.

I have the ingredients lined up on the counter when Shell walks by. "What's all this?" She picks up the flour, sniffs it, and makes a face. Gluten-free flour doesn't have the best smell—it smells sort of like old radishes. "Where'd it come from?" She sees the huge bag in the corner, finally, and her mouth opens.

"Stuff for gluten-free pie. Suzanne got it for me." I hum as I get out the food processor and plug it in.

"Cady." Shell frowns, puts her hands down on the counter. "I've already told you—we shouldn't be doing any other kinds of pie."

I spoon flour into a cup. That's the way you're supposed to do it, instead of scooping the cup right into the flour, by the way—it's more accurate. I wish Mr. Miniver were here. He said he'd "lay out the facts for Shell," but it's up to me right now.

Maybe she'll listen to me. "That's not true. We should be." My heart pounds. I think of the plans Mr. Miniver's drawn up.

Shell does a double take, her eyes bugging out. "What do you mean, it's not true? Do you think I don't know what's best for me, for the business? Did Suzanne put you up to this?"

"No. I mean, she got me the stuff. But she didn't tell me to talk to you about gluten-free pie." I tap the cup on the counter, making sure the flour's settled, and scrape the top off with a knife. "Mr. Miniver said he'd invest. The shop next door is available. And Mr. Miniver says you have to spend money to make money."

"I've already spent money making those new pie flavors," Shell says slowly. "What do you think is going to happen if I expand and it fails? Mr. Miniver will lose his money, too."

"The gluten-free pie isn't like the others. I've got stores lined up and ready." I tell her about my market research. All the details.

"Wait a minute. You called stores?"

I nod. "Of course, we'd have to get a delivery truck and someone to deliver the pies."

"Cady, I'm very impressed with your planning. I don't think any of this is a *bad* idea. But there are lots of great ideas that can't happen without the right conditions." Shell shuts her eyes and sighs. "Really, I'm so tired of saying this. Let's get through this summer."

"But—"

"I don't want to hear it!" Shell slams her hands on the counter. Tom runs away. The dogs look worried.

I stick out my chin. Shell doesn't scare me. This is like when I shoved the pie. She's not mad at me—she's mad at the situation. And she probably needs to take a nap, judging from the bags under her eyes. When Suzanne's not here, Shell barely takes care of herself. Once I woke up at two a.m. and she was still down in the living room, paying bills before she had to go to work. "I'm trying to help." I put the flour into the food processor.

"I know you are, Cady. I know." Shell looks ferocious. "But I don't need to drag everyone down with me." She turns on her heel and goes into the yard. The dogs and I watch her leave.

"It's going to be okay." I crouch between them, put my arms around them. I'm with Suzanne. This will work. We've got to make Shell see it with her own eyes. No matter what I have to do.

The pie dough is as sticky as the recipes promised it would be. But I roll it out onto greased parchment paper, and it comes off just fine. I'm careful and slow. I keep ice in the water and I let the dough rest.

When the pie is done, it smells good. Like regular pie. No more of the icky smell. I let it cool, then cut out a piece. It's exactly crispy enough.

I take a piece to Shell, who's in the living room, working through yet another pile of paperwork as she watches a TV game show. "Is this it?" She barely looks up.

I hand her the plate. I used apple. The apples are already gluten-free, because we mix them with cornstarch instead of flour to thicken them. "Yep."

I sit down in the armchair and take a bite from my own plate. The crust is surprisingly good. It's not as flaky, but it pretty much tastes like a regular crust.

Shell chews thoughtfully. She takes another bite. She chews some more. Someone on *Family Feud* cheers and I look at the TV. When I glance back at Shell, her pie plate is empty.

Finally I can't stand it anymore. "Well? What'd you think?"

Shell taps her fork on the plate. "Not bad, Cady."

And that feels better than the time I got 100 percent on a science chapter test.

CHAPTER 33

I never thought I'd like getting up so darn early every day, but somehow it's easy to wake up in the bedroom that used to be my mother's, my feet swinging down to touch the floorboards that she touched, too. Only Tom the cat tries to stay in bed, giving me an *are you crazy?* stare. Maybe I am.

It's the end of the second week of August and Jay and I are going fennel hunting while it's still cool. And it will get hot again, I can tell. Heat rises up from the earth, evaporating in sweaty layers all over us as we hike into the woods with our canvas bags for the fennel, Jacques and Julia trailing us on their leashes.

We slog through a field. Wind blows hot and dry, sending my hair into my eyes. Thunder sounds in the distance like a far-off car playing loud hip-hop beats. "Look at those." Jay points. Above us there are actually no clouds at all, but dark flat-headed thunderheads hang low over the distant forest and the hillsides. "This weather is weird."

"It hasn't rained, but it looks like it's going to."

"My mom says this is a dry thunderstorm." Jay shrugs. "It tries to rain, but it dries up before it hits the ground."

"Should we be outside?" I try to remember what I've heard about storms. Get to low ground? Don't be in a tree?

"Eh." Jay continues walking. "It's way over there. If we stayed inside every time there was bad weather, we'd never do anything around here. Come on." He jumps off the path suddenly, through dense bushes. A small flock of quails flies out, the single long feather on their heads bobbing like a fishing lure. If I were a cat, I'd definitely hunt those.

As we hike, I start our knock knock jokes. That's what we do while we wander around, try to remember the funniest jokes we've ever heard. "Hey, Jay. Knock knock."

"Who's there?"

"A broken pencil."

"A broken pencil who?"

"Never mind. It's pointless."

Jay giggles. He holds some brush steady so I can get past. "Hey, Cady. Will you remember me in a year?"

"Yes."

"Will you remember me in a month?"

"Yes."

"Will you remember me in a week?"

"Yes." I haven't heard this one. I wonder where it's going.

"Knock knock."

"Who's there?"

Jay turns and grins at me. "You already forgot who I was."

I let out a snort, but then wrinkle my nose. Because I already know. Even if my dad comes back for me and I have to move away, I'll never forget him.

Late in the morning, I make another strawberry basil pie and put it in the oven. Then I go to the pie numbers and scratch out another mark. Yes.

I'm getting closer. By next month, I should be done.

I inhale deeply, feeling like I'm getting close to the end of a good book. I want it to keep going forever.

Right after lunch, I bring ice cream and pie to Señora Vasquez, Esmeralda, and Claudia. They're hanging out because Mr. Miniver's taking them on a city college visit in a little bit. Claudia's arguing. "I don't see what the point is." She kicks her legs out and Esmeralda imitates her.

"There's a program where you can go to school for free," her grandmother says in a tired voice, like she's said this a hundred times. "We're going to get you registered with the DREAM Act. That way they can't kick you out of the country."

"Are you kidding? It'll put me in an official system. If things go bad, we're the ones who'll get deported first. Besides"—she lowers her voice—"even if I get a degree, it won't help me become a citizen." Claudia sticks out her jaw.

"The government wouldn't trick you like that, would they? For something that was supposed to help you." I wait for Señora Vasquez to tell me Claudia's wrong, but she just looks at the table. Claudia gives me her patented *Come on, you know better* stare that she gives me when I'm sloppy with the coffee.

For a minute, the only sound is Esmeralda happily slurping her ice cream, but soon even she catches on to the mood and stops, her eyes as huge and innocent as an anime character's. "Why are you mad?"

Claudia picks up her sister's hand, kisses it. "We're not mad at you, *mi querida*."

"Claudia's . . . got a point," Señora Vasquez says in a low voice.

"People like us—we're nothing to politicians. Just chess pieces they play with to buy votes." Claudia sounds like she's choking on a twisted piece of lemon. "They don't care if they use us to pick their fruit. Or that they need us for the economy." She wipes at her eyes with a trembling hand.

A kind of hollowness fills me. An awful hopelessness.

I search for a way to fix it. "Is there *any* way you could get, um, documented?" I ask. "Like, could you get married or something?"

"She's not getting married," Señora Vasquez says sharply.

Claudia shakes her head. "Yeah, marriage won't help. To become a citizen, even if I were married, I'd have to go back to Mexico and apply to come back. Which has a twenty-year wait list."

Twenty years? She'd be thirty-nine years old by then. That's even older than my dad. "That's crazy!"

"That's how it is." Claudia twists up her mouth. "Plus, I can't just walk out of the US. I'd have to sneak out, because I don't have a passport."

Like with Jay, I don't know what to say. "I wish there was something I could do." Instinctively, I touch Claudia's arm, half expecting her to make some kind of sarcastic remark.

Instead, she puts her hand over mine and takes a big breath. "I'll be okay, Cady. Thanks."

"You going to eat the pie?" I nudge it toward her. Pie makes me feel better.

She shakes her head.

"What's the downside of going?" I ask her. That's what Mr. Miniver had me do with the bakery addition: make a list of the "upsides" and "downsides" of the project. He said this helps people make up their minds and also makes you think about any potential problems.

Claudia looks at me, thinking. "I guess, if I don't sign up for that program, nothing." Some cloud seems to lift and she pulls the pie toward her. "Maybe I should do it before Jay. Be the guinea pig." She half grins, spooning pie into her mouth.

"Finally, some sense." Señora Vasquez looks out the window. "Where is he? I hope Mr. Miniver remembered to put those doors on his car."

"Pretty sure you told him five hundred times." Claudia twists a straw wrapper into a rose for Esmeralda and wipes the vanilla ice cream off her face. It looks like there's more of it on her chin than went into her stomach.

"You never know. Old people and their memories." Señora Vasquez shifts nervously. "Claudia, take Esmeralda to the bathroom again."

"She just went."

"You never know."

Claudia disappears into the back with Esmeralda.

Mr. Miniver pulls up and parks in the handicapped spot, and Señora Vasquez breathes a sigh of relief. "Finally!"

A big white work truck follows Mr. Miniver. It says JULIAN COMMUNITY SERVICES DISTRICT on the side. A man in an olive uniform gets out.

"Oh crud." Shell goes pale. She pushes her way out through the line of customers, slamming the door as she goes. I follow, as do Mr. Miniver and Señora Vasquez.

"Can I help you?" Shell asks the man.

He takes off his cap, scratches his bald head. "I'm here to turn off your water." He holds up an orange piece of paper.

Shell flushes a deep scarlet. She looks like she wants to go hide under the earth. I remember the feeling all too well. It happened every time my dad came to school. "I only got one notice."

He checks the paper. "You're three months behind." He seems almost apologetic. He hands the paper to Shell, then gets a padlock and some kind of tool that looks like a metal walking stick out of the truck. People are staring.

Shell's red turns to ash when she sees the total. She gulps, visibly. "I can have that in two days. Is that possible?"

"I still gotta turn off the water." He walks over to something in the ground and sticks the metal thing in. "Then you have to go pay the bill in person. Then we have to schedule someone to come back out. That will be at least four days from now." He sounds flat. "And we don't count the weekend, so it'd be Wednesday."

Jay and I exchange a horrified glance. That's a week. We can't be open without water. It's unsanitary. And four days closed means no money coming in. That means we can't pay for more supplies.

We're done this time. For real.

CHAPTER 34

"You can't do that!" Señora Vasquez waves her cane at him as if it's a club. She would have made a great angry villager in medieval times. "We have rights."

"Abuela!" Jay says sharply. "She's going to get us deported," he whispers into my ear.

Mr. Miniver puts his hand over hers. "The man's only doing his job. They don't give him the authority to fix anything, now do they, son?" he asks the man. The man shakes his head no. He looks like he'd rather be any place but here.

Suzanne's black car pulls up and she pops out like a vengeful Tinker Bell. "What's going on?" She marches over, her small hands clenched into fists.

Shell tilts her head at the ground. I've seen that look before. Shame. I've had it on my own face when we couldn't pay a motel bill. I step forward and speak for my aunt. "It's the water." I take the bill and give it to

Suzanne, praying she can fix it.

Suzanne doesn't roll her eyes or sigh or tell Shell she's a dope. She looks at the bill and takes out her wallet. "Can I pay by credit card?"

"No, ma'am. You've got to go there in person." He goes to some exposed pipes at the side of the building, turns a lever. Then he sticks the tool into something and twists. He slides the lock through the metal.

We're all quiet. I feel ashamed, like I did something wrong on purpose and got called out. I look at my aunt. Her cheeks are deep magenta, and she stares unblinkingly at the ground. Suzanne stands next to her, stiff, her arms crossed, glaring at the man.

The customers peek through the windows, whispering. Are they going to visit the Candy Mine next and say, "Shell's Pie is going under"?

I wonder what Mary Berry would do under these conditions. Would she yell at the man or somehow try to make things a tiny bit better?

I blurt out, "Would you like a slice of pie?"

Jay gives me a sideways glance. "Are you crazy?"

The man's face stretches in surprise. Shell practically snarls at me. This guy's turning off our water and we're going to have to close and now I'm giving away our profits. But I can't back out. "We have apple, apple cherry, strawberry basil, or apple fennel raisin," I rattle off.

Jay coughs pointedly. I ignore him.

"Strawberry basil sounds okay." The water man turns

his cap awkwardly in his hands. Shell glares at him. She's thinking, *Say please.* I race inside and get him a piece. Pile it high with whipped cream. Add a scoop of vanilla and grab a napkin and plastic fork.

I hand it to him. "Here you are, my good man." I present it to him with a little bow.

He bows back awkwardly. "Thank you." He tucks into the pie. "I've been meaning to come here."

Shell's lips thin into a straight line.

Señora Vasquez thumps her cane. "If you had been coming here to *buy* pie, we might not have this problem."

His face has an expression like Jay's grandmother is a rattler he almost stepped on. I don't blame him. If he knows what's good for him, he'll stay out of reach of her cane. He eats some more, fast. "It's delicious." He scrapes up every last bit of crumb. "I never would have thought to put these flavors together."

I shrug modestly. "I'm not the first one to come up with it." I think every possible pie flavor is on the internet already. It's just my own spin.

"It's Cady's recipe. She's going to be a famous baker one day," Señora Vasquez chimes in. "You wait and see."

I look at her in surprise. She nods at me and my cheeks flush. Yes. Wait and see.

I'm a long way from the first pie I made and threw into the garbage. Now people are saying I'm going to be famous. I grin.

"This little girl?" He puts his cap back on his head

and takes a knee. He holds out his hand. "Thank you, young lady. That was the best pie I've ever had."

I stick out my Bennett chin as I pump his hand up and down. "That's because we use butter and all-natural ingredients."

"Yup. Everything's better with butter." The man glances at the lock, then at Shell. I expect him to say, *Thanks for the pie! I'll give you more time.* But he only hands the empty plate to Jay. "I'm sorry you're going through this."

Now Shell swipes her hand across her face. "It's not your fault."

"Still."

Shell turns away. Suzanne puts her arm around my aunt. "We know you're just doing your job."

The man tips his hat to us, then gets in his truck and drives off, the wheels spinning granite dust into our eyes.

"Can't we clear out these last pies?" Suzanne asks inside the store. All the customers have left during this, as if they sensed everything happening. "We could mark them down."

"Jay and I could tell people on Main Street about it." I count the pies in the case. More than a dozen. My heart sinks.

"It wouldn't make a difference to our bottom line,"

Shell says. "If I don't have *all* the money, I might as well have none of it. We'll take the pies to the shelter."

Suzanne has nothing to say to this. Suzanne being speechless—that's a bad sign. She goes in the back.

Shell turns over the sign in the door. CLOSED.

CHAPTER 35

Suzanne knocks on my door to wake me. Tom howls angrily at her. "I know, Tom. It's too early." Suzanne comes in and sits on my bed. "Hey, Cady."

"What's wrong?" I can tell by her face something's up. It's been four days since we closed the pie shop.

She massages her temples. Her eyes are so swollen she can barely see. She's been crying. "Um. Shell and I are driving to the bank in the city. See if they can delay a little."

I sit up. That sounds hopeful.

"Otherwise, we've got to be out of here in thirty days," Suzanne continues.

Every function in my body stops. I hold my breath. "What about Jay?"

"They're going to stay with Mr. Miniver for a little bit, until María finds a new job." Suzanne fidgets with the hem of her shirt. "My parents in Washington are going to let us stay with them. I can work for my dad's auto shop. In the office, not as a mechanic." She sort of pats my leg. "But we have to go to court and get approval to take you out of state."

I'm still holding my breath. I don't want to leave California. I don't want to leave Shell's house or Julian.

And Dad. I'm still mad at him, but the thought of moving out of state makes my heart panic. How will he get better if he knows I won't be here when he gets out? "What if the judge says no?"

"They won't." Shell stands in my doorway. "As long as your dad doesn't object."

My throat squeezes. "Do you think he will?"

Shell doesn't say anything.

"What if my dad says no?" I ask.

"He won't." Shell shifts. "We'll go visit him. Make him see how important it is."

My dad's definitely going to say no. I'm his only kid, his only relative. He won't want me to move away. And maybe I'll be more upset if he says yes, because that will mean he's given up.

This is so unfair. Why did they have to bring me to Julian and make me love it? For the first time ever I have a lot of friends. Now they're taking it all away. I stand up. "This is your fault," I say to Shell. "You should have never gotten me."

Shell blinks at me hollowly. I know it's a mean thing for me to say, but it's also true.

Jay and his family. Mr. Miniver. Each of the locals

I've met, the ones who say hello and ask me how my aunts are. The chickens.

It'll be like I'd never met any of them at all. I wish she'd left me at the children's center, where I could be miserable by myself. Knowing them all and then losing them—this hurts so much worse.

Suzanne folds in half on my bed, covering her face. I've hurt Shell. I hate myself. I hate everything.

I get up and walk out of my bedroom. Down the stairs and through the living room.

I don't really have a plan, except I need to get out of here, fast. My mind's all muddy. I put on my shoes and leave the dogs whining by the gate and take off down the road.

It's only seven, so it's not hot yet. But the clouds are burning off fast and I'm already sweating under my pajamas. A car honks. I probably look kind of silly. I don't care.

My stomach growls. I skipped breakfast. I decide I don't care about that either.

To my right is the Culvers' farm. Their horses wander near the fence, sucking grass into their mouths. The white one, Miss Daisy, nickers at me. I stick my hand over and pet her. It's hard to stay mad when you're petting a horse, but I try. "Bye," I say to her. "Good luck."

I keep walking. Another car beeps at me as I trudge along the road. I ignore it.

"Hey, you!" The car pulls up beside me. A Jeep. It's Mr. Miniver.

I stop and shake my head. "I'm fine."

"You're telling me that you're out here in your pajamas and you're perfectly fine?" He beckons to me. "Get in."

"I don't want to go home." My heart twists at the word. Home.

"I won't take you home," Mr. Miniver promises. "Come on, now."

Mr. Miniver takes me to his house, a one-story ranch accented with stone walls, on three flat acres on top of a hill. Or mini-mountain. I've never been here before.

Our steps echo as we walk across the honey-colored wooden floors. Almost all the furniture is wood or has wooden elements; even I can tell it's the kind that you need to use coasters with. It's a big house, at least twice the size of Shell's. "Don't you even have a pet or anything? Like a goldfish?" I'd be lonely here. It's kind of lonely with just two of us.

Mr. Miniver shrugs. "Eh. We used to have animals. I've done my share of cleaning up the poop of other creatures."

I snort.

"Have a seat." He indicates a stool at his kitchen counter. His kitchen is kind of small for such a big house, with oak cabinets and older white tiles lined with brown grout on the counters. "Want a bagel and cream cheese?"

Do I? My stomach momentarily drowns out the sound of his ice maker. We both laugh. He hands me the bagel package and the cream cheese, and I get to work.

He takes out a saucepan and sets it on his stove. "I'm going to make you my famous hot chocolate, invented by my great-great-grandmother. Known to heal all ills. You're lucky. I happen to have all the ingredients."

I sigh. "Chocolate can't fix everything, Mr. Miniver."

"You're right. But it can help ease the problems. Like shocks on a car." Mr. Miniver gets a chocolate bar out from his cupboard. "High-quality chocolate. That's the key."

I lean my head on my hand, watching him melt the chocolate in a saucepan over another pan of boiling water. Watching him cook and smelling the bittersweet candy is settling me down.

At last he pours the chocolate concoction into two cups, then squirts some canned whipped cream on top. "If I were serious I'd make this from scratch, but this isn't so bad." He clinks my cup. "Cheers."

I tell him what Shell and Suzanne told me. When I'm done, he doesn't say anything. The sun's climbing into the sky and shines hot into the kitchen, his hanging potted plant with its tendrils making a squid shadow on the wall.

Finally he speaks. “Cady, let me tell you the one thing I’ve learned from life.”

Uh-oh. I brace myself. So many adults want to tell you about the things they’ve learned. They never seem to know how I feel, though.

“The only constant in life is change,” Mr. Miniver says.

“Yeah. I know,” I grunt. I’m already turning back into old Cady. I decide I don’t want to be like that—old Cady wasn’t that happy—so I’m going to stay quiet. For now.

“But people are naturally afraid of change,” Mr. Miniver continues. “And true, not all change is good.” He takes a sip of hot chocolate. “When my wife died, I thought my life was over. I wanted to curl up and die. But if I became a hermit, if I just gave up on life, why, it would have been like spitting on Ginny’s memory.” He indicates my mouth and hands me a napkin. I wipe. “She’d want me to live with hope.” He points to some framed photos on the wall.

Ginny has a big smile and a fluffy sweater, exactly like what you think a grandma would look like. Like a woman who hugged you a lot and gave you candies and five-dollar bills. “So you volunteering and all that, is that how you keep her alive? Her spirit, anyway?”

His eyes get as bright as headlights. “Yes. Yes, I’d say that’s right.”

We sip our hot chocolate for a while. It’s creamy and

rich and not too sweet like the packages of hot chocolate are. I want it to last forever. Then Mr. Miniver speaks again. "Life has highs and lows and it never stops throwing things at you." He smiles. "What I've learned is to enjoy the good times while they're here. And the bad times never last, either."

I swallow. "I think I've had bad times for at least the past seven years."

"What about the good parts?" he says.

I close my eyes. Jenna. The pie shop. Jay. Mr. Miniver. My tears return. "I would have rather never had those."

"You're wrong." Mr. Miniver taps my empty cup with his spoon. "What about this?"

"It was delicious."

"But it's gone forever." Mr. Miniver widens his eyes. "Do you wish you'd never had it?"

I shake my head. "Of course not."

"Of course not," he echoes. "So you don't really wish you'd never met Shell or Jay or your father, do you?"

My eyes sting. I shake my head no.

"You're going to be okay." Mr. Miniver picks up my mug. "Better than okay. Excellently okay."

I nod. I want to believe him.

"And it's not done yet, is it?" Mr. Miniver winks. His phone buzzes and he picks it up and reads the text. "Shell's on her way over."

"You told her where I was?"

"Of course. I didn't want her to worry."

I stare at Mrs. Miniver's smiling face and realize two important things.

One. I don't want Shell to worry, either.

Two. Being bitter and ignoring my dad won't solve anything. It's not helping me at all. I can be happy here and still want him to be better at the same time.

I want to see him.

CHAPTER 36

The arched metal detector buzzes, and the man in the guard uniform tells me to hold my arms straight out from my sides. I do, and his wand beeps. "Do you have something in your pocket?"

I dig into my jeans. Some coins tumble out. "Oops." I throw them into the plastic bin he holds.

Shell told me to empty them, but apparently I didn't do a good job. She's already ahead of me and waiting, and I expect her to scold me for not listening. My face gets hot. "Sorry, Shell."

"No worries." Shell stands there patiently as the guard finishes and I pass through.

She holds out her hand. I hesitate for a second—I'm twelve, do I need to hold anyone's hand?—but then the fluorescent-lit hallway opens up in front of us, the guard's work boots clumping on the linoleum, and I wish I were a little kid who could be carried.

I grip her hand tightly.

"You okay?" Shell asks.

"Yeah."

She raises an eyebrow.

"No. I don't know." I pull up the collar of my T-shirt and chew on it. "What if—what if he's different?" Or worse, the same?

Shell stops walking and faces me. "Tell you what. Let's have a code word. Say it and I make up an excuse for leaving."

I cast my eyes over the hallway, looking for something to inspire me. Just a bunch of locked doors.

The guard taps his boot. "You guys coming or what?"

"Boot," I say. "That's the code."

"You got this." Shell winks. We follow the guard all the way to the end.

My dad has to stay here for one year. Then he'll have eighteen months to prove he can be an upright citizen or whatever. Shell explained it all to me. He'll have to take parenting classes, get a job, prove himself. If you add the year in jail to the eighteen months, I'll be halfway done with eighth grade by the time he's ready to take me back. Almost in high school.

I hadn't known what to say, exactly, when Shell told me that. We'll be in another state. I'll be used to my life there. She looked at my face and knew the question even if I didn't say it out loud. "We'll make it work.

Don't worry. I will always take care of you." Shell's jaw clenched, so I knew she was serious. Well, I mean, she's pretty much always serious, but this way I knew she was extra-super-duper serious.

I believe her.

This room has a bunch of tables and chairs in it, sort of like a classroom. The light's the same greenish hue as it was in the hallway. Shell sits next to me. Her breathing's raspy and—wait for it—there's the jaw twitch again. She might be even more nervous than I am. I grab her hand and squeeze it.

Shell squeezes back. "This is going to be fine, Cady." She's talking to herself as much as to me.

Dad shuffles in. No handcuffs, thank goodness. But an orange shirt and pants. His hair looks neater than it has in a long time, combed straight back, and his eyes are clearer. "Cady!"

I don't have any words. I stand up and he grabs me in a hug, patting my back awkwardly. He feels different, a little heavier. And he seems shorter. Or maybe I'm taller.

Dad kisses the top of my head and I sit down next to Shell again.

"Hello." Shell lifts a hand, the corners of her mouth turning down, until she forces them back up.

"Michelle." Dad nods at her. He doesn't even try to smile.

"Shell. Dad." I look at both of them. Make up. Do something.

Shell puts a heavy hand on my shoulder. "I'll let you have some time with your dad." Shell gets up and retreats to an empty table in the corner of the room. I'm glad she's still here.

Dad sits there looking at me, and I have a hard time looking back. I stare at the tabletop instead. "I've missed you, Buttercup. I mean, Cady. Sorry."

I nod. *I missed you too,* is what I should say. I should tell him about Shell and Suzanne welcoming me into their house, about Jay, about pie, about the shop closing, about Washington. All the things a parent might want to know about. I can't. Acid churns into my throat. *Why weren't you different?* I want to scream at him. *Why couldn't you get better, for me?*

Suddenly I remember Señora Vasquez's story about her husband crashing their car. *I was so angry at him. . . . But blame and anger don't get you very far.*

And what Mr. Miniver said. If I could build a time machine, would I travel back and set everything different? Make it so I never met Aunt Shell and Suzanne and Jay at all?

I raise my head and look straight into my father's eyes. No. I would not. I don't want to wish away this summer, or these people. Ever. Even with all the bad stuff. I'll take it.

My throat clears. I reach across the cold metal table to take my father's hand. "I'm glad you're better. I've missed you too." I squeeze his hand. "You can call me Buttercup. It's okay."

At this, my dad's eyes well up, and then mine do too. This time, I let them. Before long, I'm for-real-no-*joke* crying, snot coming out of my nose. Dad gets up and comes around the table and Shell arrives at the same time.

They pause for a second, then both of them, on either side of me, put their heads on my shoulders and hug me.

The guard puts a box of Kleenex on the table.

"Thanks." I blow my nose so loud other people look over at us. It sounds like a car horn.

Dad straightens. "Shell."

"Jim." Shell stands up.

"You've taken good care of my girl. I owe you a lot." Dad's voice is low, rumbly.

Shell puts her hands on my shoulders. "You don't owe me a single thing. I love Cady."

At this, I get a warm bubbly feeling, like pie when it's ready to come out of the oven. This is the first time Shell's said this. Love. She loves me. It makes me brave enough to ask the questions I need to ask. "Dad, why did you lie about Oregon?"

Dad purses his lips. "You know about that, then?" He sits down at his side of the table. "I don't suppose I got a real good reason for that. Except I wanted Shell to leave us alone." He shrugs. "But I knew, deep down, if we ever needed help, she'd be there. Waiting."

"So that's why you put her on the form?" I ask.

He nods, then puts his elbows on the table, resting his head in his hands. "I'm sorry, Buttercup. About everything."

I almost ask him about Mom next. Why'd he pretend she was perfect? I already know the answer. He's Dad, and he's not perfect. Far from it. He needed something to hold on to.

I think about what it'd be like to not forgive him. About how bad I've felt.

But I don't want to. I'm tired of holding on to this. I lean against Aunt Shell, and she's there for me, an anchor to keep me from getting swept away. I have to keep moving forward. Isn't that what Dad always told me to do anyway? "It's okay, Dad."

And it really, really is.

"Good news," Shell says as we walk to the car. She holds up her phone. "María got hired at another restaurant. Still working on a place to stay, though."

"That's a relief." My feet feel like they're floating as I bounce along the asphalt.

"Yup." Shell unlocks the car. "That's what I love about living in Julian. Everyone helps each other." She gets in.

"Love*d,* I guess." I can barely hear these last words.

I freeze, my hand on the door. Everyone helps each other. Everyone loves Shell.

I hop in. "Can you take me to see Mr. Miniver?"

CHAPTER 37

Jay and I meet three times over the next week at Mr. Miniver's house. Once, when Shell dropped me off, so I could tell him about my idea. Again, with a few community leaders who know Shell. And the last time, to write emails and call people.

I was kind of hoping that Mr. Miniver and the other adults would take over and do everything. But I also have to admit that I should've known better. Of *course* Mr. Miniver made me and Jay do most of the work.

Deep down, if I think about it, I would've been disappointed if Jay and I could only watch. I didn't know how much I like helping, until now.

During our final meeting, Jay and I sit in Mr. Miniver's kitchen writing emails to everyone in Mr. Miniver's address book. Which is basically the entire town. "What should it say?" Jay asks. He's typing, I'm dictating.

"'Your presence is requested at a very important meeting. . . .'" That sounds nice and formal and sort of British.

"Nah." Jay purses his lips. "It needs to sound more exciting. Like they can't miss it because it's the most important thing that has ever happened."

"We're not writing the Declaration of Independence. It's just an invitation." But he's probably right, I have to admit. I don't want people to skip reading it.

We sip the hot chocolate Mr. Miniver made us. He's sitting in his living room, reading the paper. "Mr. Miniver," I holler. "What do you think?"

"It's your show, Cady. I'm just the adult who's providing you legitimacy." He turns the page.

I sigh. He's sure had an opinion about everything else in the history of time. I close my eyes, trying to make my brain work.

"How about a rhyme?" Jay gestures in the air like he's putting a sign up. "'We need a fleet of people to meet.'"

I can't help but giggle.

Jay blushes and laughs. "Hey, I'm going to be a video game designer, not a writer."

I snort, but his bad idea gave me a new one. I gesture at him. "Move over." He gets up and I sit at the keyboard, my fingers flying faster than they ever have for any school assignment.

Jay reads it over my shoulder. "Yup," he says.

I lift my right palm up and he slaps it in a silent high five.

*

On Saturday afternoon, the church bells chime twelve times. I'm making my aunts go to the town hall. Mr. Miniver told them there was a special vote about another big franchise trying to come into town, and that got Shell pretty amped up.

I don't have butterflies in my stomach—I've got a swarm of june bugs. This was all my idea, and if it doesn't work . . . well, I don't know what will happen.

"Don't worry," Jay whispers as we go up the steps. I nod, but he might as well be telling the sun not to rise.

"I wonder which franchise it is now," Shell says. "Mr. Miniver didn't say."

"It's a big one," Jay pipes up. "Like one of the major ones." Shell glances at him curiously and Jay nods as if he really knows something, stroking his imaginary beard. Shell chuckles.

I take Shell's hand and she automatically squeezes it. That's something I never would have done a couple months ago, but now it feels as natural as breathing. Her touch makes me feel brave. If the Julian pioneers could survive slavery and come out here, then I can darn well talk at a meeting.

I stop at the placard outside and point at it. "Surprise!" FUND-RAISER FOR SHELL'S PIE.

"What in the world?" Shell puts her hands on her hips. "Cady, what have you done?"

I gulp. "Nothing, yet." With shaking hands, I push open the door.

We enter the auditorium. There are maybe two dozen people sitting on folding chairs, with tables full of doughnuts along the sides of the room. Mr. Miniver knows how to make people happy.

I scan the room. Jay's family sits in the front row, and Jay goes to join them. Gable's there with his parents. I see every person Mr. Miniver's introduced me to. The shop owners from the general store. Adam, the candy store clerk who gives us free taffy. Mrs. Showalter from the museum. The lady who sells pie right up the street. The man who plays the guitar. The Culvers, whose horses I petted when I was feeling sad. Mrs. Moretti from Grandma's Pies. Miss Mia, the youth group leader. The parents who chaperoned the trip. The man who turned off our water. All of them are here.

Shell walks shakily up to the podium. "Folks. Thank you so much for coming today." Her eyes fill with tears, and she grips the front of her shirt. "It means a lot to me. It really does. But this is all my fault. One hundred percent. And I'm not going to take your money to fix my mistakes."

The crowd murmurs. Mr. Miniver takes the mic back. "Come on, Shell. We're here for you."

Shell shakes her head, retreating off to the side and sinking into a chair. Suzanne pats her back.

A bonfire erupts inside me. Shell sounds like my father. My father, who always turned down help, even when we badly needed it. I think about how close Shell is to losing everything. For different reasons, but with a similar ending.

Not again.

I go up to the front. I wait for my legs to quake, but they don't. "I've got something to say," I tell Mr. Miniver.

Some of the people in the audience nod at me. For some reason I'm not afraid. I guess I know they all want to help me. Everyone here wants me to succeed. And that makes a big difference.

"I'm Cady Bennett." My voice is too quiet.

"Speak up!" an old man in the back yells.

I try again, loud, pulling the mic down toward me. "My name is Cady Bennett. And I want to tell you about my aunt Shell." I grip the sides of the podium. "Aunt Shell is the hardest worker I know. And the kindest. If it weren't for Shell, I'd be in some stranger's home. Shell took me in when my dad . . ." Now my voice quivers. "When my dad went to jail."

I hear gasps and murmurs. But it doesn't matter how they react. This is my story. I can tell it. "My dad's had problems for as long as I can remember." I'm aware of folks looking at me with sympathy, or maybe pity, but still I don't care. "He pushed Shell away. He pushed everyone away. Bad thing after bad thing kept happening, until nobody could fix it.

"But I keep thinking. What if my dad had let someone help him? What if people had given him a hand up, out of the hole we were in?"

Jay gives me a thumbs-up to continue. I look across the room at Shell. She's holding Suzanne's hand tightly. Suzanne's crying. Does she want me to say this?

She gives me a tiny nod.

This helps me say the next bit. I look right at my aunt. "What if today—just today—you take the help?"

Shell doesn't blink, but her eyes look bright.

She shakes her head no, as stubborn as ever.

There's a pause and a murmuring. Then the water man stands up. "Anyone who's ever had your pie won't want that shop closed down." He gives me a warm smile, and I return it.

"Your family has been here for years," Mrs. Moretti says. "We can't handle all the pie business alone."

"Your mother was my best friend," Mrs. Showalter adds.

"Your father gave my father a job when he got laid off," a man says.

"A few years ago, when Gable was headed down a bad path, you were the only one who could get through to him," Gable's father says. Gable gives a quick nod.

"You helped me get the job at the youth group," Miss Mia says.

"Mrs. Vasquez watched my children after school when I couldn't afford child care," a woman adds.

"Jay takes care of our horses when we go out of town," says Mr. Culver.

"Suzanne cooked for our football fund-raiser for free," a burly man adds. "Not to mention all the pies that Shell donates."

"When my wife died and I was too depressed to leave the house, Shell brought me a pie and ate it with me every week," Mr. Miniver says. He takes a breath and smiles at me. "They're not strangers, folks. They're part of us."

The crowd goes quiet again. I hear air moving back and forth through my nose, into my lungs, out.

Then somebody starts applauding, and finally the room erupts into raucous noise. My face goes warm again, but it's a good warmth. I stand with my head bowed over the wooden platform.

And then Shell has her arms around me, and the top of my head is getting wet from her tears. This time, the hug feels like it'll keep me from breaking. Not like it will break me.

CHAPTER 38

At home, Shell, Suzanne, and I enter silently. The dogs bark and Tom howls. Shell turns on the lights.

The fund-raiser earned enough to pay two months' worth of mortgage, plus the water bill. Mr. Miniver is taking care of the rest. We're caught up. Barely.

I feel like I just ran a marathon. Or maybe two marathons. I don't know what that's like, exactly, but probably a lot like this. It's like every drop of energy has been drained out of me.

"I could use a snack." Suzanne puts away her purse. "Cady?"

"Yes." When can't I?

But Shell doesn't say anything. She goes into the kitchen and turns on all the lights. Then she goes into the master bedroom and turns on those lights. Then the bathrooms.

Suzanne and I follow her wordlessly.

Shell goes upstairs. To my bedroom. To the other bedroom and bathroom. The hallway.

I remember when I first came to this house. I can admit to myself now that I was plain scared of everything in it—Shell and Suzanne and how being here meant I might not be with my dad for a long time.

Now it's easy to call it my home, too.

Finally all the lights are on.

We stop as she stops at the end of the hall, looking out the small window where there's a view of the apple orchard. "I almost lost all this," Shell says in a low voice. Her shoulders sag. "I should have let the business fail instead of risking everything."

"It won't fail again." Suzanne's face is set in determination.

"You can't promise that." Shell sounds like me.

Suzanne and I go on either side of her, putting our arms around her.

"No. But you'll always have us." I squeeze Shell extra tight, and she kisses the top of my head. We look out the window at the land. The apples will be ripe in two months, and each tree's branches are heavy with them. Beyond, through the leaves, the lights from Jay's house twinkle like stars.

Dear Jenna,

I hope you're ready to eat pie. Because we're going to make a lot of it for you.

Love,

Cady

SEPTEMBER

1,000 Pies Down

0 to Go

CHAPTER 39

"Who can tell me another method of getting this answer?" Mr. Simon, our math teacher, taps his marker on the board.

Two hands shoot up. Mine and Jay's.

Mr. Simon closes an eye and points to me. "I saw Cady first."

I walk up to the front and take the marker and turn to the whiteboard. A year ago, I would have hated coming up and trying to solve math problems. In this class, it's no big deal. I start writing.

I know everyone in this room is hoping I'll get the right answer. And if I don't, someone will help me.

The bell rings and Mr. Simon shouts out the homework pages. Jay and I walk out together. I pat my backpack. "I have something for Claudia before she leaves."

Jay nods. "What's the math teacher's favorite dessert? Pi!" he says, and chortles at himself.

"What do you get when you take the sun and divide its circumference by its diameter?" I counter.

Jay shrugs.

"Pie in the sky!" a girl shouts from behind us.

I hold out my hand and she high-fives it.

Everyone says middle school's the worst, but for me it's the best. This school is small, maybe a hundred kids at most. And because of Jay, I met pretty much everyone in school before the end of summer.

I have a new backpack printed with silly pictures of sloths riding unicorns over rainbows. Shell let me text a picture of it to Jenna's mom. Jenna texted a picture of the same backpack. *Twinsies!* I sling it over my shoulder, heavy with textbooks. "What's 1.57?"

Finally nobody answers. I've stumped them. Then a grown-up voice chimes in, "Half a pie!" It's Mr. Simon, passing us on his long legs. "You guys are even cheesier than I am. Have a good weekend!"

Jay and I bike to the pie shop. Because I am now the proud owner of a purple mountain bike with a shelf on the back for my stuff. Shell spent two days teaching me how to ride, letting me coast along the grass until I got it. The bike lets me go wherever I want, whenever I want. I've never been able to do that before.

Mr. Miniver paid for all the equipment for the gluten-free addition. It didn't take long to install the new ovens and counters next door, connected by a door. Suzanne calls Mr. Miniver our "angel investor," which is a perfect term for him.

Jay and I park our bikes outside the shop and go in. It's full of customers, ordering the specials. Shell added two savory pies, chicken pot pie and a beef stew thing, plus a couple salads, so people eat lunch here as well. "Diversify to survive," Mr. Miniver said.

My stomach growls as soon as I open the door. I thought I might be sick of pie by now, but it turns out it's a hard thing to get tired of. Especially when you can change the filling.

To advertise, we've been handing out flyers like mad. GRAND REOPENING. Plus, almost every restaurant in town has ordered gluten-free pie for the menus. And we got thirty stores in San Diego to stock us, too.

Suzanne looks up from the counter as we enter. "Hey. How was it?"

"Okay," I say.

"Just okay?" Suzanne arches an eyebrow. "You're turning into a teenager, Cady Bennett." Suzanne took a leave of absence from her job to help, since Claudia's going away to college and I'm back in school. It's been different having her around every day. Different in a good way. She balances out Shell.

I get two plates of pie, and Jay and I sit down to eat. "I bet I can do my math faster than you," he says.

"So what?" I say. "Better to get them right."

"And I'll do them right."

"Fine."

We race through the problems. Sure enough, Jay wins, but I don't care that much. I look at the clock. "Isn't Claudia leaving soon? I want to say goodbye."

"She's moving to downtown San Diego, not to another planet," Jay says.

Shell comes out of the back, balancing five bakery boxes on top of each other. "Beep, beep! Hey, kids. How was school?"

"Okay," Jay and I chorus in low tones. Everyone asks the same thing.

"That's very descriptive." Shell laughs. She looks lighter. She stands up straighter and her forehead isn't wrinkled in worry all the time. Best of all, she's more relaxed. She's kind of a different Shell. The old Shell, Suzanne says. Though to me, she's the new Shell.

All of us are walking taller these days. When so many people believe in you, it really does seem like you've got a superpower. It makes me feel like I can accomplish anything now.

And I am accomplishing something important today. I put on my apron and hairnet and wash up. Jay does the same.

He holds up his dripping hands like a surgeon. "Ready?"

I nod.

Ceremoniously we get out the flour. Today I make the crust by hand. It's too important not to. Carefully I cut in the butter and water and put it into the refrigerator.

Then I peel Granny Smiths and Galas by hand. I cut them up and add the spices. Jay watches with a serious expression. María comes over, too, and puts her arm around her son.

I take the dough out of the fridge and dust the counter with flour. Shell and Suzanne come in now.

I roll it out in the clock pattern. The butter stays perfectly chilled. I drape it over the pie tin and cut away the extra. I put in the apples and add the top crust, then make slits in the center like spokes on a wheel. They all watch me like I'm about to win a big chess tournament or something quiet like that.

This will be the thousandth.

I put the pie in the oven.

Nobody moves from the perimeter of the table. "Do you remember when Cady first came here and she ate like two pounds of pasta?" Suzanne says.

"And when she burned the cake?" Shell ruffles my hair.

"And when she, like, saved the shop?" Jay says.

My neck and face warm up, but not from embarrassment, because my stomach doesn't hurt with butterflies. Instead, it feels like butterflies are on my skin, beautiful ones dancing around.

This is the first time people have told stories about me. I'm practically like Paul Bunyan. And this is only the beginning. I lift my head and smile at them.

"I heard there was an important thing going on." Claudia comes in, followed by Mr. Miniver and Esmeralda and Señora Vasquez.

"Make the mark." Jay points at the paper.

"Not until the pie comes out," I say.

The bell in front tinkles.

"Hello?" Gable calls. "Anybody here?"

"In the back!" Claudia yells.

Gable comes in, followed by his dad. "What's going on? We need to buy a pie and you've got customers!"

"I'll help you." Claudia starts for the front.

"What are we waiting for?" Grant asks.

"Cady's thousandth pie," Claudia says. "Remember, I told you about it."

More people talking about me. Somehow I don't mind a bit.

"Oh!" Grant nods. "That's important. Tell you what. I'll man the counter for a bit until you come back."

"You sure?" Shell squints at him.

"Of course." Grant goes out front.

I swallow, watching the timer count down like I'm waiting for a rocket ship to take off. Finally the buzzer pings. I put on the mitts and use the paddle to take out the pie.

It looks sheer perfection.

Now I walk over to the sheet and make the final mark.

A thousand pies.

Everyone yells, "Woo-hoo!" and claps.

"Leveled up!" Jay shouts. "Go, Cady!"

I turn and wipe at my eyes with my sleeve.

Shell lifts me up and I laugh wildly as she spins me around. We take up the whole space together. "You did good, kiddo."

Shell takes us home after that. Mr. Miniver comes to Jay's house with his Jeep. Claudia's going to the community college downtown.

Mr. Miniver's securing boxes. Esmeralda is sitting on the porch, crying as she watches her big sister load her stuff. "I'll see you all the time, I promise," Claudia's telling her, pushing strands of sweaty hair off her little forehead.

"I have something for you." I take a small bag out of my backpack. It's a pretty notebook, covered in hummingbirds and flowers.

Esmeralda holds out her hands. "Ooh. I want it."

"Thank you, Cady." Claudia beams at me. "Hey, Ezzie, let's draw together. Okay?" She whips out a pen and draws a sun. Esmeralda takes it and draws a face on the sun, then holds the notebook out for Jay.

Jay draws sawtooth blades of grass. I draw a person with a giant, goofy happy face.

I want this moment to last longer.

"I'm going to college for you guys, you know," Claudia says in a low voice. "I want to change the law for you before you turn eighteen." She frowns at the page, then lifts her head. "I'm not going to be quiet anymore."

"I know," Jay says softly. He draws a flying cat.

Mr. Miniver comes over, his eyes fiercely lit. "That's right. You protest. I'm going to write so many letters to Congress their eyes will bleed from reading them. It's time for them to fix the mess they made."

Esmeralda hands him the drawing and the pen. Mr. Miniver sketches something for longer than any of us; we're all fidgeting worse than Esmeralda.

He flips the book to show us. A house. A house with a wide-open front door. "If any of you kids ever need a place to stay . . ." Mr. Miniver taps the door on the picture. "You know where I am."

Claudia's face crumples. She stands up and hugs him. "Thank you, Mr. Miniver."

Señora Vasquez limps out of the house. "Are we ready, Claudia?" She takes a look at the packed Jeep and her lip starts trembling.

Jay pipes up. "Don't worry, me and Cady and Esmeralda are still here."

She ruffles his hair, then makes a face. "Ay, Jay, you smell like a locker room filled with cattle! Go take a shower."

I burst into laughter.

CHAPTER 40

When I step through the gate, Jacques and Julia go crazy, barking and jumping around as if I've been gone for a hundred years instead of half a day. I have to pet them for five minutes before they calm down. Inside, Tom howls at me and I pick him up and stroke his fur.

The house is quiet, but not too quiet like Mr. Miniver's. It's more of a waiting kind of quiet, because soon Shell and Suzanne will be home. Anyway, I'm not scared to be by myself now. Not with so many people in town that I know will come help me in a second.

I get a granola bar out of the kitchen and tear into it, Jacques and Julia vacuuming up the crumbs. I break a piece in half and give it to them. This reminds me.

I run up to my room and get the laundry basket of food and bring it downstairs. Then I put everything away. Except for another granola bar—that I'll keep, in case of a snack emergency.

"There." I stand back and look at the pantry, waiting

for my old familiar panic to come back. But there's nothing. I feel the same as I did a minute ago.

Smiling to myself, I pick up a Red Delicious apple and crunch into it. Then I go into the living room, plop down on the couch, and turn on *The Bake Off*. I'm still not done with all the episodes. Luckily, there are more on Netflix.

One of the contestants, a girl Claudia's age named Ruby, puts her pile of buns down in front of the judges. She looks upset. "I'm sorry," she says. She lists all the problems she thinks they have.

They tell her not to apologize, because they haven't tasted them yet. It makes them not want to eat any. But she's so sure she's messed them all up she doesn't care.

A pile of mail sits on the coffee table with a letter waiting for me. Dad. I pause the show.

I hope you're well, Buttercup. I'm doing much better these days. They say people usually lose weight in here. I'm gaining.

I know Aunt Shell and Suzanne are taking good care of you. I don't want you to worry about me. You did too much of that before. It's time for you to worry about yourself. Got that?

Talk to you real soon.

Love,

Dad

I put it down, waiting for a big wave of sadness to knock me over, the way it always does when I hear from Dad. To my surprise, it doesn't.

I feel . . . settled. As if things will work out. I don't know if my dad will do enough to get me back. Maybe I'll live with him again, maybe I won't. Nobody can tell the future. Claudia doesn't know if she can ever get a green card, but she hopes for the best. So do I. All we can do is keep working. Like I did with the pies.

I hit play.

Mary and Paul eat the buns the girl thought she'd ruined. "It's scrummy!" Mary Berry tells her. They tell her not to come in apologizing when they haven't even tasted anything yet.

The girl smiles. The judges were right. You shouldn't assume things are awful before they've had a chance to really finish.

Sometimes things are scrummy even if they look bad at first.

We stand in the parking lot under a shade cover. The pies sit in neat rows in white boxes with Mr. Miniver's cartoon face printed on them. Today we're at a store near Jenna's house, by my old school. They're having a gluten-free fair, with stores offering samples of all kinds of different foods under tents. This is the first store to agree to carry Shell's, and we're hoping it will take off from there.

I watch the crowds sampling the gluten-free and vegan goods, my stomach pinched with excitement. Lots of people take postcards from our table. *Aunt Shell's Gluten-Free Pies, now available at a store near you,* says the postcard, with Claudia's art on it. It's the same one I sent to Jenna.

> *Ask your mom if she'll take you. Shell says you get a free pie. An ENTIRE pie. But you have to get your own whipped cream.*

Jay and I wear plastic gloves and hairnets to look official and less like kids. I don't think anyone would trust a kid to wash her hands. Suzanne and Shell stand nearby, chatting with the store manager. Suzanne catches my eye and winks. I wink back. Which probably looks more like a twitch, because my wink's not very good. But whatever.

Across the parking lot, a black SUV pulls in and heads in our direction. I recognize the blond head of Jenna's mother.

I clutch Jay's arm.

"Is that her?" Jay says. "Ow, what's with the death grip?"

"Sorry. I'm excited." I watch as Jenna climbs out of the car and begins running in our direction.

"Wait!" her mother shouts.

"Yep." I wave at her, not caring if I look like a dork

in my net and rubber gloves. Jenna stops running and waits for her mother.

"I'll cut her a real slice of pie." Jay cuts her a strawberry piece. The recipe's the same, just the crust is different. He cuts her an enormous slice, way too big, almost a quarter of a pie, but it's fine because I'll eat what Jenna doesn't.

Shell comes and puts her arms on my shoulders. "You doing all right, kiddo?" she whispers. Her warmth is as comfortable now as a sweater I didn't know I needed until I put it on. We're long past the awkward silence phase.

"Better than okay," I whisper back.

"What's going on over here?" Suzanne steps next to us and puts her face right next to mine, lowering her voice. "What are we whispering about? Are you talking about me?"

"Yes," I whisper jokingly. "Gosh, Suzanne. What an ego!"

"We're saying that we hope you make your famous fish tacos tonight," Shell whispers too. "This store has a pretty good seafood department."

"Hint taken." Suzanne heads off toward the store with a wave. Suzanne's thinking about making her leave of absence from the boat a permanent thing. I hope she does.

But if she has to go back to work again, it'll be okay.

It'll be okay if this gluten-free pie thing doesn't work as well as we want.

Because I'm Cady Madeline Bennett, and I can pretty much get through everything.

"Cady!" Jenna shouts. Running again. "I'm here! I'm here!"

A grin about as big as the Grand Canyon comes over my face. "I want you to meet someone!" I grab Jay with my left arm, Jenna with my right. I pull them together in a huddle-hug. My new friend and my old friend.

And you know what? Hugs might have handshakes beat, sometimes.

CADY'S
RECIPE
BOOK

Note: This part involves very hot ovens and knives, so please, please, please do not try these recipes without an adult around.

RECIPES

9-Inch Double Pie Crust, with Notes from Cady

Ingredients

2½ cups unbleached all-purpose flour

1 teaspoon salt

1 cup (16 tablespoons) unsalted butter*

½ to ¾ cup ice water

*If you use salted butter, reduce the salt in the recipe to ½ teaspoon.

You can use a food processor, a pastry cutter, or just a plain old butter knife (no steak knives necessary!). If you're doing it by hand, you'll also want a fork or wire whisk. And you'll need a rolling pin to shape the dough.

Directions

1. In a food processor, pulse the flour and salt together. Or you can mix them together with a fork or wire whisk.
2. Cut the butter into 1" cubes. Pulse (food processor) or work it into the flour (with a pastry cutter or knife) until pieces of butter are scattered throughout. Be careful with the food processor—it works super-fast!
3. Now get the ice water. Pulsing or tossing with a fork or your fingers, drizzle in a little of the water, paying attention to the dough texture. How much water depends on a lot of things, such as the temperature of the room—so go by the dough, not the actual amount of water.
4. The dough will start sticking together, at which point *stop*. You still want to see pieces of butter—if you do this too long, the butter will melt instead. If the dough's still crumbly or there are dry spots, continue to add ice water and mix.
5. Form the dough into a big ball, then divide it in half. Shape each half into a disk. Cover w/ plastic wrap while in fridge.
6. Chill the dough for at least 30 minutes before rolling. You could roll it right away if needed, but you should really let it rest.
7. If your dough's too hard when it comes out of the refrigerator (because it's been in there for longer

than 30 minutes), let it sit out at room temperature for about 10 minutes. Then it will roll out easily. If it's too warm, the dough will be too sticky.

8. Next, roll your dough. Make sure the surface where you're rolling is nice and clean. Then sprinkle a little flour onto the surface. You could also roll your dough out on a pastry mat (a canvas mat sold in stores) or a piece of waxed or parchment paper. The papers are nice because they control the mess and the dough won't stick.

   How do you not overwork your crust? You try to roll it as little as you can.

9. Roll out the dough into a circle, trying to keep an even thickness. To do this, pretend that your pie crust is a clock. Roll the pin toward an imaginary number 12, then 6, then 3, then 9.

10. Roll in only *one direction at a time*—this will help you not overwork the crust. So, roll to your imaginary number, then pick up the pin and roll it again.

    The dough should be about ⅛ inch thick, and about a 12-inch circle, to fit into a 9-inch pie pan. Get down low and see if it seems to be the same thickness throughout—sometimes the edges get really thin.

    Do you still see pieces of butter throughout the dough? Yes? That's what you want.

11. Repeat with the other dough disk, for the top of your pie.

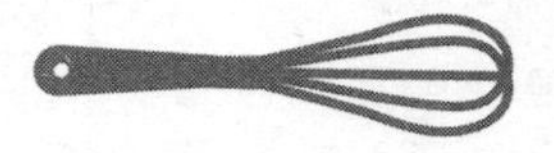

Apple Pie, with Notes from Cady

Ingredients

3 Gala and 3 Granny Smith apples, medium sized—peeled and cut to about the size of the apple slices you take for lunch. Make sure there's no core in the slices—it'll taste like tree bark!

½ cup white sugar

½ cup packed brown sugar

1 teaspoon ground cinnamon

½ teaspoon ground nutmeg

3 tablespoons cornstarch

Pastry from 9-Inch Double Pie Crust recipe on page 357 (make sure you have two crusts!)

1 tablespoon milk (any kind)

Other stuff

9-inch pie pan

Butter knife

Pastry brush (a barbecue brush could work as long as it's really clean; you don't want barbecue sauce taste on your pie)

Directions

1. Look inside your oven and make sure nobody's storing pans in there. Put the oven rack in the middle.
2. Preheat the oven to 425 degrees.
3. In a large bowl, mix the apple slices with the sugars and cinnamon and nutmeg. Sprinkle the cornstarch over everything and mix it in, too. The cornstarch will help absorb the moisture—no soggy bottoms!
4. Put one crust on the bottom of the pan. Pour in the apple mixture. Yes, the apples will look like a hill and be a little taller than your pan. That's okay—they'll cook down.
5. Put your other crust on top and crimp the edges together by pinching the crusts between your fingers. Try to make sure there are no spaces.
6. Take a butter knife (or any knife) and make two to three slits near the center of the pie. This lets the steam out. (The apples let off a lot of water when they cook. Again, no soggy bottoms!)
7. Now dip the pastry brush in the milk and paint the top of the pie with a light coat. This will help the top crust get a nice, even brown.
8. Bake 15 minutes in the preheated oven.
9. Reduce the temperature to 350 degrees. This will keep the crust edges from burning. The higher temperature helps brown it.
10. Let it bake for 35 to 45 more minutes. How long it

takes depends on your oven, your altitude, and the exact mix of dough you made. So turn on the oven light or open the door and peek in.

When the top of the pie looks an even, golden brown, it's ready.

This part is the hardest. You have to let it cool. Probably for an hour, or you'll burn your tongue.

Eat it with whipped cream, ice cream, or even cheddar cheese! (Apparently, there's an old law in Wisconsin saying restaurants must serve a slice of cheddar cheese with apple pie. That's usually not on the menu in California, though.) It's up to you.

Now that you know the basic recipe, you can adjust the spices. Want more cinnamon? Add it. Want a little bit of sharper spice? Try a dash of ground ginger. You can also use different kinds of apples or fruit. Invent your own pie!

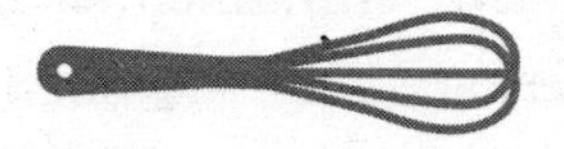

Cady's Fennel Apple Raisin Pie

(makes one 9-inch pie)

Ingredients

1 fennel bulb

3 Gala and 3 Granny Smith apples, medium sized, peeled and sliced

⅔ cup raisins

¼ teaspoon ground cardamom

1 teaspoon ground cinnamon

½ cup white sugar

¼ cup brown sugar

2 tablespoons all-purpose flour

Pastry from 9-Inch Double Pie Crust recipe on page 357 (make sure you have two crusts!)

1 egg, beaten, or 2 tablespoons of milk for wash (optional)

Directions

1. Preheat the oven to 425 degrees.
2. Cut the fennel bulb into slivers.
3. In a large bowl, stir together the fennel, apple slices,

raisins, cardamom, cinnamon, sugars, and flour.

4. Place one pie crust at the bottom of a 9-inch pie pan and pour in the apple mixture.
5. Top with another layer of crust. Crimp the edges together by pinching the crusts between your fingers. Use a fork to poke holes in the middle to allow steam to escape.
6. Use a pastry brush to apply egg wash or milk to the crust, if desired.
7. Bake for 20 minutes at 425 degrees.
8. Reduce the temperature to 375 degrees and bake for 30 to 45 more minutes, until the top is golden brown.

Note: Buy the fennel bulb at the grocery store.

Lady Baltimore Cake

Ingredients

3 cups flour, sifted

3 teaspoons baking powder

½ teaspoon salt

¾ cup ~~shortening~~ butter

2 cups sugar

½ cup milk

½ cup water

1 teaspoon vanilla extract

6 egg whites

Directions

1. Preheat the oven to 350 degrees.
2. Grease two round 9-inch cake pans.
3. Sift together the flour, baking powder, and salt.
4. In a separate bowl, cream the butter with the sugar until fluffy.
5. Mix the milk, water, and vanilla extract together in a small bowl.
6. Alternately add the mixed dry ingredients and the liquids to the butter-sugar mixture, beating well.

7. In a separate bowl, beat the egg whites until stiff and then fold into the batter.
8. Pour the batter into the pans and bake for 25 minutes. Let cool for 10 to 15 minutes in pan, then put the cakes on a wire rack to cool.
9. Place one cake layer on a plate or platter. Spread about a quarter of the icing over the cake, using an icing spatula or butter knife.
10. Place the second cake on top of the first frosted layer.
11. Pour the rest of the icing over the cake, spreading it down the sides to completely cover. If you're feeling fancy, try swirling it with your knife or spatula.

Never-Fail or Seven-Minute Icing

(will make enough to frost a two-layer 9-inch cake)

Ingredients

2 egg whites

1½ cups sugar

⅓ cup water

Few grains of salt

¼ teaspoon cream of tartar or 1½ teaspoons corn syrup

1 teaspoon vanilla extract

This icing is kind of like making a candy. You'll be working with hot liquids here, so you'll need an adult to help. Wear an apron to protect against splashes.

This icing is very sweet, so it's better if the filling between the layers of your cake is something that's on the tart side. If using jam, try to use something that's a little bit tart—preferably without corn syrup, which seems to make things taste sweeter than usual.

Another idea is to use the leftover egg yolks from this and the Lady Baltimore Cake to make a custard filling.

Directions

1. Fill the bottom of a double boiler with water and put heat on high.
2. In the top of the double boiler, combine all ingredients except the vanilla extract. Using a hand mixer, combine these ingredients.
3. Place the pan over the boiling water and use the hand mixer to beat for 7 to 10 minutes, or until the mixture holds a point when the beater is lifted.
4. Remove from heat, add the vanilla extract, and continue beating until cool enough to spread, about 5 more minutes.
5. Good for the tops and sides of two layers.

Tres Leches Cake

Ingredients

1½ cups all-purpose flour

1 tablespoon baking powder

¼ teaspoon ground cinnamon

6 egg whites

1½ cups sugar

3 egg yolks

2½ teaspoons vanilla extract

½ cup whole milk

1 cup evaporated skim milk

1 cup heavy cream

1 cup sweetened condensed milk

Directions

1. Preheat the oven to 350 degrees.
2. Grease and flour the bottom and sides of a glass 13 × 9-inch baking dish.
3. In a large bowl, whisk together the flour, baking powder, and cinnamon.
4. In another large bowl, using an electric mixer, beat the egg whites until firm peaks form, 7 to 8 minutes.

5. Gradually beat in the sugar. Add the egg yolks one at a time, beating to blend between additions.
6. Beat in 2 teaspoons of the vanilla extract. Add part of flour mixture, then the whole milk, then the rest of the flour mixture, beginning and ending with the flour mixture.
7. Pour the batter into the baking dish; smooth the top.
8. Bake for 25 minutes.
9. Reduce the temperature to 325 degrees; continue baking until the cake is golden brown and the middle springs back when pressed, 20 to 25 minutes more.
10. Let the cake cool in the baking dish for 15 minutes; then invert the cake onto a wire rack set inside a rimmed baking sheet.
11. In a mixing bowl, whisk together the remaining ½ teaspoon vanilla extract, evaporated skim milk, heavy cream, and sweetened condensed milk.
12. Poke holes all over the top of the cake with a skewer. Slowly drizzle half of the sauce onto the cake, letting it soak in.
13. Invert a platter on top of the cake. Lift the rack and gently invert the cake onto the platter. Drizzle the remaining sauce over the cake.

Strawberry Basil Pie (makes one 9-inch pie)

Ingredients

2 pounds strawberries

8 basil leaves, chopped

Juice from 1 lemon

3 tablespoons sugar

2 tablespoons cornstarch

Pastry from 9-Inch Double Pie Crust recipe on page 357 (make sure you have two crusts!)

1 egg, beaten, for egg wash

Sugar, for sprinkling

Directions

1. Preheat the oven to 350 degrees.
2. Hull and slice the strawberries.
3. In a large bowl, combine the strawberries, basil, lemon juice, sugar, and cornstarch.
4. Lay one of the pie crusts into a 9-inch pie dish and leave a little overhang.
5. Pour in the mixture. Top with the other pie crust

and crimp the edges together with your fingers, then use a fork to poke holes in the middle to allow the steam to escape (or you can make a lattice-top crust by weaving together strips of dough).

6. Use a pastry brush to brush on the egg wash, and sprinkle the wet crust with sugar.
7. Bake for 45 minutes.

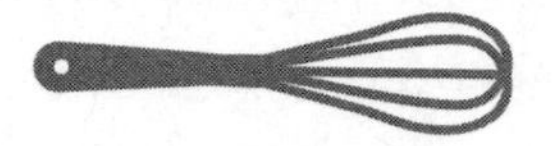

Gluten-Free Pie Crust

Ingredients

2 cups gluten-free flour (any brand)

½ teaspoon salt

2 teaspoons sugar (for sweet pies only)

½ cup unsalted butter

1 egg

⅔ cup ice water (approximately 11 tablespoons)

Before you start, cut the butter into small pieces (about 1/2-inch) and stick them into the freezer for about 15 minutes.

Directions

1. Combine the gluten-free flour with the salt and optional sugar. Use either a food processor or a fork, mixing until the flour is aerated.
2. Add the butter. Mix with the fork or pulse the processor 10 times, until it looks crumbly.
3. Add the egg, pulsing or mixing until the egg disappears. The mixture should still look crumbly.
4. Stir or pulse in 1 tablespoon of ice water at a time,

just until the dough will hold. Being on the wet side is better than being too dry. It should look like dry cottage cheese curds.

5. Divide the mixture in half and roll into two balls. Cover each ball in plastic wrap and put in the refrigerator for 30 minutes to rest.
6. Gluten-free dough is very sticky, so make sure everything is floured or lightly oiled so the dough doesn't stick to your surface.
7. With floured hands, shape the balls into disks.
8. Place each disk onto a piece of floured waxed or parchment paper. Cover with another sheet of floured waxed or parchment paper. If you want, you can very lightly oil your paper instead (use a spray such as PAM, or a tasteless oil, as opposed to olive oil).
9. Roll the disk while it's sandwiched between your floured paper until it's slightly larger than the pie tin.
10. Take off the top piece of paper. Put your hand under the bottom paper and flip it into the pie tin. Peel back the paper as you press the crust into the tin. If it breaks apart, press it back together.
11. Poke the bottom slightly with a fork (not all the way through).
12. Repeat with the other disk for the top of your pie.
13. Use your choice of filling.

You can make the crust ahead of time and keep it in the refrigerator or freezer, empty or filled, until ready to bake.

ACKNOWLEDGMENTS

To my critique partners on this: Karina Glaser, Casey Lyall, Ki-Wing Merlin, Laura Shovan, and Timanda Wertz. Your encouragement and insight helped more than I can ever say. You ladies rock.

To Brenda M. Villalpando, Esq., thank you for answering my immigration law questions about a fictional character. Any mistakes are my own. To Genevieve Suzuki, Esq., thanks for referring me to Brenda and for all the coffees, omelets, burgers, fish-shaped cakes, and general emotional support.

To Steven Torres of Pop Pie Company, thank you for showing me the inner workings of a pie shop, feeding me too much pie and coffee, and giving me some small-business insight. Here's to living your dream.

To Stephanie Lurie, thank you for your generous early insights and direction.

To Laurie Jamrok and Abbie Stevens, thank you for being my test kitchen.

Thanks to Mary Pender-Coplan, my United Talent film agent, for your support.

To my agent, Patricia Nelson, thank you for interrupting me midpitch to tell me you loved it. Thanks for believing in me.

A very huge thank-you to my editor, Kristin Daly Rens, who has shaped this book into what it was meant to be. I've learned a lot from your patience and wisdom.

To my family, for (mostly) respecting the "closed door" rule and not complaining about all the grilled-cheese sandwiches for dinner.

And thanks to the young person I can't name.